Awaken Me

Awaken Me
A Connected Novel

Emily Gossett

iUniverse, Inc.
Bloomington

Awaken Me
A Connected Novel

Copyright © 2011 by Emily Gossett.

All rights reserved. No part of this book may be used or reproduced by any means, graphic, electronic, or mechanical, including photocopying, recording, taping or by any information storage retrieval system without the written permission of the publisher except in the case of brief quotations embodied in critical articles and reviews.

This is a work of fiction. All of the characters, names, incidents, organizations, and dialogue in this novel are either the products of the author's imagination or are used fictitiously.
iUniverse books may be ordered through booksellers or by contacting:

iUniverse
1663 Liberty Drive
Bloomington, IN 47403
www.iuniverse.com
1-800-Authors (1-800-288-4677)

Because of the dynamic nature of the Internet, any web addresses or links contained in this book may have changed since publication and may no longer be valid. The views expressed in this work are solely those of the author and do not necessarily reflect the views of the publisher, and the publisher hereby disclaims any responsibility for them.

Any people depicted in stock imagery provided by Thinkstock are models, and such images are being used for illustrative purposes only.
Certain stock imagery © Thinkstock.

ISBN: 978-1-4620-3825-1 (sc)
ISBN: 978-1-4620-3826-8 (hc)
ISBN: 978-1-4620-3827-5 (ebk)

Library of Congress Control Number: 2011917808

Printed in the United States of America

iUniverse rev. date: 10/20/2011

CONTENTS

One 1
Two 7
Three 22
Four 31
Five 40
Six 56
Seven 65
Eight 72
Nine 83
Ten 91
Eleven 107
Twelve 116
Thirteen 123
Fourteen 126
Fifteen 130
Sixteen 142
Seventeen 147
Eighteen 152
Nineteen 157
Twenty 174
Twenty-One 184
Twenty-Two 190

*For my sister, Aimee,
who was my inspiration for this book, and my parents, who
support me unconditionally.*

IF YOU HAVE FAITH AS small as a mustard seed, you can say to this mountain, "Move from here to there" and it will move. Nothing will be impossible for you.
Matthew 17:20

One

THE COOL SPRING WIND BLEW my waist-length, blonde hair around my face as I stood on the bow of the yacht. I shut my eyes tight as I leaned my head back, enjoying the coolness of the wind on my neck. Taking a breath, I opened my eyes. It was a perfect night, not a cloud in the sky, the stars glowing brightly. I glanced down at my left hand and admired my sparkling canary diamond. This was exactly what I had wanted, to get married and have a family at 23. I was, after all, marrying a man that any girl would dream of, not to mention one of Palm Beach's most eligible bachelors. Having been with Derek Sladen for six years, I couldn't imagine marrying anyone else.

For as long as I could remember, which isn't very far back, my life seemed like a roller coaster of emotions. I was always easily angered or on the verge of an outburst. How Derek put up with my moods was beyond me. And yet, I have to say that my feelings of angst and moodiness were always justified.

Apparently I had spent my youth growing up with my mother. We worked at a local bed and breakfast. That was before the car accident. I was told, afterward, that I lost my mother, along with all my memories. The only thing I remembered was waking up in a hospital. That was where I first met Elizabeth, Derek's mother. She was the only witness of the accident. She gave me my "new life," and she introduced me to Derek.

Everything seemed wonderful, full of possibilities. I inhaled deeply, taking in every moment of this perfect night. It was, after all, my engagement party. I was so deep in my thoughts that I didn't hear the door open.

"Aimee, are you out here?"

I turned around and saw Krissy, my best friend, peeking from behind the door. She looked sleek in her tight, navy blue dress. Her short brown hair was neatly pulled back, her pale blue eyes squinting against the wind.

"It is seriously cold out here!" She walked to the bow and stood, arms crossed, with an annoyed expression on her face. Typical Krissy behavior. "This is your engagement dinner! When are you going to grace everyone with your presence?"

Laughing, I put an arm over her shoulder and sighed. I was more of the reckless kind of gal. You know, the jump-in-before-looking or simply-run-away-when-things-got-hard kind of girl. And, of course, Derek was always the person to bring me back.

"I can't believe I'm getting married in two days," I said, almost wistful. "In Greece!"

I was pretty excited about the location of the wedding. Derek's family had endless amounts of money and had spoiled me accordingly.

Smiling, Krissy looked up at me with concern in her eyes. "This is what you want, right? I mean, Derek is a great man, very good looking, and his family is nice. But are you happy?"

Her eyes were soft, yet I could see the worry etched on her face. But I had thought hard about this. I couldn't imagine how I had actually hooked a man like Derek Sladen. Sure, I'm pretty and curvy and all that; and Derek loved my hazel eyes. Elizabeth's kindness had certainly helped. She was the very reason Derek and I had met in the first place. But was I *happy*? His family truly loved me, and when I looked into Derek's green eyes I felt safe. In fact, I wouldn't know where I would be if I hadn't met Derek. That thought scared me. I gave Krissy a wide, confident smile.

"Yes, I am happy. And, yes, I want this," I said, reassuring her.

Krissy was shivering slightly from the cold breeze, but she smiled back at me.

"Lead the way, Obi Wan Kenobi," I said sarcastically.

She just shook her head at me. I mustered as much confidence as I could and followed her back inside.

Once I entered the room, Krissy motioned her hand toward the bar. Of course, she would head in that direction. I gave her half a smile as she walked away.

The room was beautifully decorated with red orchids, lilies, and crystal. The piano sat to the far right side of the room, and a little bald man played gracefully. The room was filled with so many people I didn't know.

I looked anxiously for Derek, my eyes scanning the crowd, but was interrupted by his mother, Elizabeth, who gently touched my arm. She looked elegant in her black cocktail dress. Her pale green eyes met mine with warmth. I always admired how beautiful her face was. She was like a mother to me.

"Aimee! I was beginning to worry. Derek went upstairs to look for you," she said softly.

"No need to worry," I said, trying to reassure her.

"I just haven't seen you for quite a while." Elizabeth looked relived almost. I wondered if Derek's family really thought I would bolt.

"Is Derek still upstairs?" I asked.

"I believe so; you should go find him."

Elizabeth was smiling as she nodded toward the back stairs. I squeezed her arm as I snuck through the back of the room undetected, thanks to my awesome Ninja skills.

Why on Earth would a yacht, especially one of this caliber, have annoying spiral stairs? I was constantly hitting my arms on the railing, leaving my elbows bruised. This time, thankfully, I made it through unharmed. I reached the top, my heart beating a little faster in my chest as I saw a light in the room across from where I stood. It was dark in the hallway and the door was slightly ajar. I quietly peeked in, anxiously waiting to see Derek. What I didn't expect to see was Krissy. I had almost pushed the door open; thankfully I froze. Derek was there with her. Something about this scene was wrong, surreal. Derek moved in closer toward Krissy; she responded instantly. Derek gracefully traced her neck with his fingers. Krissy had this intimidated look in her eyes.

His perfectly chiseled features, which gave off the essence of masculinity, mixed with his solid build and his dark grey suit, looked so sexy on him. His green eyes stared intently at Krissy. The corners of his lips curled to form a smile, but something about this smile wasn't friendly. Derek ran his hand through his jet black, cropped hair, making it a little more unruly. My arm hairs prickled up, and my breathing became a bit uneven.

"I'm not afraid of you. You may have her fooled, but I know exactly what you are!" Krissy said fiercely.

"Awww!" He said sarcastically. "It won't matter for long though, and I doubt you will say anything."

Derek was calm and collected as he took a swig of whiskey. My inner self wanted to barge in and demand to know what was going on. But I needed to be a new Aimee, one that listened and waited before jumping into something I knew nothing about. Still, an unsettled feeling crept through my body. Was it fear, or anxiety about the wedding? Whatever this feeling was that was growing within me, I wanted to find out what was going on.

"What makes you so sure I won't say anything? You know what I am!"

"That I do. And you should know how fragile your life is. So wouldn't you think it wise not to antagonize me?"

Derek placed his glass down on the nearby table. Krissy's eyes flashed as she continued to glare at Derek. I was about to open the door, until Derek made a move so quickly I almost didn't catch it. With one swift motion, Krissy's neck was in his hands. Krissy's confidence was gone; she looked terrified beyond words. Derek's face was malicious, with an excited smirk playing at his lips. In one swift movement of his wrists, Krissy's life was gone. Derek remained calm and cool as her body hit the floor with a light thud. Derek adjusted his suit and picked up his glass.

A scream was building within me. Holding it in was hard. I backed away from the door, hoping he wouldn't look up. Pure, petrified terror swept through me. Oh God, I could feel it, that same burning fire in my chest. Anger, fear, these emotions poured through me uncontrollably. Derek left the room. Fortunately for me, he exited through the back door while I was frozen against the back wall, with my hands covering my mouth.

My heart stopped beating as I looked at Krissy's body. Taking uneven steps toward her, I hoped, maybe she was just knocked out. I approached her.

No pulse. She was gone. My hands started to shake slightly. Was this real or a bad dream? Derek wasn't a murderer. He had always been so gentle. My mind began to race. The sound of soft footsteps was coming from the direction in which Derek left.

I was already backing away, exiting the room, trying to escape somehow. Hot tears were blurring my vision as thought after thought raced through my brain. The life I painted with Derek and his family. How would I face his family, well, Elizabeth in particular? What could she possibly do or say to fix this mess. I felt so betrayed. And I realized I did not know the man I was about to marry.

On the brink of hysterics, my breathing was staggering. I couldn't see where I was going. I was numb from the shock. I heard the yacht's horn blow near me, jolting me back to reality. Glancing around, I ended up back at the bow of the ship somehow; the cool air drying my tears. I held my arms close to my body, trying to comfort myself. I began to think again. How long did Derek . . . I stopped my thoughts and pushed that image and those thoughts to the back of my mind.

Glancing around, I realized we were docked. My small clutch was still lying where I had forgotten it earlier. Picking it up, I thought about what I had in it. I had my cards and some cash. And then I thought to myself, *I'm sure I can pawn this ring.*

Could I actually run away from all this? I would not just be leaving Derek, but I'd be leaving his family and Elizabeth. I was such a coward. I would fear for my own safety. And with this much pain that began to grow inside me, I just knew I would never be able to face them.

Being as quiet as I could in heels on a wooden deck, I passed the main ball room with all the windows. I could make out Elizabeth waiting by the same spiral staircase I had walked up earlier. I began to wonder if she would be waiting much longer. Feeling sick, I abruptly turned to the dock. The bridge wasn't set up yet, and the gap between the dock and the yacht was fairly large.

"*Great.*" I thought aloud sarcastically as I realized I would have to jump. I glanced down at the red satin, floor-length dress I wore. I knew

Derek would have loved this dress. Just the thought of him even liking this dress made me want to rip it off and throw it in the ocean. With a burning anger tingling in my fingers, I took off my heels and tossed them onto the dock along with my clutch.

"*Well, here goes nothing.*"

Taking a deep breath, I jumped and landed on my knees.

Very gracefully done! I thought, almost laughing to myself. I was about to stand when I felt a pair of firm hands grip my arms and help me up. Shocked at the touch, I snapped my arms out of those unknown hands. Fearful of it being Derek, I quickly brushed my hair out of my eyes. I was met with an amused grin and grey eyes that bore into mine. There, in front of me, stood this man. His chin length, brown, wavy hair was beautiful as it lay against his pale skin. He was literally a Greek god. Realizing my mouth was open, I closed it. His cool eyes just watched me.

"Are you okay?" His thick, Italian accent thrilled me.

"Fine," was all I managed to say; with his eyes never leaving mine.

Breaking eye contact and remembering why I jumped off the yacht, I gathered my clutch and put my heels back on. I needed to leave this place before Derek could notice I was gone.

Making sure not to look back at the tall man, I headed toward land.

"Do you know where you are going?" the handsome man asked as he followed behind me and kept my same pace.

"I do," I lied. I had never been to Greece before.

Realizing that this stranger was still following me, I stopped and turned to him. His face looked down at me and still had that same amused expression.

"Can you leave me *alone*?" I tried to put as much rudeness in my voice as I could, when in fact I didn't have a clue as to where I was going and his presence was comforting. But, for all I knew, he could have been sent by Derek.

He simply nodded. "As you wish," he said with one last smoldering look and then disappeared into the crowd. I was mildly surprised that he listened without much hesitation. Standing at the edge of where the land met the dock, I glanced back looking at the elegantly lit yacht one last time. Then, as I turned myself onto my heels to leave, I exhaled, trying to calm myself.

Two

AS I STOOD THERE, I could see that Greece was really beautiful. It was such a mix of old and new architecture; all of the buildings that I could see had rustic white smooth walls with delicate details surrounding the doors and windows. So much history surrounded me. I stood in front of a fountain that must have been around when Julius Caesar was on earth, that's how ancient it appeared. It was a man holding a naked woman in his arms as water bubbled out, trickling down their bodies.

The people, the town, it all seemed unreal, a foggy haze as I walked through the crowds. The women really knew how to dress, with their clothes layered stylishly. I wasn't sure I would be able to pull it off.

I wandered around for God only knows how long, until I decided to ask a European man, "Hi. Do you by any chance have the time?"

He smiled as his eyes checked me out. *That's a bit creepy.*

"Never mind," I said as I hastily turned away from him.

Finding out the time proved to be a challenge in itself, as it appeared not many people understood me. I wasn't in Florida anymore. Stupid language barrier. Frustrated, I walked into a cozy little coffee shop, chiming the bell over the door as I entered. The sales guy behind the register glanced up at me, a clock hung behind him, reading 8:40. The guy behind the register did a double take, and then spoke in Greek. I shook my head, gesturing that I didn't speak Greek, and he asked again in broken English.

"Can I help you?" his accent was thick as he looked at me with a hopeful expression.

"Uh, no thanks," I told the disappointed coffee guy.

My tearing eyes and bared arms unwelcomed the cold air as I walked down the cobble stone street. It was getting colder, and my dress provided me little warmth. I could feel the anxiety begin to build up within me.

"Okay, Aimee, you can do this. Sure you just ran away from a life of luxury and a man who just murdered your best friend. Oh and not to mention you were supposed to get married in two days. But, life could be worse." I thought out loud, startling a couple that was sitting close together on a bench.

The piercing pain in my feet and nearly frozen body made me almost pass by a nice looking hotel, with gigantic white marble pillars, and a large gold-plated sign above the entrance, engraved with the name "The Enclave."

I walked inside and saw that the main lobby was luminous, with red velvet sofas and chairs clustered together around a grand fireplace. The floor was a deep grey marble, and I could see my reflection in it. I sure knew how to pick expensive things. One of God's gifts, I guess. The bell boy smiled at me as I passed by him. I received a few looks actually, as I walked toward the front desk. I probably looked like a call girl in this satin dress.

The girl at the front desk raised an eyebrow as I approached the long white marble counter that stretched along the back wall. She would have been prettier if her snobbish expression had been a smile instead. Her brown eyes narrowed in on me as I approached her.

"Welcome to the Enclave. My name is Natasha. How can I help you tonight?" I flashed the rock on my left hand and her expression faltered into shock. My smile grew, it was caddy of me.

"I would like a suite!" I said with confidence. I debated whether or not to charge Derek's card. He wouldn't know until he went back to Palm Beach anyway. A smile grew on my lips at the thought of his expression when he would get the bill. The more I thought about it, the more I realized it would only cause him to come look for me. So, I decided to give her my personal card instead.

"How many nights did you need?" Natasha asked, pulling me out of my dream.

"Three nights and I'll need to go shopping in the morning. Or is there a service for that?" I asked.

"Yes, we can arrange a ride for you or if you make a list we have personal shoppers who can bring back clothes for you to try on."

I didn't want to walk out looking like this tomorrow, so a personal shopper wasn't a hard choice for me to make.

I finished with Natasha and followed the eager bellhop to my suite, passing by people that didn't hide their curious stares. This hotel was exquisite, with marble flooring and elegantly detailed angels painted on the ceiling, with walls of rich gold and deep blues. My heels echoed loudly in the hall as we approached the elevator.

The elevator we stepped into took me straight to my room, using a special key.

Nothing would prepare me for how gorgeous my room would be. Facing the sea was a canopy bed with a living room in the center around a fireplace. The dark grey marble continued in the room. It was beautiful. The bellhop cleared his throat as he turned to me expectantly. I happily handed him a large tip. He smiled and left the room.

Walking to the window, I looked out at the ocean. It really was hard to see clearly, the glare on the window hindered my sight. But the moon was very visible. Luckily, I wasn't near Derek's yacht.

Feeling truly alone, I began to contemplate what I was going to do and where I was going to go. All my belongings were in Palm Beach, Florida, and at Derek's house nonetheless. I began to realize that I had done what I always do, and acted on emotions and fled. Letting the reality of my grief sink in, my tears began to erupt like a volcano. I couldn't control them. A knot grew in my chest. I felt such despair, an aching pain. Clutching the wall for support, and feeling like the wind had been knocked out of me, I blindly made my way to the bed.

After what seemed like hours of crying in a curled ball on the bed, it felt like I ran out of tears. My eyes stared blankly at the high ceiling as I began replaying the night. Krissy and Derek and how his eyes looked at her. Derek taking Krissy's life. All I could see was her falling to the floor. I would most likely have to suffer in silence. Why couldn't I escape my head? Tonight wasn't what I planned, what a mess of events. It was supposed to be a happy memory, one with family and friends. Instead I was left trying to figure out what I was going to do now. Do I go back to Florida? How could I face anyone back home? Especially after what I saw Derek do to Krissy. Could I have stopped it? Would Derek have killed me?

Aimee, just breathe, I reassured myself. I was beginning to have an anxiety attack; my breathing was staggering and I could feel the warm fire growing in my chest.

The room began to move around me. I sat up thinking this would help to cure my madness, that I was just dizzy from crying, but it got worse. The room felt like I was in a warped tunnel. I quickly started opening and closing my eyes, hoping the room would stop. But it wasn't the room, it was my vision. Everything present became blurry and I drifted to sleep, or so it felt. Blackness surrounded me.

I felt the warmth before I saw the scenery before me. The beach was warm as I sun bathed. Well, I would have been sun bathing if I had worn a bathing suit. But, I just stood in the sand. It was a perfect blue sky day, with a slight sea breeze. I was on Derek's private beach, and it was so peaceful. It was one of my favorite places to escape for a day. The palm trees blew gracefully in the breeze, and the sound of the waves brought a sense of peace to me. This was a nice dream. An odd reality it brought me, something unusual. I felt a soft touch, I knew instinctually that it was Derek's hands that glided up my side. Derek's eyes were examining me. I smiled at his approval. Why was I smiling? I should be terrified, at least I was earlier. But my feelings were muted. The moment passed, as did the ocean.

The scene quickly changed and I was standing on the cobble stoned street in Greece. I was alone, though. The gold-plated Enclave sign shone with an unusual brightness. Derek appeared by my side again. The hair on my arms rose.

"The Enclave, Aimee? Of all places to go!" Derek said with his arms crossed and eyebrows raised.

"This is my dream! Why are you here?" I asked. His smile curled up the sides.

Wasn't I supposed to be angry at him? The small fragments of my night unraveled before my eyes and I couldn't stop it. It felt like my brain was being pried open, like a bad headache; I grasped my face in pain. This was the weirdest dream I ever had. I was more exhausted. My eyes could no longer see; instead his voice surrounded my blackness.

"I found you." Derek said softly.

"What do you mean you found me?" I asked, getting mad. All of the stress from the day must have given me some psychotic warped dream. The headache lifted and Derek's face appeared.

There was something about his smile that was bothering me. "Don't worry, I will see you soon enough." He said so confidently. He touched my face and terror seared through my body.

"Oh, really? I think not!" I said angrily. His green eyes just watched me with amusement. Oh, how I loved his eyes. And I still do. What conflicting emotions I felt. How can I hate someone that I loved? What a curse to be that good looking. My eyes began getting heavy and the dream became hazy, like a thick fog. Derek was gone, but slowly my mind became blank, as I finally felt exhaustion take over me.

I woke up to a soft knock on the door. My eyes became alert and I sat up too fast. Glancing around the large room and remembering where I was, I got up and sluggishly moved to the door. I was still in the satin red dress. My head pounded with a serious headache. Passing a mirror, I caught a glimpse of my horrific morning face, mascara smudged all under my eyes, looking like some creature from a sci-fi movie.

"Coming!" I yelled as I used my hand to wipe some of the mascara away. Peeking in the peephole, I saw a tall beautiful woman standing there with a rack of clothes. I excitedly opened the door.

"Hello, Miss. My name is Iva." She said with a smoldering Italian accent, as she glanced at my state while rolling the cart in. "Hello," was all I replied. She smiled at me, and something about her reminded me of someone I once knew. Maybe it was just her ice grey eyes, the same as the mystery man I met last night. She neatly unzipped the bags in the living room area, revealing the clothes. Surprisingly, she had great taste. I immediately began taking the red satin dress off as she helped me into a more casual day dress. Her hands briefly touched my arm and I had a sense of deja vu from her touch. She winced at the touch.

"I'm sorry, Miss." She said politely. Her face was gentle and elegant, but had a fierce edge to it, like Iva could kick some serious butt. Her brown hair was in a tight bun.

"My name is Aimee. No need to be formal." I said. "How long have you been a personal shopper?" I asked curiously as I examined the dress she put on me.

She hesitated a moment before answering. By now, she was zipping the back of a sexy black dress up for me. "A long time . . ."

"Oh. You have really good taste." I said.

Iva smiled. "What happened to the dress you were wearing? I noticed rips by the knees."

I glanced in the mirror to admire what I was wearing. Turning my attention back to Iva, I answered, "I jumped off a boat onto the dock." Her eyebrows rose. "I didn't want to stay on board any longer." A smile crept over her face; I could tell she tried to hide it.

"What is so funny?" I couldn't help the smugness in my voice.

"I'm sorry. It's not funny, just curious as to why."

The horrible image of the man I was going to marry snapping Krissy's neck, played in my mind again. I shook my head, trying to erase it. A cold chill ran down my spine. "Long story. My wedding was tomorrow, but I just couldn't marry him anymore." I replied, a bit sad. My life had seemed so right and in a flash, things quickly changed. I felt an overwhelming sadness.

Iva's smile shifted a little. "Oh. Well, better to realize that now before you married him." She said softly, as she gently helped me into the next dress. I wish I had done something. Maybe expose him to Elizabeth.

Iva soon finished and began packing the unwanted garments back into the bags. She was heading toward the door with the almost empty clothes rack, but stopped just before. "It was nice meeting you, Aimee. I hope your stay gets better." Her eyes just stared at me, and her words sounded sincere. I nodded, afraid of what I might say. I almost felt like crying. Iva left and I sat on the bed. What was it about Iva that made me feel so comfortable? At that thought my stomach growled and food became a dominant thought.

The main hotel lobby was buzzing with happy tourists. The woman at the marble check-in counter was the same one from last night. Natasha was her name and she glanced over at me smiling, clearly she did not recognize who I was in this conservative outfit, jeans and a cute, long sweater. Surprisingly, the air was warmer as I walked outside the hotel. It was partially overcast, and the breeze was mildly cool. At least I was prepared now for the temperature.

Walking causally down the sidewalk, the tourist shops were alive with people. I would have loved to sit and people-watch, but my stomach told me differently. A breeze rustled through my hair and I caught wind of something that smelled heavenly. Following the scent led me to a pastry shop. I wasn't even sure how I got there.

The tiny hole-in-the-wall shop was cute and intimate, couples were sitting outside under tiny yellow umbrellas drinking coffee; this setting was like a movie, and a pang of jealousy flared in me. Derek.

Having bought pastries I couldn't pronounce, I ate quietly as I continued to walk back outside, oblivious to the surroundings as my mood lifted with each bite, sending my taste buds wild and watering with each tantalizing bite. Being completely absorbed with my pastry, I didn't realize I was rounding the corner into an ally. It was darker, I noticed, and above me hung clothes lines that were streaking in between the peeling, off-white buildings. I was so taken with the scenery above me that I ran right into something, or someone. Almost choking on the pastry, familiar hands grabbed my shoulders, sending an electric current through my body. My eyes widened as I looked into those same grey eyes from last night. It was such a feeling I never felt before and pure horror filled me.

"Hello again," said that same Italian accent. He looked at me expectantly, what he was expecting was beyond me, and he smiled a crooked grin.

"Hi." I said swallowing the piece of food I was chewing. "Can you release me now please?" I asked.

He smiled and released me, slightly jumping from the tone of my voice.

"Why are you following me?" I asked as I snapped my arms out of his reach, while I examined him with uncertainty. He still looked like a Greek god with his wavy, brown hair, ice grey eyes and pale skin. His lips were still in a half smile. Could I really be attracted to a man so soon after leaving my fiancée?

"No, I just happen to be in the same places as you at the same time." He said as he glanced around the ally before returning his piercing gaze back on me. "You really shouldn't be wandering around by yourself." His voice hid something I couldn't quite figure out, concern maybe?

"For your information, I can go wherever I please. And why shouldn't I call the police on you? You could be some dangerous villain or something for all I know!" I said sounding utterly ridiculous.

He just raised his eyebrows in a perfect arch, ignoring my last comment. "Where are you going now?" He asked calmly.

"What's with the questions? I don't even know you!" My voice went up a notch, my sudden burst of anger always seemed to get the better of me at times.

His smile grew. "My name is Alec. And you are?" Alec didn't offer his hand to me, and even if he had, I wouldn't have taken it. Instead I crossed my arms like a pouting child. He seemed to bring out this character in me, which was a bit unsettling. I was so used to trying to be controlled when I was around Derek and his family.

"What no last name? I don't need to tell you my name, anyway." I felt snarky and annoyed by him.

"Last name is irrelevant and I already know who you are. You're Aimee. Everyone is looking for you. Actually, I'm surprised they haven't found you yet, considering you're staying at the Enclave." His voice held such a fire. I turned my face away from his. I felt the color leaving my already pale face. Searching? They were looking for me? Of course they were. I felt terror enter me. It was so much more potent. I leaned on the white light post, to stabilize me.

"How do you know any of this? And even if they find me it doesn't matter because I'm a free woman!"

"If you go back to the hotel, HE will find you." Alec said. I searched his eyes for signs of deceit, but from what I could sense, there wasn't any.

"What about everything I just bought?" After uttering those words, I realized how dumb they sounded. What did I care more about? I knew I couldn't face Derek, the murderer.

"Okay." I said. "What do I do? You obviously know something that you aren't telling me!" My anger was seeping out of my words like venom.

His smile continued to grow. "You don't have to worry about your clothes. Iva has them for you." He said.

Astonished, my mouth dropped open. How did he know Iva?

"What is going on here? Who are you?" Fear started to seep through my veins. I slowly backed away from him, reaching a brick wall. I felt trapped. And scared.

"Aimee, I can help you. If you want help, then believe me when I tell you that you can trust me."

Words from a stranger, I knew better. Yet there was something about Alec. I couldn't place it. I felt comfortable with him, maybe I really could trust him. Or maybe it was me being careless and allowing myself to trust a complete stranger out of fear of Derek.

My two choices were these, go with a stranger or be confronted by my ex who killed my best friend. Looking into Alec's eyes, I made my decision. His eyes bore into mine, like he knew what I was going to say.

"If I go with you, will you explain how you know everything?" I asked.

"When the time is right, things will reveal themselves." He said.

I didn't have any clue what he was talking about, so all I did was nod.

Alec smiled and nodded toward his heavily tinted car. How did I not notice his BMW sooner? Am I actually getting into his car, like some stupid common-senseless girl? The type I would make fun of? I glanced around, hoping that someone might see me get into his car. But, I was in an alley with nobody around. Only a fool like myself would get into these situations.

"Of course," I said to myself.

Alec was already in the car waiting for me patiently. The inside of his black, 750 series BMW had black leather seats that smelled new. I glanced at his navigation system in the dashboard, hoping I would see a destination. I noticed that he was dressed nicely. He wore a form-fitted, buttoned down, long-sleeved, dark blue shirt paired with dark denim jeans. I really began to wonder who this man was. Or what exactly he does. He peeled the car out of the ally and I scrambled to put my seat belt on. I wondered if I was going to die from his driving alone.

Winding through the streets of Greece, everything was a blur, we began heading, well, I didn't know where. I peeked from the side of my peripheral vision; his hands were gripping the steering wheel, keeping his eyes on the road. He was so tense.

"Where exactly are we going? And why are you helping me?" I asked, trying to be as polite as I could be under the circumstances, even though every ounce of my being cried out in outrage and anger.

"You leave me no choice but to help you. And you'll see where we are going." His straight face was bothering me. He seemed so controlled.

All my life I ran away from things, anything complicated. Derek, a number of times, would find me and bring me back. I don't know why I would run. Maybe I just didn't feel content or maybe I was looking for the unknown. Thinking about Derek made me sad. Would I ever see him again? And was my dream really a *dream*? Or was it something else? Every time I would ask Elizabeth about the accident, she would avoid it. I always let it slide. I had been okay with not knowing details. But now, with things unfolding right in front of me, Derek's cruel behavior, what indeed would be my sentence? What scared me the most was that I still loved Derek. I was horrified with what he did, but that part of me was still consumed by him. Maybe it was just something I would have to outgrow.

The awkward silence in the car grew thick. So thick, you could cut it with a knife. Alec's face softened as he took a deep breath.

"Aimee, do you remember anything from your past?" His face was now hiding behind his soft waves.

Feeling a bit uneasy, I kept my eyes on the road. "Nothing before the accident. Why don't you tell me what you know? Because I know something is going on here!" My voice got loud, but Alec just kept that smooth expression. The fact was, I didn't know what kind of accident I was in. I was alive and should've just left it at that. I always knew there was something missing, but I never pushed Elizabeth for answers.

"I'm curious to know what you were told about the accident." Alec said, locking eyes with me briefly. I caught myself staring at his perfectly proportioned face. How deceiving my emotions were. In fact, I began to worry about what he knew, which was likely more than I knew.

"I don't know anything except waking up at a hospital." Soon after I met Derek, he pursued me immediately. Thinking of him now only made the visual of him breaking Krissy's neck more present. I gulped as I closed my eyes for a second. The aching, why wouldn't it stop? Alec stayed quiet as I battled my feelings.

"Who are you?" I asked. I didn't mean for my voice to be rude, but I couldn't control it. I was on the edge of insanity.

"It's not important who I am." Alec said.

"Yes, it is important! I got into this car with *you*! I don't even know you or why I listened to you! I have no clue where we are going or what is going to happen to me when we get there! And you just sit there with that stern face, and what, I'm supposed to be okay with all this?"

The amused expression returned to his face. "Yes." He answered calmly.

I was on the verge of jumping out of the car or screaming at him. But, by the looks of him, I wouldn't have made it very far. So instead I sighed deeply and dug my back further into the leather seats.

I noticed a dark horizon when I woke up. I didn't even realize I had dozed off. I quickly wiped the drool from the corner of my lip. *How embarrassing*, I thought to myself. I glanced over at the God-like man sitting next to me; Alec. His expression hadn't changed.

"We are almost there," was all he said.

We began to descend underground. I wasn't paying attention and somehow missed seeing an entrance. My eyes narrowed as I tried to capture the dimmed light. Alec parked the car next to what would seem to be a parking lot, if it was normal. These cars would make Palm Beach cars look like shams, with every kind of exotic car you could imagine surrounding me. A green Lambo with matching green rims was next to me.

This garage was made of silver walls, actual sheets of silver, I could see the cars' reflections in them. The ceiling looked low and was black concrete. The floor was also black concrete.

An electric current shocked me when Alec touched my arm. I jumped, startled.

"So, I guess we're here?" I asked, my voice was low, almost a whisper. I was afraid and cold, even though I had worn a sweater.

"Yes." Alec said quietly.

He opened my door and I hesitated for a moment, almost debating if I should get out of the car. My legs moved, but my body felt like I was floating. Alec led me to an elevator. It appeared to be made of some type of strong steel, like something you would see in battle, or like a safe house. What did they keep out? Alec pressed the third level and it didn't even feel like we were moving further underground. The doors opened and my eyes tried to gather as much as they could in the dark hall. It smelled earthy and was warm.

Silently, we walked together as the light got brighter. What I didn't expect was what the third level looked like. It was an underground palace or fancy mall. There were shops of all sorts lining each side. Even though it was clearly upscale with black sparkling granite floors, the structure of this underworld had an ancient feel. Almost like a small Rome, but more modern. It was surprisingly bright and cheery, even with no windows. If I didn't know we were indeed underground, I would have thought it was a normal place. We crossed a bridge that went over a coy pond that divided the two main sides of this place. I had never seen anything like this before.

Where was I exactly? Everyone was dressed so nicely, like in H&M or Forever 21, or maybe the real deal clothes. And boy they were good looking. Men, women, and children. I realized that most of the people, minus the younger people, all had pale skin and icy, grey eyes, but their hair were different lengths and colors.

A small grumble of uncertainty mixed with fear began to corrupt my mind. It was hard not to feel this presence of fear when everyone around me caused the hair on my arms to prickle up. Alec was swiftly moving as we walked through the crowd. I received mixed looks from some of the passers. One girl my age almost stopped as her eyes went wide; she raised her hand, as if to point at me.

I ran up to Alec, touching his arm. As I did that, I felt the return of the electric current go through me. Surprised that the hair on my head didn't stand straight up, I let go of his arm. Alec turned, not fazed by the touch. Looking into his eyes, a piece of his soul was revealed to me. He had more than a deep sadness etched on his face. There was also a haunted look that lurked behind his grey eyes that I could see

"Yes Aimee?" Alec asked.

Whispering, I asked, "Why are these people looking at me? Do I have something on my face?" I felt insecure by the gawking.

"No your face is fine." He said, as he quickly glanced over me and then began walking again. He turned down a small hallway that had one door in front of us.

We walked through the plain white door. Walking into some room, but it wasn't just any room, it was large and like a council room, with white walls surrounding me. Long stone benches engulfed this room, with dark red velvet drapes hanging on the walls, where windows would be if there were any. On the front wall was a large portrait of a woman with hazel eyes, wearing a long silver dress. She was very regale. There in the middle of the room stood a woman I did know. Shoulder length brown hair pulled back into a low ponytail, her grey eyes narrowed on me, statuesque stance, Iva. She was smiling as if she knew I would see her again after this morning.

Who are these people? That was the question of the night.

"Hello again, Aimee. Long time no see." She nodded at Alec who crossed his arms, but her eyes never left my face.

"Yes, long time indeed. Maybe you can tell me what is going on, because this guy over here hasn't said anything productive to me," I said as I got closer to Iva. Iva continued to smile, but addressed Alec.

"Hasn't changed much since the last time, has she Alec?" Her Italian accent was smooth.

My mouth dropped. Last time? What did that mean?

"No, she hasn't. Her tongue is still sharp." Alec said laughing. His laugh was deep and exciting.

How was I beginning to have feelings for a complete stranger?

A new door opened and an older man entered along with a woman. He was mid-fifties, with greying hair and a grey suit. The woman wore a long-sleeved dress. She looked very statuesque. Their eyes showed joy and I noticed that it was the same woman in the portrait on the wall.

"Does she remember anything?" The man asked curiously. His Italian accent was just as strong as Alec's.

"I'm afraid not. All she remembers is waking up at the hospital." Alec said.

The man turned to face me. I could feel the color drain my already pale face. Something about this man, I couldn't place it, made me feel uncomfortable. The woman placed a hand on his shoulder.

"Be careful, we can't explain things to her yet!" said told the older gentleman.

"I'm standing right here if you have forgotten and I can understand English perfectly. And since no one seems to tell me anything, why are we underground? Better yet, who are all of you?" I asked as my voice rose an octave. I was boiling in anger mixed with fear. They just stared at me, not saying a word. "Hello? I'm tired and annoyed. Can I please get some answers?" My patience and tolerance were never good to begin with, but they were really waning at this point. I felt that same burning sensation in my chest, the one I usually got when I'm angry. I felt like I was on the verge of losing control. The death of my best friend, the betrayal of my ex fiancée, everything seemed to mix into one giant festering pool in my brain and I couldn't stay calm.

The older woman walked toward me. "You haven't changed much since I last saw you." Her voice was soft. Her accent sounded somewhat French. It was very mild and she was well spoken.

"Meaning *what*?" I asked, a bit rudely.

"Meaning your temper, as well as a few other things," the older woman said as she touched my shoulder.

"ROSEMARIE!" The older man scolded.

"I'm sorry, Ralph." Her eyes filled with tears and she turned from me.

This night just was getting more and more bizarre as it progressed. How much more I could digest was beyond me.

"Perhaps I should take her to her room to get some rest?" Iva said in a reassuring way, along with changing the subject.

I just glared at them all because I wasn't getting any answers.

The man nodded as he began to guide the older woman out the door; the woman named Rosemarie glanced over her shoulder back at me. Her hazel eyes were deep; I could see pain and happiness at the same time etched in her face.

What secrets did they know? I thought I had been confused in the car, but now I was a hundred percent more confused. The only thing I knew for certain was that Iva was right—I was really exhausted.

Alec stood in that very still way that he was good at; I don't think he was planning to move at first as he continued to look into my eyes. Iva cleared her throat, and Alec broke eye contact. Alec was so mysterious, yet he was a familiar presence.

"Goodnight, Aimee, I'll see you in the morning," Alec said, although he didn't move.

"Goodnight, Alec; she will see you tomorrow." Iva took my arm and I followed, unable to speak.

Why had Alec looked at me that way? So many thoughts raced through my head. I had so many new feelings I never felt before. Feelings I didn't know even how to register.

Iva led me back out into the main court, and I was still getting mixed glances from passersby. The crowd of people were more my age; some were sitting on the stone benches, while others stood in groups, eyeing me as I passed.

The stores were closed as Iva led the way.

Iva soon turned down a hall that had many doors, having the look of a hotel hallway, with off-white walls and dark blue carpet that smelled like it was just vacuumed. The doors even had numbers on them. Iva abruptly stopped in front of 156.

She turned toward me. She looked uptight with her arms crossed. Was this how she always was? She reminded me of Krissy in a way. Something about them was the same.

"Aimee, I know you must be confused about everything that is going on. But try to get sleep tonight, okay?" Her Italian accent was smooth and soft.

That was easy for her to say, I thought darkly.

Iva opened the door for me, reveling the room. It was very clean and looked like it was lived in once; the bed was to the left. It was a canopy bed; it looked so welcoming. The walls were a pale blue color, and the dresser in front of my bed had a plasma TV on top of it. A small living room was in front of what I assumed was my bathroom.

My eyes continued to glance over the room. I was trying to take it all in but couldn't, due to how tired my mind was; instead I muffled a "'Night" to Iva and flung myself onto the puffy white bed, slipping my shoes off. Sleep at last

Three

WAKING UP WITH NO LIGHT coming in the room was a strange feeling. There weren't any windows here. I didn't have a clue as to what time it was, either. But where I was, exactly, would be a better question to ask. My mind almost immediately began replaying the previous events. First, my ex fiancé was a murderer. And not only that, but he killed my best friend, Krissy. Second, I got into a car with a complete stranger and ended up God only knows where, with no answers to any of my questions. This whole endeavor had become a very annoying predicament to be in.

My feelings were still there for Derek. I tried not to think about him, but it was hard when those thoughts consumed me. Then there were these new feelings for Alec. What did Alec even know about me? And let's not even mention the attraction that was there. Yes, Aimee, you've really done it this time, I thought to myself. Driving yourself mad must be your specialty.

After taking a much-needed shower, I proceeded to the closet. Alec was right about my clothes. They were all here. I pulled out a pair of jeans and a cute tank top. Looking at my reflection, I noticed something different about my eyes, but maybe I was just imagining it. It wouldn't be the first time.

Shaking the towel off of my wet hair, I began combing the knots out. That was one thing I really hated about long hair, the knots.

Hopefully today I would be getting some answers about everything. It was highly unlikely, but I could still hope.

Going over to the king-sized, canopy bed, I sat down to put socks on and I noticed a picture on the nightstand. Nothing out of the ordinary about the picture itself, but it was something behind the picture that caught my eye; the first picture was slipping enough to see a second behind it. Opening the back of the frame, the picture that had been hiding fell to the floor. Reaching down and turning it over, I just froze; the girl in the picture was Iva, but next to her was . . . me?

I looked at it more closely, the same sandy blonde hair, hazel eyes, and soft curves. Was that possible? Had I been here before like the older woman, Rosemarie, had suggested? Why was everything so complex? I didn't have time to dwell on that thought because a knock at my door startled me. I put the picture under my pillow and ran to the door.

Iva stood there, smiling at me, looking a bit more relaxed as far as Iva went. Something else was strange about her, but I couldn't quite place it.

"How did you sleep last night?" she asked solemnly.

"Great. I passed out as soon as I lay down," I said, crossing my arms.

"I see you found your clothes," she said, glancing at what I was wearing. "You must be hungry."

Until she suggested it, I hadn't realized just how hungry I was. Iva gestured toward my grumbling stomach; I hadn't even heard it. Iva continued to smile at me as she turned to leave the room.

Iva shut the door behind me and I followed her closely. "What do you feel like eating?"

"Anything. I'm not a picky eater," I said as I stifled a yawn. The hall still had the fresh, vacuumed scent.

I had almost forgotten how extraordinary this place was. We entered the main court area and the chandeliers that hung from the ceiling gave off bright light. It was so cheery, yet it made me feel on edge and unsure of my surroundings. The old, white brick walls surrounded this place; one would never think it was underground. The floor was made of dark granite, and it sparkled as the lights shone on it. The ceiling was brick, like Chicago brick, old. Some of the structures, like the school, had an older feel to them, with their large wooden doors and smooth walls. The school gave off the essence of an antique horror movie. I personally wouldn't go inside.

This place seemed to have a little of everything as far as shops; I noticed more clothing stores than anything else. I felt like I was in a mall, a very upscale mall.

The food court area was buzzing with people. This place also had a homey feel. At least that's the vibe I got. Seeing everyone saying hello or hugging, it was a community.

One thing about me is that I'm unable to conceal my facial expressions. So, I was sure I had a look of awe, mixed with anxiety, all over my face.

We ended up at a bakery, and it smelled wonderful. It was a tight fit, not exactly cozy, more stifled than comfortable;, the walls were painted deep brown and made the place seem smaller than it probably was.

I sat at a table close to the entrance as Iva went in to fight the crowd of kids. I was hoping she would order me a variety of things.

It was strange to me, the no-windows thing; I didn't know what time it was, if it was day or night. I glanced at Iva, who came out of the bakery with a number of bags in her arms. She had on an annoyed expression as one of the small boys nearly tripped her. She reached me and began organizing the food bags in front of me. Iva seemed to be OCD, and I probably wouldn't be far off in that assumption.

As soon as Iva took the food out of the wrappers, I forgot my woes and dug into the closest croissant. She chuckled at me, amused. My usual self would have made a face, but the croissant with the chocolate filling was delicious! Nothing could distract me from it. I sighed deeply. Iva's smile broadened as someone approached behind me.

"Alec," Iva said. As Alec moved into my peripheral vision, he just nodded and sat next to her, looking at her. His perfectly proportioned face was relaxed as he sat across from me; his brown locks were damp from the shower he probably just took. Alec was a fine specimen for me to admire.

It was nice seeing him; there was something deeper about him I couldn't ignore, besides the obvious looks. Alec's grey eyes looked at me confidently. I didn't realize I was smiling, my heart fluttered mid-chew. I heard a soft chuckle. Iva sat there watching me also. Why was she laughing? Maybe she could read thoughts. If that were the case, she would be utterly confused with mine.

"So what's on the agenda today? Any hope of getting answers?" I asked, hopeful, as well as avoiding the subject that most likely would have come up after Iva caught me staring.

"Some things will be answered. But not by me, I'm afraid." Iva's voice was soft and sweet, mixed with her heavy Italian accent. She had her hair pulled into a tight bun and her black pencil skirt was really cute. I wanted to shake her, to make her more relaxed instead of so uptight-looking.

"Aimee, I wish I could tell you everything. Please be patient. I can read your expression, and it's telling me you're going to either run or have a tantrum," Alec said in his deep Italian accent.

In fact, I had been debating those thoughts while I sat there. Alec was really good at reading me, for someone who just met me. I sat up a bit straighter.

"Don't act like you know me! Neither of you does! And now I'm thinking I should have just faced my ex fiancée!" After those words left my mouth I saw a change in Alec's expression. Was it anger, hurt, annoyance? I couldn't read his face as well as he did mine. But did it matter? They didn't know me!

"Then why did you come with me?" Alec asked quietly.

Iva moved uncomfortably. Now she looked like she was going to bolt. I scowled at Alec over my hot chocolate, putting as much intimidation in my eyes as I could. His eyes widened as he focused on mine. Iva, I realized, was also looking at my eyes. They started to freak me out a little and my intimidation went out the window. I sat, slouched, and leaned back into my chair.

"What's wrong?" The words left my mouth uncertainly.

Shaking his brown hair away from his eyes, he placed his guarded look back up.

"Nothing is wrong," Alec said. His lips went into a hard line. Was he lying to me?

"Right. I need to use the rest room, are you going to escort me there or can I take myself?"

"I trust you will be okay to take yourself. Do you know where it's located?" Alec said as his eyebrow rose, making a perfect arch.

"Yes, I think I can manage," I said, wondering if I could actually find the bathroom.

"It's past this bakery on the left-hand side," Iva said. Simply nodding, I set off in that direction. Most likely I'd end up lost. Some things are inevitable with me. One thing being that I have always seemed to attract danger to myself and, two, I usually wind up getting lost.

I passed small children, who eyed me cautiously; one brave little girl smiled at me. A very attractive, dark-haired guy flashed a crooked grin at me, and I revealed my pearly whites to him.

I turned down the hall, hoping that the bathroom was here. I noticed this hall was dark and creepy, almost like the alley I met Alec in, except it was enclosed and had a strange smell I couldn't quite figure out.

There were three different doors to choose from. I didn't see any picture of a woman on a door; all I saw were words, but in another language. "Wonderful," I said aloud. I guessed I would have to check all three.

The middle door turned out to be a broom closet. So, door number one it was. Possibly. Opening the door, I got a rush of cold air in my face. It felt like a refrigerator. The blue light was dull and it took a moment for my eyes to adjust. The hair on my arms started to prickle when my vision became clear. I gasped in horror, a silent scream building in my throat, unable to come out. Shock rushed over me. Blood, bags of blood like what you would see at a hospital or a blood mobile, or a crazy horror movie. My body froze at the sight around me. This was a refrigerator. A refrigerator filled with blood.

I began to back away, and I scurried out of the room, shutting the door behind me. Horrified at what I had just seen, an overwhelming terror swept over me. Leaning against the wall in the hall, for support, I tried to calm myself; taking deep breaths didn't work. The question was there, planted in my brain: These people—what were they? Was I in danger? I could feel the light shivers that ran through me; I was petrified.

The hall I stood in still led to somewhere and anywhere was better than waiting for my sentence. Whatever that would be. I decided it was time for me to run away, again. Walking seemed awkward as my heart pounded in my chest. So, I began running down the hall without caring if anyone saw me, not that they would anyway. My breathing became heavier. I realized the floor started to slant. Was it possible to be going further underground?

The hall split into a cross. Making a sharp left, I followed it further. My pace became less urgent and I slowed to a walk, trying to focus on where I was going. Everything about this hall was strange; the lights began to flicker as if winds were sweeping across them. I stopped walking to catch my breath, and I noticed a door at the end of the hall. This door was made of the same metal as the elevator in the garage. I slowly made my way toward it.

The walls were rough, mixed with dirt and concrete, some tree roots peeked out, the temperature was warmer and smelled earthy, and even the floor was dirt. I was almost to that door when a hand grabbed my shoulder and turned me around. I felt a scream building in my chest, and that warm heat deep within me returning. The person placed a warm hand over my mouth swiftly.

"Be quiet!" The man said, almost like he sensed the scream that was coming as well as something else. He was tense as he held me close to him.

"What are you doing down here?" the unknown man asked me in a husky voice. His accent was Romanian.

"I, I got lost." I told him some of the truth. "But, I didn't know where I was, and I was trying to leave."

"It isn't safe down here; Ill escort you back." The light grew brighter as we walked. I finally got to see what this mystery man looked like, and good God! His tight black T-shirt defined his muscles. His hair was messy, short, and dark brown. His eyes were a brown, honey color. A smile slipped up from somewhere inside me.

"Who are you?" I asked. Once again, the question of the day. All I had been asking was who these people were!

Glancing at me briefly, all he said was, "Marcus."

"Nice to meet you, Marcus. I'm Aimee." His fast-paced walking stopped and he turned quickly toward me. My breathing also stopped. He examined my face for the first time and his features lit up. A tiny smile was sneaking up the corners of his lips. Unlike Alec, he didn't try to hide it. He had a casual way about him.

"I thought I had heard wrong, but the rumors are true, then," Marcus said.

People were talking about me? I became intrigued about what people were saying, but decided not to ask.

"Do you work down here?" I asked.

"I was on guard today. But it's not my usual post." We entered the opening and Alec stood there along with Iva. Both of them looked angry with me, nothing new. It really irked me. I was a grown woman, for heaven's sake. I kept my face calm as I waited for them to interrogate me.

"Aimee, you passed the bathroom," Iva said, making a point. A smart remark was at my lips but I decided to behave.

"I knew after a while you went down the wrong hall." Iva's concern caught me off guard; there was warmth behind her ice-grey eyes.

I still wouldn't give into them. And why would I? I wasn't sorry. These people could be killers for all I knew.

Alec just nodded at Marcus, not even looking at the sexy man next to me. I felt another grin cross my lips.

"Thank you, Marcus, for bringing me back," I said, in a sassy kind of way. Alec had disgust written all over his face and openly shared it, his eyes narrowed on me.

Marcus smiled at me before turning to leave; I watched him as he disappeared around the corner. Alec was suddenly in my face.

"Do you have any idea the danger you were just in?" Alec said, holding my shoulders. His calm attitude was on the verge of snapping. Alec was pretty tall and I felt short under his gaze. And I was a tall girl at 5'9".

"No, I didn't, because no one seems to tell me anything. I was lucky, then, to run into Marcus," I said, backing away from Alec, remembering why I had run in the first place. In fact, I should have been terrified of them.

"HA. Yes, he wasn't dangerous just now, but there are things you should be aware of, Aimee. This place has certain dangers. One of them, you just walked in on. Some things never change." That haunted look returned to his eyes. "Just, please, next time think before you run."

I leveled my eyes with Alec's. "Can you explain the bags of blood?" I blurted out, catching Iva and Alec off guard. "I think I have a right to know what dangers you speak of." I crossed my arms and leaned against the wall. Iva and Alec exchanged looks.

"That is something I can't tell you!" His eyes softened.

"You can't tell me? Right, this is why I'm so confused and angry, because you won't tell me things! Why should I stay?!" I could feel my anger escalating as well as my voice; a few passers glanced at me curiously.

Iva and Alec glared at each other, clearly not knowing what to do.

"Perhaps we should take her to see Rose?" Iva suggested, taking a breath.

"Rose said she would summon us when the time was right . . . but what If we just showed up?" Alec pondered that thought for a moment. Running his hands through his tresses, he clearly was frustrated. "Okay," he said, and Alec abruptly began walking; it took a moment for his actions to sink in. Iva, however, in sync with Alec, was moving. The sudden turn in events made me worried; did I want to see Rose? Why couldn't they just tell me what they knew?

Before I knew it we were on the other side of the court when Alec motioned to Iva with a nod. She disappeared into the crowd. Facing me, Alec looked straight into my eyes; my breathing stopped. I should have been terrified of Alec, but I wasn't.

"Aimee, I cannot go with you. I will speak with the secretary at the front desk, but you will be going alone." In Alec's eyes I saw more than concern.

"I have been alone most my life, I doubt whatever the old lady has to say to me will change anything."

His lips went into a hard line. "You haven't been alone your whole life!" he said as he went to speak with the secretary at the desk. I stood next to a large koi pond, with a fountain bubbling in the middle. The desk where the woman sat was in front of a large glass door. All the buildings had unique forms. There were different names on the front of each store. My fingers were going numb due to me squeezing my hands so hard. I had no idea what was to come. Alec caught my eye and signaled me to come to him. I took unsure steps toward him.

"Beth is going to escort you now. I'll be waiting for you here," Alec said.

"How long will I be in there?" My voice was shaking a little.

"I don't know. Everything will be okay." He squeezed my shoulder, and the electricity returned with his touch, along with a flood of emotions. How I could feel, safe, terrified, and attracted all at the same time when I was with Alec was beyond me.

"Aimee, I'm ready for you." The short woman named Beth was standing near the glass door. She wore a very arrogant expression, and even was more smug than Iva.

Four

I NEVER FELT SUCH EMOTION RUSH over me. This place felt strange but also gave me a sense of belonging. Everything was just so confusing. What waited for me inside this room before me? What answers would I find? Sitting outside another door, in a glass hall (yes, glass), I could see the fish swimming below my feet, and there were white lilies in vases all around. It was my favorite flower, the same I had had at my engagement party.

I wondered what was so important about this woman I had met so briefly the night before. What could she possibly tell me? My thoughts were interrupted by Beth. She was shorter than the other women in the . . . well, I didn't know what this place was, but she was gawky and her crazy, untamable, curly, auburn hair was pulled away from her face. She looked at me with a cold stare. Whatever I had done to her that made her stare at me like that was beyond me. I just glared back at her.

"Mrs. Bazile is ready now. This way."

I stood up and walked through the open door she held for me. Her icy grey eyes lingered on me a bit longer than I felt comfortable with.

The room was lit dully, the windows that showed the real outside had a UV ray resistant glass. Or at least it appeared that way. I almost wanted to go to the window and feel the warmth on my face and see the outside.

The floor in this room also was glass with swimming fish. It was quite beautiful. White sofas and lounge chairs were scattered over the room in clusters. Flowers were painted on the walls, lilies to be exact, and there was a large desk off to the side. The woman I noticed was putting her book down on her desk as I entered. Standing, she gracefully walked towards me.

"Aimee." She placed a shaky hand on my shoulder. It took every ounce not to brush her hand off; my pulse was racing. Her hands were pale white, her hazel eyes soft and confident, her greying hair in an intricate braid.

"Please come and sit with me."

Moving toward the couch, taking a seat close to her, I felt comfortable. I couldn't explain why. I wasn't as afraid of Rosemarie as I thought I would be.

She was watching me. "I know you have many questions to ask me, Aimee, about who we are and why you're here. But, I must know first, what is the oldest memory you have that you can think of?"

She studied me for a moment longer and I turned my head to stare at the wall. Why did these people always ask me that question? I wanted to tell her to leave me alone, but she hadn't shown me any reason to be rude.

Thinking about it, I wondered, what did I actually remember?

"Well, I remember waking up in a room; it was the hospital. A woman told me they didn't know who I was. They just knew my name, because the bracelet I wore had my name engraved on it. She said I had serious head trauma from an accident. My mother had died in the crash. I didn't stay there long."

I had met Derek soon after Elizabeth took me in. Rosemarie's hands lay gracefully in her lap. She nodded to herself; I guessed at something she was thinking.

"Do you know where you are now, as we speak?" she asked.

"I don't," I said, wondering if she would actually tell me.

"Good. Unfortunately, we cannot tell you this location. The things that have happened to this community—I can't risk it."

I didn't know what she was talking about; I sat quietly trying to be respectful, even though I was surging with anger and confusion that was boiling my inner core. I didn't want to unleash the angry Aimee, even though I had every right to be mad.

"I tell you this for your protection and the protection of the community."

"What happened to this community?" I asked.

"A long while ago, this community was broken into by a race that threatens our very existence, in order to ensure the survival of their race. By the time I realized that the community had been breached, my daughter was gone. Everyone else was otherwise unharmed and all were accounted for. They came, just for her. It was planned, and I don't know how they were able to get in undetected."

She spoke with such sadness. Her eyes looked past me.

I felt my arm hairs prickle up; that seemed to happen a lot being around these people. "What does this have to do with me?" I asked. My voice was raspy.

"It has everything to do with you . . . ." Rosemarie's eyes rested on me. "I wish there were an easier way to tell you this, Aimee, after everything you have been through over the last six years. I can't even imagine, but I cannot put it off. I must tell you." Rosemarie paused a moment. "You're my daughter." Her voice was strong, yet had a gentle demeanor.

Shock, anger, and confusion, washed over me, but mostly shock. This couldn't be the truth; wouldn't I feel a connection to my so-called mother? During the last six years I had tried to deal with the fact that my mother was dead and that Derek's family was my family, maybe because he had been telling me that since I met him. Why, Lord? Looking back into the eyes of my "mother," I inhaled deeply.

"I'm from Florida! My mother is dead! None of this makes any sense," I said, trying to reassure myself.

"For six years, yes, I suppose you spent those days in Florida. It was a lie they told you. I'm your mother. For the earlier years of your life, you spent your days here with me and with your father. That was up until the Rogues captured you. I'm amazed you did not turn—grateful, actually. Do you know who the Rogues are? The ones who took you, by any chance?"

"I don't have any idea what you are talking about! Rogues? Turned into what? And how would I end up in Florida?" My voice went up an octave and my collected self began to unravel.

"I'm not sure how you ended in up in Florida. I assume the Rogues lost you along the way; to start the turning process they erase the memory of your previous life, so you can start new with their twisted ideas. That's what they did to you. You weren't in an accident. Rogues are what we call wild werewolves. They are cruel, killing out of lust to take lives!"

Werewolves? Was this woman on crack? There is no such thing. I was sure my face showed my exact feeling, as it always does Suddenly, like a light bulb, I understood—blood, pale skin, all of them having the same grey eyes. Of course, all the signs were right in front of me; I knew what these people were. If I asked, though, would she tell me? I wondered. Did I want to know? Could I believe it? I was grasping the cushion that I placed in my lap. I wanted to scream; I was terrified beyond comprehension.

"What are *you* exactly?" I asked. I needed to hear it. I needed to make sure I wasn't going crazy, not that I could believe this nonsense anyway.

"I think you already know . . . I can see it on your face," she said, smiling.

Could I say what I was thinking without screaming? If she was my mother, how come I wasn't one of them? How did everything get so twisted in two days? I was really reconsidering my jumping off the yacht now, but which was worse, a murdering fiancé or these creatures? The word was at the tip of my tongue.

"Vampires." The word came out of my lips softly and had a sour taste. I think sickness had truly come over me. Feeling a bit woozy, I glanced at the ground. Then I looked into her face.

Rose's face wasn't shocked. Instead, she sat there, peaceful, while I wanted to get as far away from this place as I could.

"Yes, the new age likes to think of us as the keepers of night. But, more or less, we are vampires."

My mouth hung open and I pointed a finger at my so called vampire mother. "If I am your daughter, why am I not one of you, then?"

"We never awakened you. We were born with the genes of our ancestors. We were raised in communities, like this one, with the already awakened vampires. When we mature to a certain age, we make the choice to be awakened as a vampire, or we can stay as we are. Humans cannot be awakened unless they possess the genes of vampires. In the communities, it is unlikely to meet a human, since we are all vampires here."

"Are you immortal?" I asked, still not believing what she was explaining.

"We do live longer than humans; we age more slowly, but eventually we die of old age. We are mortal. Just with a few more perks. We aren't easily killed."

My brain became overloaded. I couldn't process what Rosemarie was telling me; I didn't want to. Everything that I believed conflicted with what she was telling me. Alec and Iva, both were vampires. Luckily, in some twisted way, I wasn't. My so-called vampire mother was watching me; most likely she was waiting to see if I would combust, which wouldn't be a bad thing at this point. It would save me from this nightmare. I was on the brink of jumping out of my seat.

"Why are you telling me this? Why couldn't you let me be?" I asked.

"Because I'm not one for waiting long. Six years is a long time to be away from your daughter, Aimee, too long. You needed to know the truth no matter what state your mind is currently in. Everything you were told was a lie."

"I don't know if I believe it, any of it! I never even met these so-called Rogues. I don't even know what one would look like." Had Derek lied to me all these years? Did he let me believe I was alone and needed his family? The room became blurry; everything around me felt as though it were speeding up. My breath was uneven; the fire in my chest was heating up. That's one thing that had never changed, the burning flame, which I always felt in me, warming my fingers.

"Rogues, or if you prefer the term werewolf, look like normal people. When they change form, that's when you know their true identity. That, and their eyes, they change color." She touched my hand; I lifted my eyes to her. "I know this is a lot of information to digest. It must be scary and you must think of me as a monster. I won't harm you. And you have choices to make. I hope you stay. I have missed you so."

I was skeptical still. I couldn't believe the things I was being told, or maybe I just didn't want to believe them. It was utterly ridiculous. I wasn't even sure if I was mad still or just numb.

"I do believe things happen for a reason, which is why I think you're back. It's been six years since I saw you last. I hope I don't lose you again."

The door opened and the mass of curly, auburn tied-back hair stood quietly at the door. Rosemarie acknowledged Beth was back in the room and nodded at her.

"Your highness, the council has arrived from Spain," Beth said.

Highness? Was she royalty? Am I royalty?

Rosemarie stood, glancing down at me. "We shall speak again soon. Beth will show you the way back to Alec."

I nodded to her. Rising from the couch gave me a feeling of floating. My mind was spinning as I began to leave. I was almost at the door.

"Aimee?" Rosemarie said.

"Yes?" I said as I turned toward her.

"I am truly happy you are back home." With that said, Beth led me back to the entrance. I could see Alec standing, still waiting for my return.

I kept my eyes down as I approached him. How could this be real? Why couldn't I be ignorant to all this? What's worse was that my life for the last six years could have been a lie. Surely Derek didn't know any of this. And what about Elizabeth? I wanted to drown out these emotions. I didn't know if I wanted to cry or scream in rage. Maybe both. I nearly forgot Alec was standing next to me. I turned my unfocused gaze toward him.

"Aimee?"

I wasn't sure what I looked like to him at that moment. I could only imagine my shocked face was most likely green.

"Aimee, are you all right? Do you need to lie down?" Alec asked as he touched my shoulder. I jumped slightly from the touch. He was after all, a vampire. That is, if Rosemarie was telling me the truth.

"I'm not sure, Alec."

He gasped when I spoke his name for the first time aloud. I looked at him, puzzled, as I continued to speak. "I don't know where I belong or if this is just a bad dream and I can't wake up. All I know is two days ago my life was planned out for me. I thought I knew everything only to find out now that my mother isn't dead. Instead, she is a vampire, and I could be one as well. What exactly am I?" I said, still unsure I believed these shenanigans.

"Before you awaken, you are called a Yurnling. Meaning, as children we yearn to be vampires. The age of Awakening is 18. It's part of the graduation ceremony," Alec said. I still was caught up with his Italian accent. He could be cursing at me and I still would've listened to him speak. I shook my head as if I could clear everything out of it.

"Oh. Well, what am I supposed to do now? Why didn't you just let Derek's family find me?"

"You don't have to do anything at the moment. Your mind has been through a lot, and you need to rest." Pausing, he tried to either steady me or comfort me. "As for leaving you to Derek, I couldn't do that. Knowing who you truly are, I couldn't walk away from you."

Alec's eyes were full of such warmth as his eyes bore deep into mine; I couldn't help but smile.

Changing the subject, my mind was running a million miles an hour, and I thought of how food was beyond me. Actually, it wasn't so far out of my mind, because I loved food.

"Do you eat food?" It was a question that didn't surprise him; it was also a concern I felt. I was horrified, and yet, here I stood, talking to a vampire.

"I can eat food, but I survive off blood. Most of the people here have never seen a real human; all they know is this . . . ." He pointed around the court. "We have a blood bank."

"Blood bank? And who exactly donates?" I asked.

Alec smiled, trying to conceal his laughter. "We have fake blood mobiles that go around, quite a few, actually."

"And who are the drivers? Vampires?"

"Not vampires, werewolves," Alec said.

"Right, werewolves. That makes total sense. I'm assuming they're the good werewolves?" I asked sarcastically. "And people just donate blood?"

He cocked his head to the side as he took hold of my face, which sent chills through my body. I could have sworn my heart skipped a beat. Every fiber of my being told me to be afraid, to panic, run away. Yet I trusted him. He hadn't harmed me. Everything I learned was unreal, but my body wanted to know the truth.

"Yes, the humans donate."

"And the werewolves?" I asked.

"Yes, the good ones," Alec said giving me a crooked smile.

"Were we friends before I got kidnapped?" I asked, still not one hundred percent believing the story. However, I was intrigued with what Alec's role was in everything.

"Yes. You could say that," He smiled, but the smile quickly faded. "You and Iva used to be very close."

That thought wasn't so farfetched. There was something about her that I felt so connected to even though she was a bit uptight. She and Krissy seemed a lot alike. That thought made me really sad. My mood quickly became dark.

"I wish I could remember something, anything." I said.

"For now, I think you should rest; I will get you for dinner later."

Could I really eat with all these feelings and emotions flowing through me? Thinking hard about it, the answer was yes. Food and I were pretty close. That was a surprise to most considering my figure never changed. It was always toned.

"What do I wear?"

"Anything," Alec said, not taking his eyes off me; we made our way to my room in silence.

Everything was a blur to me; I couldn't focus on anything in particular. I wished I couldn't feel anything at all. I was so confused with the overload of information I received. Before I knew it, we were standing in front of my door. Alec motioned to leave, but I saw him hesitate.

"Will you be okay if I leave for a while?" he asked, as his fingers lightly caressed a wild strand of hair and tucked it behind my ear a little uneasily; his hand was shaking. My heart nearly jumped out of my chest. His fingers were so close to my face. He was, after all, a vampire, yet deep down I knew I could trust him. My attraction to Alec seemed to grow.

"As well as I can be." I said.

He turned on his heels gracefully with one last smoldering look.

"Wait, I have one more question."

Glancing over his shoulder, he said, "Yes, Aimee?"

"Can you go out into the sunlight?" It was a dumb question, but I was known for not thinking before I spoke.

His smile grew, showing me his teeth for the first time. And there they were. Fangs. They weren't as scary as I'd imagined, though.

"Can't you tell by our tans?"

"Tans? You're pale." Realization dawned on me. Duh. "So that's a no."

"It's a no." Amused once more on my behalf, Alec reached out, almost brushing his fingers against my cheek. He stopped abruptly, pulling back. My body, standing so close to him, became alive. I wanted him to touch me. I braced myself, but the touch never happened. I felt a little disappointed, and my breathing faltered.

"See you soon," was all he said, and he was gone.

Five

DEREK STROKED MY FACE GENTLY.
I was drowning in his deep green eyes. They held a secret waiting to be unlocked. My hair blew fiercely in the wind. The moment was peaceful as we sat on his porch in Florida. It was a gorgeous day. These were days I craved. Derek caught my attention by touching my shoulder. His touch teased me, leaving me wanting more.

"Aimee, I miss you so much. Why did you leave me?" Derek's voice almost sounded as though he was hurt.

I could hear the subtle sound of the waves breaking on the shore. I loved his house. We shared a hammock and sat very close together. My heart ached for him. But it didn't just ache for Derek. A new feeling had grown. One I didn't believe quite yet.

The ocean was the best feature of the place. His hand felt warm as he laced his fingers with mine. I couldn't remember a time when he was so relaxed with me.

"You don't remember why I left you?" I asked. I was surprised he couldn't remember that night, when it haunted me so much. But then again, he didn't see me.

"No, I don't. I can come get you. Where are you?" His voice was soft, like silk. His lips were close to my ear. There was something missing. He felt so real holding me. It reminded me of the night I left him, when I was at the Enclave Hotel.

"I don't know where I am, Derek. I found out a lot of things, things I don't know if I believe are real," I said softly.

He got off the hammock and kneelt in front of me holding my hands.

"I meant it, Aimee; I want to spend my life with you. I love you." His eyes showed the kind of love I always felt for him. His lips moved oh so close to mine, but the world around me became hazy. I was waking up. This was all just a dream.

My eyes opened as I heard a phone ringing close to my head. Rubbing my eyes, I reached for the phone blindly.

"Hello?" I answered angry.

"Aimee, dinner is in an hour," came Alec's voice.

"Okay," I said, hanging up the phone. I sat up, a little disoriented.

My dream, it felt so real, Derek was so real. I felt the pang of his lost touch. I'm so stupid! He murdered my best friend! God only knows how many others he's killed and I'm dreaming about him? I'm really pathetic! Kicking the sheets off me angrily, I scampered over to my closet, thrusting the doors open.

A yellow, satin dress hung in the back of the closet. It caught my attention immediately. It was pretty and scandalous-looking. I wasn't sure how dressy the dinner would be, but a wearing a scandalous dress never killed anyone. My smile grew. Slipping the dress on, it fit in all the right areas.

I managed to put my thick hair up in a loose bun. It was a bit challenging. Then I added the finishing touch with some gold shadow around my eyes. My makeup pulled the look together. All of a sudden, I heard a knock at the door. I almost dropped my mascara in the sink. My heart immediately began pounding.

"Coming!" I shouted. I took one last look at the dress I wore.

I opened the door slowly. Alec looked as though he was holding his breath as he stared at me. His grey eyes went wide. I felt a bit uneasy under his gaze.

"Is this all right to wear? I didn't know if it was fancy or casual," I said, knowing I would've still worn the dress anyway.

He cleared his throat and closed his mouth. "If you want to cause an outburst, then it's perfect." His gawking made me smile.

"Then let's get going," I said, a bit too excited.

He looked rather dashing himself in his black slacks and black, long sleeved, button down shirt. His hair was loose and, for the first time I noticed that entwined in his locks he had barely visible gold metal beads, very much like something you would see in a movie based in Rome. It looked sexy. As I watched him all I could think of was "Greek God." Alec looked at me and I was sure he noticed me staring at him; he instantly tensed up. He didn't seem to like it when I watched him, or so it seemed.

The dinner hall doors were wide open and had what appeared to be very tall deep cherry tree trunks for pillars and, as we got closer, I noticed engravings in them of moons and vampires. I didn't see any werewolves. I traced my finger over the engravings, just to admire the detail. Someone cleared her throat next to me; I looked up and Iva was smiling at me. She looked breathtaking. She wore a simple off the shoulder, knee length, black cocktail dress; her hair was tousled and looked fresh.

"Aimee, you look fabulous. I wonder who picked that dress out?" She giggled.

Iva wasn't as uptight tonight as she had been earlier. It was refreshing.

"Uh, I believe you did. You look amazing as well!" We both smiled at each other.

The man at the entrance nodded at us, giving me an extra glance as we walked past him. I had never seen a banquet quiet like this before, except maybe in a movie. It was fit for royalty. The lights were dimmed, which gave off a seductive atmosphere. The centerpieces on every table overflowed with flowers I didn't even know the names of. They were large and deep purple with white orchids, lilies and huge white roses. The table cloths looked ivory and satin. I was dressed appropriately, seeing as many people were dressed rather exquisitely. The tables were shaped like a horseshoe; the main table, where my mother would sit, was at the head of everyone and the dance floor was in the middle. I heard soft music playing and saw a woman playing a harp. It felt like a royal reception. I noticed my so-called parents mingling with some bald man. Beth hovered close by, looking anxious. What she was anxious about being in a place like this was beyond me.

"Do I have any brothers or sisters?" I curiously asked Iva.

"No, unfortunately, it's only you."

"Oh . . . . Where do we go now?" I asked. A few guys my age strolled by nearly stopping at the sight of me, but the expression on Alec's face gave them warning to keep walking. I nearly started to laugh, but held it in.

"Next to your parents," Alec said, cocking his head to the side.

"Are you two coming with me?" I certainly didn't want to go alone. Alec, in his cool way, just nodded at me as we walked closer to them. My parents were standing on a stage. I didn't even know how I felt saying that those people on stage were my parents; I felt no connection to them whatsoever. I was left with a feeling of disbelief, and fear.

The stage was only slightly raised. Alec grasped my hand to help me up the stairs. His hand was warm and sent a wave through me. I almost didn't want his hand to let go of mine. Aimee, get a grip! I thought to myself. I shouldn't be having feelings of this kind of attraction for Alec. It was unsettling. We locked eyes for a fraction of a second until my thoughts were interrupted again. Only this time, by my vampire mother Rosemarie.

"Aimee, you look beautiful!" Rosemarie said, bringing my attention to her. My father, Ralph, looked at me and I could see the pride in his eyes. But he hadn't really talked to me since I met him again, and I would feel awkward speaking with him alone.

"How are you feeling? I'm surprised you didn't run away." Rosemarie touched my arm gently. A moment of fear passed through her eyes.

"Alec, I want to thank you for watching out for my daughter and bringing her back to us." Her gaze fell on Alec as if he was some nobleman or something. Alec's face, however, looked serious, yet his lips twitched slightly.

My father approached me, his eyes prickling with tears.

"Welcome home," was all he said, he most definitely would've started to cry if he had said more, which was obvious by the tears in his eyes.

Lost for words, I focused my eyes on the mass of people standing before us. A tiny balding vampire man came to the microphone. He tapped it lightly. He began to speak. He, too, had an Italian accent.

"Good evening. If everyone could please find their seats, dinner will be served momentarily. We have an important guest with us tonight." His voice echoed the room, filling it with his presence.

My heartbeat quickened slightly, a brief moment of unfathomable fear came over me. Was he going to announce me in public? More panic coursed through my body. I reached out and gripped the back of my chair. I was on the verge of hyperventilating and was really uncomfortable. Alec came closer to me almost like he could sense my feelings of uneasiness. I was unable to look at Alec, remaining focused on the back wall. I waited for the moment to pass by.

"Congresswoman Ivete Kroshkman from Russia has graced us with her most gracious presence . . . ."

Ivete was pleased by the gesture of the man and rose to wave at the crowd. Her black, waist—length hair was silky. Her icy grey eyes showed pure amusement as she smiled. The velvet floor-length dress she wore looked like she had made it from my curtains. She finally sat down, as did my parents.

The man was groveling for this Ivete woman. So I tuned the announcer out. I was just happy I wasn't the target of the night. More than happy, I was ecstatic!

Alec pulled my chair out for me so I could take my seat. Iva nearly smiled at the gesture. My parents were speaking with Ivete. Even thinking of them as my parents was strange. For six years I'd thought I would never see my parents. I'd thought my mother was dead. But, as I studied them, I noticed we had very similar features. Well, my mother and I had similar features. I didn't see any of Ralph in me. One thing that really stood out to me was my mother's hazel eyes. Hazel like mine and not grey like the rest of the crowd of vampires. Alec touched my leg by accident as he pulled his chair in. It nearly caused my heart to stop. Alec, for a brief moment, I could have sworn, stopped breathing. The touch sparked something within us both.

Sitting in between Alec and Iva, I wondered what we would be eating; Alec said they didn't live off food.

And so, dinner was served. It was a type of steak. I didn't seem to be really cooked. It was so rare, it might as well have still been mooing. Luckily, they made my dish medium rare. I sighed in relief.

Iva leaned in close to me. "Not what you expected, is it?" Iva asked.

"Well, no. I thought you might be sacrificing a human or something," I said sarcastically. Her lips tightened as she held in her laughter.

When dinner was finished, Iva and I excused ourselves to go to the restroom. I began following Iva afraid of what I would find if I went alone again. I shivered slightly at the memory of the blood.

A very built man stood by the door. I recognized him immediately. Messy, dark brown hair, very rugged face.

"Hey Marcus," I said. He looked around before he acknowledged me. Marcus gave me a sly smile. His eyes were a lovely shade of green. Wait, green? I could have sworn they were honey brown when I saw him this morning. *Maybe it was the light*, I thought to myself.

"Are you staying out of trouble?" His smile was taunting.

"As much as I can, trouble sort of finds me," I said. Iva poked my back clearly not wanting me to speak to Marcus.

"We need to get going," Iva said in her polite voice.

"Maybe we will meet again?" He asked, hopeful. I began to open my mouth, but Iva pushed me forward. So all he got was a half-smile.

Walking out of earshot, she gave me a warning look.

"Aimee, did Rose speak of Rogues?" Iva's voice was a whisper.

"Yes. Why?"

"Then you should know, they hunt Yurnlings, and kill the innocent . . . Marcus is a werewolf. He may not be a Rogue, but he is still dangerous. Some werewolves choose to live among us. They act as protectors and have the freedom they wouldn't have living among the Rogues. He is dangerous! Don't speak to him again," Iva exclaimed. Her very calm and uptight demeanor faltered a fraction.

Who was she to tell me who I can or can't speak to? She doesn't own me! I thought before saying anything aloud.

"Well, what can I do in this underground cage?"

"It isn't a cage, Aimee. Rose told you, you can make your own decision. We would like you to stay."

"If this is freedom, then I should be allowed to speak to whomever I wish, wolf or not!" My temper always got the better of me. "What's there to do down here, besides not talking to the werewolves?" I asked sarcastically.

Iva brushed off my mood. "Lots of things. You have only been here a day. You should wait until you're out of shock before we throw you into the lifestyle of this CAGE." Iva smirked then turned her back on me as we walked into the decked-out bathroom. Well, actually, decked out was probably an understatement. Everything was marble and pristine, unlike a public bathroom. A chandelier hung from the ceiling over each individual sink. It was a bathroom that would be in a master suite bedroom.

Iva waited for a vacant toilet as I washed my hands. I wasn't in shock anymore as Iva had said. Maybe I was just numb to everything around me. Derek was so far gone. I missed his green eyes. The ache of him being gone was still pounding in my chest. I loved him, as hard as it was to come to terms with. I could feel my eyes prickling with hot tears. I had to keep myself together.

Derek and Marcus actually had the same colored eyes, I realized, while I stood there thinking to myself. I shook my head to drown Derek out.

I knew it; I was going to end up old and alone. That thought scared me. I didn't want to die a virgin or unmarried. And, yes, I was a virgin, or so I thought, I couldn't actually remember.

"Come on," Iva said impatiently.

A tall vampire woman glared at Iva as she exited the stall; apparently she'd overheard Iva's remark. Iva simply rolled her eyes at the woman as she finally entered the stall; I took that opportunity to sneak away from Iva. I knew it was wrong to try to ditch her, but she was killing any chance I would get to meet guys. I was desperately trying to forget Derek and I thought Marcus could make a great substitute.

I walked back into the dinner hall and anxiously scanned the crowd for Marcus. I spotted him across the room along the back wall. He wasn't hard to miss.

I couldn't walk across the room to him because, unfortunately, everyone was here and walking across the room would be a journey in itself. I decided to creep along the back wall, figuring it would be more effective. I was almost there when I felt those known hands gripping my shoulder and suddenly turning me around. Alec stood there with an amused expression and his arms crossed. He was so stealthy, a true ninja in disguise.

"Ditching Iva, huh?" His eyebrows rose.

"She needed her space, I think, no need to babysit me." Alec gave me that "don't lie to me" face.

"I'm not under house arrest. Rose said I was free to make my own choices," I said, exasperated.

"That may be so, but not free to wonder off to go speak to the werewolf."

How did he know what my intentions were? I had no response, so I just glared at him. Why couldn't he just leave me alone?

"Can you just take me to my room then? If I'm not allowed to mingle with people, then I'd rather go to bed and dream!" I said, being overly dramatic.

"You can mingle, just not with werewolves." His voice sounded low and dangerous, all that amusement vanished. His eyes narrowed on me.

"If they are so dangerous, why are they in the hall with us? And you're treating me like a child." My voice was escalating and a few passing girls glanced at me.

"Because you are acting like one. All you do is argue with everything I say. I . . . your family cares about you and they are worried about your mind being scarred or in shock from what you've learned in a day. Werewolves won't guard your feelings and their moods can change in an instant. One emotional outburst and they transform into a monster, which is why it is not safe." His face showed such an intense look. The electricity was flowing between us. In the heat of an argument, why did my attraction to him come out more? I was supposed to be angry, not thinking about how good-looking he was. And that's when it happened. My eyes became unfocused, almost like a feeling of the lights being turned off. I could hear Alec's voice in the distance, but it was tuned out. There was a small light in the distance. It was getting brighter.

The feeling that was happening to me was strange, almost like an out-of-body experience. I started envisioning things. Was this real? I was standing in the same dinner hall, but my outfit was less dressy.

I was wearing black, high-waisted, skinny jeans with a silky top and heels. I liked this outfit. It was like a movie. I watched myself stand in the empty room and I stood waiting expectantly for someone. Even though I was viewing this scene before me, I could feel everything the past Aimee was feeling: anxiety, excitement, and love. The door behind me opened, and my heart was beating rapidly in excitement and anticipation.

"Aimee." I heard this soft Italian accent behind me. His breath was at my neck, shooting chills down my spine. Turning my body to face him, Alec was smiling as he was leaning against a wall. His eyes, they were blue, like the ocean. He wasn't awakened yet. The way he looked at me, my heart was pounding through my chest. Could he hear it?

"Have you been waiting long?" he asked, leaning into me. His body was warm.

I could feel my answer, but I didn't have time to speak. Outside the door, I heard some kind of a commotion. Not even a moment later, the doors swung open and Iva came running in, terror on her face. She wasn't awakened yet, either.

"Aimee, we have to leave now! They are coming!" Her voice was shaking in fear as she took my hands in hers. She was almost pleading with me.

"What's going on?" I asked. Alec straightened up. His face looked serious now.

"The Rogues, they breached the building! Please, we have to leave now!"

Still holding my hands, Iva began pulling me toward the door. Responding immediately, I released her hands as I began sprinting behind her. Alec then grabbed my hand, like he was trying to keep me safe.

The hall was empty as far as we could see. My neck hairs began prickling up.

Our pace slowed as we rounded the corner, Iva ahead of us, like the warrior that she was. She glanced around before making the cross. She then gave an all clear signal. We crossed the main court as quietly as we could. I was so close behind Alec. But, even then, I wasn't safe. I felt a sudden pain, a pain so sharp in my legs, I stumbled and fell. My ankles had chains around them. It had happened so fast neither of them had had time to respond to it.

That's when I saw them, the Rogues I assumed. Somehow they had fired the chains at me. We hadn't even seen them coming. Looking up, Alec's eyes were full of shock. He was being held by two Rogues. Their faces where full of malice and they had blood at the corners of their snouts, growling at us. They stood tall, muscular, and had greyish brown skin. Eyes blood shot, they stood on their back legs; it didn't look normal. The terror ran through my body. I was completely helpless.

Iva was pinned to the ground and crying. One came stealthily behind me, taking his stance in front of me. Kneeling, his eyes looked into mine. My heart stopped as his lips curled into a terrible smile. He took the chains off my legs. I stood still, afraid to move. The Rogue's smell was so potent, like the smell of rotten meat. It was horrible. I was taking staggering breaths as I just waited.

"Aimee, we meet at last," he said in a cruel tone. His bloodshot eyes bore into mine. Like I weighed nothing, he picked me up, throwing me over his shoulders as he calmly made his way to the exit. I twisted my face up for one last glance at Alec; I saw the terror in his eyes. Alec was watching and there was nothing he or Iva could do about it. Our eyes locked one last time.

I suddenly got a throbbing headache and I felt like the room was spinning. Someone was shaking me and my eyes tried to focus on my surroundings while my body reacted in complete shock.

Alec was calling me; he sounded so distant and he was blurry. Still, I was unable to focus on him.

"Aimee?" Alec was shaking me gently. His voice sounded worried.

"Stop shaking me; I'm going to be sick," was all I was able to say; my voice sounded so distant.

Blinking back tears, I was violently shaking. Not because he was shaking me, but because I was full of terror from the memory. I just closed my eyes and began to sob.

"Aimee? Aimee? What happened? Iva, I think we need to bring her to Jules!"

I felt my body being lifted off the ground. Alec was carrying me, but that's all I remember. I was falling, into a blackness that engulfed me. Everything around me blacked out.

I heard voices before I opened my eyes. Waking up, still dizzy, my eyes trying to adjust to the light, I was surrounded by white colored walls. The deja vu of being back in the hospital where I met Elizabeth washed over me. It appeared to be a hospital or psychiatric room. The moment of when I woke up six years ago began to plague my mind. The day my life became a lie.

I was lying on a bed. I sat up slowly and cautiously. Alec had his face in his hands, looking paler than usual. Iva sat close by, glancing out of the little peephole in the door. They were both frozen at the sight of me.

"Where am I?" I asked, somewhat groggy.

Alec shot up gracefully and with two strides he was next to me. Worry was etched in his face. He wore the same expression as the day I was taken.

An odd realization came over me. The Rogue's cold, bloodshot eyes; there was something about them that I recognized.

"Jules will be here in a moment. Are you okay? The way you looked-"

I pushed my thoughts to the back of my mind. I was trying to appear strong now. I needed to escape this hospital room.

"I'm fine. Really I'm fine. I don't know why you are making such a big fuss," I said, trying to reassure them. They weren't buying it, I could tell.

Even though I tried to push the memory away it was consuming me, the anxiety was creeping in on me again. Could I tell him what I saw? Was the vision even real? How could I even comprehend that everything I believed the last six years was a lie? I had so many questions. The first question was, who was I? The second was why me, why did the Rogues want me? I didn't want to think anymore. This was just a bad nightmare that I so badly wanted to wake up from. I pinched myself. This caused Alec and Iva to raise their eyebrows at me.

"You are clearly not all right, pinching yourself?" Iva said as she crossed her arms. This gesture of Iva's was beginning to be her trade mark.

The door behind Alec opened, cutting off any comment I was going to make.

A short, older woman came forth, her hair pointed in all directions. She reminded me of an elf, like from Lord of the Rings.

"Hello, Aimee, my name is Jules," she said in a dreamy voice. She had such a gentle presence. She obviously was a doctor.

I sat there unable to say anything to her. Overwhelmed with emotion, I just stared at the floor. I was hoping they would all disappear.

"Aimee, do you want to talk about what happened?" She was sitting on a stool close to me, clipboard in hand. I was eyeing that board. As though Jules could read my mind, she set it down on the table near her.

How could I talk? This woman sure did cut right to the point. How would I even begin to express what I just saw without them thinking I was mental? But who knows? Even I thought I could be slightly off the rocker at this point.

"I'm fine, really. I think this was blown out of proportion." Pulling the blanket closer to me, I felt cold. Jules nodded as she waited patiently, glancing at Alec and Iva.

"Can I go back to my room? I'm tired," I said, without meeting their eyes.

"Yes, you can go. When you are ready to talk you can come to see me." She stood up. "Don't be afraid to come back," Jules said and left the room. Alec was about to protest, but it was Iva who gave him the death stare and Alec swallowed whatever remark he was going to make.

"Come on, Aimee; let's get you to your room," Iva said, soothing me. She was gently helping me off the bed. I was still woozy. Who was this weak girl? I felt like a coward. *This wasn't me*, I thought, silently protesting against myself. Alec was on the other side of me, trying to help guide me.

"Can you take her back? I'm sorry Aimee, I'm really thirsty." Iva looked really sorry. Thirsty meaning blood, I assumed.

Alec barely moved his neck.

"I'll be fine," I told Iva.

It felt like a long walk. Alec and I were close to my room and the silence was thickening around us. Silence and I didn't do so well together. People were most likely asleep and the hall had an eerie feel to it. I really didn't want to be in my room alone tonight. I was afraid of what I would see if I closed my eyes. *I'm being such a child right now! Why couldn't I just snap myself out of this rut and pull myself back together?* I realized Alec had stopped walking and, sure enough, my door was in plain view, number 156.

"Thank you for walking me back. I'm sorry for being so difficult. You have to understand that I'm feeling lost; I don't know who I am or where I belong anymore. And I feel stuck between two worlds." Tears were trickling down my face. Alec touched my shoulder in a soothing manner. His touch excited me more than soothed me.

"Aimee, I'm here for you; I always will be. Iva and I care about you. You can trust us," Alec said, softly.

I averted my eyes to the ground. I couldn't face him. I felt so weak.

"I know I can trust you . . . ." And I knew I could. But could I actually tell him what happened? How was it even possible to have a memory come back to me? Wasn't it erased? Nothing anymore seemed realistic. Or made any kind of sense.

"It was you, I saw you with me in my memory. You and Iva."

"Memory?" Alec asked.

"It was when the Rogues took me. You both were with me . . . ." I slowly raised my eyes; he was still, and I could see by his expression he was trying to grasp what I was telling him. "I do trust you."

Alec's hand was still on my shoulder. Like it was frozen there. His eyes looked haunted. He really was perfect looking, his pale skin and brown wavy hair, his lean body, built like a tennis player. God-like. If Rome saw this man in front of me, its statues would be carved after him.

He was so vulnerable looking, so sad. I needed to comfort him. It wasn't his fault I was taken. Reaching up, I pulled him into a hug. I held onto to him tightly. He was stiff at first and then held onto me, embracing me, his hands grasping my back, his face on my shoulder. It felt so right, like we fit together. I liked being close to him. A new sensation was growing, it was warm and light. Almost as if it was being awakened by Alec. I couldn't grasp this new desire or feeling.

"It's not your fault Alec. I saw it all, everything. You were with me then. And you're with me now," I said into his ear. We stood there like that for a few more moments; I hesitantly pulled away from him. My lips grazed his cheek by accident and my breathing stopped. Our eyes held each other's gaze; electricity passed through me. His lips were so close to mine, inches away. I could almost taste them. How could I feel this way? It was only days before I left Derek. Everything in this community triggered something deep within me.

"And I will always be here for you, Aimee!" Alec said fiercely. I could see that he was a protector.

Footsteps abruptly became louder, coming closer with each step. Alec backed away from me. Iva came into view, stress all over her face.

"Aimee, don't ever ditch me again!" Iva said angrily.

I guess she was holding it back in the hospital room. But she sure didn't hold back now.

"I'm sorry. I won't do it again," I said, trying to calm her.

"Do you have any idea what it's like to find out you left me and when I found you, you looked like you were in a coma!?" Iva said; for someone who is very collected, she looked a bit mental at the moment, with her arms flailing around her.

I walked up to Iva and hugged her. I really caught her off guard; she was stiff, in shock I assumed. But eventually Iva gave in to the hug.

"I'm really sorry, I won't do this to either of you again! I promise! With that said, I am really tired, but I don't want to be alone; can one of you stay with me tonight?" Alec and Iva nodded solemnly at me.

"Alec would you like the first shift?" Iva asked.

Alec just glared at her. I was unsure of why.

"If it's going to be a problem, then you don't have to stay with me." I said as I shifted awkwardly. I really hoped someone would stay, preferably Alec. Nobody spoke for a long moment.

"I can stay with you." Alec's voice was a whisper. His face was completely unreadable, yet excitement washed over me. I wanted Alec to stay with me.

After I changed into sleepwear, I went straight for my bed. I curled up in a ball under my covers. Sleep could have washed over me easily. I glanced around the room for Alec. I relaxed once I found him sitting in a chair, by the door. He, of course, had his inscrutable expression on as he leaned back into the chair, allowing the shadow to cast over his face.

"Thank you for being here with me," I said. I couldn't confess how terrified I actually was or how happy I was that it was Alec who stayed with me; it even took hard effort to keep the smile from my face.

He continued to just stare at the wall, which started to bother me. Why was he being so weird? Me and awkward silence never did well together. After a long while of agonizing stillness, he finally spoke.

"Can I ask you a question?"

I was considering what he would ask. "That depends."

Alec ignored my answer. "Did you have any memories while you were gone?"

"As far as I know, this was the first memory I had. But who really knows, because maybe I have before, but thought it was a dream," I said, shrugging into my pillow. "Tonight, though . . . was something different, I have not experienced something like that. It was so real. Like I was reliving it."

Tears began to blur my vision. Everything in the last couple of days had been an overwhelming overload. Derek still consumed my thoughts, and now there was me finding out I'm a Yurnling. Yes, my emotions were running high from the aftermath of everything, mixed with all this information I found out today. The tears escaped and rolled down my cheeks. I hid my face in my pillow. I wanted to sob, to release this knot in my chest, but I couldn't. I didn't want to seem weak in front of Alec.

"Aimee, I'm so sorry, so very sorry. I can't begin to express how much guilt I have. I let you down. You were with me and they took you. The Rogues' breaching was to get you and they won." His voice was so plagued, I could hear it.

I sat up after wiping the tears from my face. I strained my neck to get a view of his face. I could barely see his expression due to the shadow he was still engulfed in.

"It isn't your fault! They held you down, you and Iva. You are not to blame," I said quietly.

Alec stayed in the same position as before.

"Everything is just so new to me now. Do you have any idea what it's like? One day you think everything is a happy ending then, moments later, your world crumbles and you are left feeling empty, alone and so scared, with an overwhelming loss. I thought two days ago that I would be married by now, but instead I find out I'm, well, a Yurnling thing among vampires. And was apparently kidnapped by Rogues." As well as Derek being a murderous fiancé.

I just needed to talk, to vent, and it felt good to just let it out. I wanted to say so much more, to scream at the top of my lungs and release this hurt.

"I can't imagine how you're feeling, but I do understand about how quickly things change. My world was planned out too, Aimee. I was graduating and with a girl I loved. We had planned our future. I wanted to marry her." His voice cracked. "But now everything is gone; my world has changed, too. Life has another plan. Life goes on." Alec leaned out of the shadows and his face was still so sad looking.

My mind became curious. Who was this girl? A bit of jealousy was lingering in my chest.

"Did she die, the girl?" I asked, trying to keep my voice normal.

Alec leaned out enough, and I could see his eyes lifted to mine; his frown grew, a small crease forming between his eyes.

"It doesn't matter what happened to her; that girl is gone now. My point is that I can relate to that feeling you have." He leaned back into his curtain of darkness. I had a feeling he was hiding from my gaze. "You should sleep now."

I kept the lamp on as I lay back on my pillow. The truth was, I was indeed tired, but so many thoughts flooded my mind. I yawned as I tried to drown out the constant activity of today. Clearing my mind wasn't as hard as I thought it would be. And, finally, sleep found me.

Six

MY DAYS QUICKLY BECAME LOST. I wasn't really keeping up with the time or day, but I knew that today was Thursday. I'd been here a week now. Iva sat cross-legged, reading a magazine. I was lying on a white shabby-chic sort of couch in Rosemarie's glass room, watching the koi swim happily under my couch. Why couldn't I be a fish? Fish had no worries and no complications. Rosemarie's room was still the same as the first time I came in here. Big flower arrangements, lilies and orchids. Her desk was still a disarray of unorganized papers. Her large windows that looked outside were my only glance at sunlight. And, of course, the glass floor. It finally hit me that the smell in this room was sweet, reminding me of Sweet Tarts candy.

It was hard not to think about everything I had learned and was still learning. I was lucky to not have had nightmares about the Rogues who took me, but I dwelled on that one memory I had about them, that memory and Alec. I wanted to talk about everything I was feeling, but I couldn't. I didn't want to raise suspicion with Iva of what my feelings could be. Especially because I didn't know how I felt about Alec. Something about him was so familiar and comfortable. He seemed to heighten my anger issues, and bring out the child in me. But I couldn't deny these feelings no matter how infuriating he was.

Since the night when Alec stayed with me, I hadn't seen him much. I wanted to ask Iva where he was, but my own pride got in the way and I was left with curiosity killing me. Alec wouldn't leave for long, would he? And why would he leave at all?

My attention was drawn toward the blue sea glass door; it opened and Rose, my mother, walked in. Her willowy figure was draped in a lovely opal floor-length dress, made of a shimmery material. I still wondered what made her important to this community. I hadn't asked, but I was sure she was someone important. She casually glided ever so gracefully to her desk. She began looking through her papers.

"Have you ladies made your decision yet?" Rose asked. At that moment I remembered that I was supposed to make a decision on whether or not I would be a part of a Masquerade ball the committee was putting together. My parents were also very much involved in event planning. Rose thought Iva and I would be good candidates to help decorate. Decorating wasn't my strong suit. It bored me to tears. Even in Florida, Derek's family was invited to the most elite of parties or events and being a part of them didn't satisfy me. The only thing I liked about these big events was that I got to play dress up.

"Well . . .," was all that came out of my lips.

Rose chuckled at my response. "I think it would be nice for you to be involved in something where you will be around others your age. Maybe you will meet an eligible young man."

Iva laughed at this statement with a smirk on her lips.

"I'm not exactly interested in anyone here," I said, a small lie because I was attracted to Alec. And Marcus was cute. But at that moment I figured my days for a serious relationship should be put on hiatus.

"Sure . . .," Iva said sarcastically, as she rolled onto her side.

"I'm not! I'm done with men!" I said sternly, but even I thought it sounded utterly ridiculous. I knew as well as Iva that I couldn't be done with men.

"Aimee, one bad experience can't cancel out all future prospects," Rose said, and frankly she was beginning to annoy me.

"Yeah, yeah." I wished I could be alone right then.

"Has Alec returned yet?" Rose asked, catching my eye. She hid a glimmer of a smile.

My eyebrows rose up. I was in fact wondering where he was and happy she brought it up.

"I'm not sure when he'll be back. He didn't tell me where he was going," Iva said.

I sat up and pushed my long hair out of my face.

"Did he go search for the girl he loved?" I asked, remembering he told me about how he lost the woman he loved, and I didn't think it would be a far off idea if he had gone looking for her. The thought of it made me a little sad. I wanted someone to love me like that, enough to go to the end of the world to find me.

They both looked at me with such confusion on their faces. I instantly felt stupid for saying that out loud. There goes my speaking without thinking again.

"Aimee, where did you hear that?" Iva still had that 'what are you talking about?' expression on her face.

"He told me that he once loved a girl and she was taken from him," I said, digging my own grave and feeling bad about telling them something he told me. Maybe he didn't want to share that info with them. Iva raised her eyebrows at me and Rose was glancing at the clock on the coffee table.

"Oh, look at the time! I have a meeting in ten minutes. Aimee, you should take your place among the court function community with Iva. Planning the last minute details should be exciting for this masquerade ball."

I was thankful that Rose changed the subject. The ball would be fun, needless to say. I just wasn't interested in the planning part. Rose gracefully left the room.

"What are you going to wear?" I asked as I sank into the couch.

"Not sure yet. Do want to go shopping for a dress?"

"Now, that sounds like something I really want to do. Can we go now?" I said. My eyes lit up as I rose off the couch in excitement. Would this mean going above ground?

"Let's go," she said, smiling, reveling her fangs.

I grabbed her hands and pulled her to her feet.

We never did leave the community. All the shops were underground. I was a bit disappointed. Actually, I was more than disappointed, I was downright distraught. What designers could they possibly have? My answer came as we entered a really nice store; all kinds of designer clothes hung on racks everywhere I looked. It had the feel of BCBG, with how large the store was, yet it was cluttered from every angle.

"HEAVEN!" I said happily. A little vampire woman came over to us; she seemed eager for us to spend money or maybe she was just bored. Maybe it was both. Which reminded me. "Iva, do they except Visa cards?"

"You of all people should not worry; now shop!" Iva said.

Iva didn't waste any time; she was taking dresses off the rack and placing them in the woman's hands. I was stunned as I watched in a trance. This was clearly Iva's element. The poor woman, she was so little that I wasn't sure if she'd be able to see over the dresses. I held my laughter in as she waddled to the fitting room.

I spotted a red floor-length dress made of silk. It was the same dress I wore the night of my fast departure from Derek. Iva, as if sensing my uneasiness, came over to me. She glanced around and quickly spotted my nemesis.

"The dress did look really nice on you," she said as she tilted her head.

"It really did. I searched so many stores for a dress for that occasion . . . . Do you want to get married?" I asked. Iva's facial expression became comical, skeptical even.

"I haven't ever really thought about it. I guess if I met someone I could love. That's one problem with living in a community your whole life. You grow up with the guys that live here, too."

"Yeah. I could see how that could be a problem. Did I have a boyfriend before I was taken?"

Iva hesitated before answering me. "Not exactly a boyfriend—he was a bit more. You were in love, both of you. Ever since he joined us, you and he were always together . . . well, I was always there, too."

"Joined us? Where did he come from?"

"His family was seized and they were killed by the Rogues. He managed to escape and was found shortly after."

"Who was he?" I asked.

"I don't think I should be the one to tell you."

I almost protested but my eyes caught someone outside the window. Alec. Iva noticed him, too. Alec came toward us, grinning.

"So you have returned and may I ask where you went?" Iva asked slyly.

Shrugging and looking like his usual Greek god self, Alec smiled at us.

"I just needed to get out for a bit. What are you ladies shopping for?"

"Dresses for the ball, of course." Iva said smoothly. She wasn't flirting, but they were so comfortable with each other that a little bit of jealousy swept through me. Deciding I didn't want to feel like that, I turned my attention to the dress rack on the other side of the room.

My mood shot up quickly as I found a dress that I liked. It was a dark red, halter-style dress with a nice cleavage line, knee length, and tight. Yes, I had fallen in love.

In my peripheral vision, I could see Alec approaching. He cleared his throat. I was feeling childish, and I didn't know why, so I ignored him. My mood changed at that point. I wasn't mad at Alec, but I couldn't justify the way I felt for him. I think that's what made me mad, and when he was gone, he left me dangerously curious as to where he was. Either way it wasn't an excuse.

Running a hand through his brown locks he stepped closer to me. Just being near caused an eruption of butterflies. *Calm down*, I told myself. I was being extremely stupid.

"Is it safe to assume that you're also going to the ball?" His eyes were ice grey; I could easily fall into his smoldering gaze.

Instead I turned to admire the dress once more. I saw a flash in Alec's eyes as he looked at the dress.

"Yes, I am going. With Iva!" I said stiffly. Alec shifted so I could pass him. I was careful not to touch him or look at him. Being so close already was making me struggle not to just melt.

"Are you angry with me?" Alec's deep Italian accent caressed my skin.

His question took me off guard. I wanted to avoid answering it. It wasn't exactly anger. I was more annoyed. The more important question was why? He didn't do anything to make me treat him poorly. Ah, the joy of being a woman and an emotional wreck.

"Why would you think that?" I asked; the sharp tone was load and clear.

He moved his arm to block me from walking past him.

"I don't know, maybe because you look hostile." He was clearly amused.

"What are you getting at exactly?" My voice was shaking slightly. My mood was at a peak. Alec looked cautious, sensing it too, and once again he studied my eyes.

"Why do you keep studying my eyes like I'm an experiment?" I snapped, nearly dropping the dress.

"Have you looked at your eyes when you're mad?"

"Why would I do that? I already know what color they are," I said, crossing my arms, while glaring angrily at him.

"This is the second time; I could have sworn your eyes changed colors. Hazel to a, well, I don't know what color it was. It happened too fast." He was still looking into my eyes.

"Okay, stop. My eyes do not change colors! And, excuse me, but I have a dress to try on." I pushed his arm out of the way and he grabbed my waist, turning me around. My breathing was staggered, mixed with excitement. Everything he did was spontaneous; I couldn't read his mysterious ways.

"Can you just calm down. I wanted to ask you something." Alec's expression softened and he started to look like the younger Alec from my memory.

"And that is?" I asked with a hard expression. Iva came out of the dressing room looking at us curiously as she came closer. Perfect timing. What a cliffhanger!

"Wow, now that's sexy!" she said, looking at the red dress I held. "You'll most likely have a few dates after they see you in that!" She smiled happily. Alec, on the other hand, well if he had had color in his flesh, it would've been gone.

"Don't you agree, Alec?" Iva asked sweetly.

His lips went into a hard line. "Maybe she'd get some dates, if she could manage to be nice and less moody," Alec said. I smacked him hard on his shoulder, which caught him by surprise.

"It doesn't matter what you think, because I may be moody with you, but I most definitely will not be toward an actual prospect!" I said passionately. His eyes flashed, and I then regretted being so cruel.

"Okay, so we have lots to do, Aimee."

Iva began pushing me over to the register while dismissing Alec in that polite way of hers, called the "nod and smile."

Sitting cross legged, I was irritated beyond words to express and baffled by the job I was asked to do. How Iva and I ended up on the committee was beyond me. We didn't even agree to it. Yet here we were in the dinner hall setting up the decorations. I was grouchily glaring at all the people scurrying around. They put me in charge of the flowers and the room was massive. I began attempting to assort and put carnations together, white and red mixed with some kind of black flower. This was a cruel punishment; my fingers hurt. I was originally assigned to the balloons with Iva, but we were playing with the helium so much that Zara, the gal who is the head of the committee, got annoyed and sent me here to put the flowers together.

"Hi, are you Aimee?" a skinny, curly red-headed vampire girl stood before me; she seemed to be one of those people who would be a loner and was uncomfortable talking to people she didn't know, or any kind of person in general. She dressed in ordinary jeans and a T-shirt that was too big for her.

"It depends on what she is needed for," I said grumpily.

"Oh, mum, Zara wanted me to help you fix the flower arrangements."

Fix? I wasn't fooling anybody with my lack of creativity, but still Zara was getting on my nerves; she should be grateful that I was doing this at all.

"Okay," I said. I was a bit offended and wanted to leave, but my chances of escape were as slim as this red headed girl helping me with fashion advice.

We sat in silence as I copied her lead in rearranging the flowers. I had to give this girl credit. She was very creative. Wanting to stretch my legs a bit, I stood and backed away from the red head. She glanced up at me, confused.

"I will be right back, bathroom," I said. I was very aware that she knew I was lying as I walked toward Iva and the hot man next to her. What I wasn't expecting was that Zara would tap me on the shoulder. Her bleached-blonde hair was cropped short and slick. Her sharp features would be pretty if she wasn't so arrogant and bossy. Grey eyes narrowed on me, clipboard in hand, foot tapping.

"Where are you going?" she asked in her annoying bossy voice.

"To the bathroom." I lied.

"Sure, the bathroom is in the opposite direction."

"Thanks, I didn't know where it was. I will be going now." Quickly turning to leave her examining eyes, I heard her "tsk" at me.

"Just because the Leader of our world is your mother doesn't mean I have to like you! I plan on having the ball perfect and the same with further events. If that includes you being kicked out of here, then I will personally escort you!"

What a witch! But, the good thing was she told me why my mother was important! My mother was the leader of this community. It wasn't a surprise.

"I'd like to see you try!" I said, in a snarky voice.

"Things can be arranged." She then made a note on her clipboard and headed off to go yell at someone else.

Mimicking her last facial expression while turning my head, I almost ran into someone. Brushing my hair out of my face, I was standing in front of the guy Iva had been speaking to. He was very nice looking, with his dark clean-cut hairstyle and his boyish face.

"Oh, sorry," I said.

"It's all right. I'm Anthony; I was just talking to your friend over there." His voice was smooth and confident and my smile broadened.

"And what were you two talking about?" I put some "Aimee charm" on.

"Well, you, of course. She told me you're single?"

"That depends," I said, smiling.

"Do you have an escort to the ball?" He was pretty forward, but it was rather nice.

"Why, are you asking me?" I asked, tilting my head.

"It depends on what you would say." His half smile excited me.

"Yes."

"Yes you have an escort or yes you will go with me?"

"Yes, I will go with you," I said.

He smiled. "I will meet you in front of the coffee shop around eight." He lightly touched my arm.

"Okay," I said. He walked away just as Alec entered the room. Why does he always appear out of nowhere?

My smile faltered a bit. Luckily he didn't stop to chat; he went to see Iva and they went into an immediate discussion.

Deciding to go back to the red-headed girl so Zara wouldn't have a coronary, I sat down in higher spirits. The girl just shook her head at me, clearly disapproving. I wasn't going to let her kill my buzz.

After being slave driven all day with setting up the room, Iva and I were finally free women. It was about five o'clock. So, Iva and I headed back to my room to get ready for tonight.

The court was pretty quiet as we hastily made our way to my room; my footsteps echoed on the granite floor. I could sense Iva watching; glancing up at her I rose my eyebrows.

"What is it?" I asked, laughing.

"So I'm assuming you told Anthony yes?" Iva asked.

"I did. He seems nice and he's pretty good looking. How did you know?"

"He asked me about you and I could tell that he was going to ask you . . . . Alec asked me to go with him," she said with a giggle. I almost choked on my spit at her statement. Why didn't he ask me? That thought caught me off guard. I was desperately trying to conceal my frown.

"That should be fun, we can double," I said as calmly as I could.

"Are you okay with that?" she asked.

"Yeah. Why wouldn't I be?" I asked, glancing at her.

I wondered if she could hear my thoughts, because right then they were screaming. I was trying to bury them. I didn't own Alec, let alone have a reason for my feelings.

"I'm just making sure, because if you have any . . . thoughts, or feelings for him, we can switch dates tonight." She was trying to get a hint of jealousy from me, but I wasn't about to let her know my true emotions. Mostly because I didn't even know what they were, or if I just had a simple crush. I didn't want to ruin the evening.

"Listen, we are going to have fun and if this Anthony guy is a creeper, then please rescue me," I said. She agreed to that.

Seven

*I*VA LOOKED STUNNING IN HER pale gold, floor-length dress, but then again, she always did look nice. I straightened her hair for her and did her eye make up like a mask with gold and black accents; mine was red and gold for a more dramatic feel. Iva helped give me soft curls with her new curler, and they made my hair look fresh and bouncy.

The dress showed just the right amount of cleavage, thanks to my fabulous bra. I sort of felt like my dress choice might not have been the best. I felt very risqué in it. Iva kept reassuring me that I looked sexy, not skanky. Yet I had a bit of regret for wearing this dress, and it was too late to change now as we left my room to make our way to the coffee shop. I kept pulling on the sides of the dress.

"Stop, you're going to stretch the dress. You look great!" Iva said, with her usual eyebrow raised at me. I stopped messing with the dress and gave a sigh.

Anthony was already there as we approached. He openly checked me out with a look of "he likes what he sees." Iva, standing next to me, was pretending to choke to cover her laughter. She elbowed me in the side.

"You look great." Anthony said, clearly pleased. His black tux went nicely with his dark hair. He held his mask in his hand.

Coming around the corner, wearing his mask and all, Alec caught my eye as usual. His smoky grey suit looked dead sexy on him. He wore his mask. This made him even more mysterious.

Alec grinned at Iva and gestured for her to take his arm, she slipped hers through. I eyed her fingers as she placed them softly on his forearm. I wanted my hand there, not hers. I quickly brushed those feelings aside as I came closer to Anthony.

Anthony did the same gesture to me and I happily took it; I could have sworn Alec's lips twitched. Or maybe I was just hoping to get a rise out of Alec. Anthony and I followed behind them. I resisted the urge to kick Alec for ignoring me.

As we approached the entrance, it was claustrophobically crowded with people trying to get in. I noticed Zara right away; she stood close to the door, with that same clipboard in her hand. She, however, looked gorgeous, regardless of how much she bothered me. I passed her, smiling; even though she wore a mask I could feel the glaring of her eyes. Did she ever stop being so controlling? I think not.

We entered the masquerade ball. And, to my surprise, it looked amazing. The light source came from torches that hung on the walls and candlelit chandeliers that dropped from the ceiling. I was happy that the red head helped fix the flowers because now they really looked nice as they sat in the middle of the tables as centerpieces, as well as lining the entrance.

"Not bad!" Iva said, also gesturing toward the flowers.

Snarky, I said, "Yeah. Thanks to the red head."

Iva smiled. "Good thing!"

People were dancing on the floor and the DJ was playing a pretty great remix of a techno song. It almost felt like a rave. Minus the glow sticks. I was surprised all around by the turn out. Well, considering that this was probably the most exciting event to happen in this underworld cage, I guess I shouldn't have been all that surprised.

We picked a table and placed our drinks there to mark our territory. I took a sip of my punch then eyed the good-looking man next to me, Alec. I felt a bit guilty; I was here with Anthony but was totally ogling

Alec. *I'm a free woman now*, I thought. I was able to look at whatever or whoever I wished.

"Do you want to dance?" I asked Anthony as excitement poured through my body.

"Do you want me to lead?" he asked laughing.

I noticed that his accent was barely there. His eyebrows rose at me asking him first to dance, but it didn't matter. I wanted to dance my crazy life away.

He took my hand and led me to the floor. I glanced over my shoulder at Iva. She just shook her head and shrugged. Alec stood next to her gripping his glass tightly with a stony expression. Clearly, he didn't like this arrangement. I felt a tiny bit guilty about making Alec jealous, but that feeling soon passed. It made me happy. I was evil deep down and I liked it.

Finding a spot on the floor was hard; everyone and their mothers were most likely here surrounding me on the dance floor.

Pushing the nonexistent space, I didn't hesitate to start dancing. I really loved the song. Laughing a bit, I thought to myself, *All I need is some glow sticks.*

One thing I did like was that Anthony had rhythm, which made it easy for me to really get into the song. We moved well together, it was getting hot and sweaty, and Anthony was getting a little too comfortable with me. His hands started to slide down to my rear end; I kept moving his hands back up. He apparently wasn't getting the hint. Next thing I knew was that his lips were at my neck, kissing it softly. His fangs brushed my skin, sending a thrill of adrenalin through me.

I wasn't sure if I wanted to kiss him, but, hey, it wouldn't hurt to have a little fun. Bringing my face closer to his, my lips inches away, everything around me went into slow motion; the music was muffled as I was anticipating the kiss. The kiss never happened. Firm hands on my shoulder pulled me back.

What the heck! I was spun around.

Alec's eyes had a fire in them, one I hadn't seen before. It scared me, actually. His eyes just continued to glare at me. Cowering under his gaze, I did not want him to disapprove. But that quickly vanished as it was replaced with burning rage. He wasn't my father, after all.

Anthony was equally as outraged as I. But Alec would win the battle if they were to fight it out. Even though Anthony was built the same, like a tennis player, there was something about Alec. He was fierce.

"Can I help you?" Anthony asked, annoyed at the interruption.

"Aimee, I think it's time to leave," Alec said, full of authority.

Just who did he think he was? The anger started to bubble within me.

"I don't want to leave! I'm having a good time!" I said with attitude as I placed my hands on my hips.

"I don't think you understand, I'm not asking, I'm telling you!" His Italian accent turned dangerous and smooth.

He was embarrassing me. Iva came to the rescue as promised, not from Anthony, but from Alec. Iva grasped my hand as she guided me through the crowd.

The hallway was deserted. My arms were crossed as I was trying to calm myself. I paced back and forth; Iva stood there watching me. I looked like a crazy person. If smoke was able to come out my ears, it would be fire.

"What is his problem? How can I ever see Anthony after tonight?" I said, with my voice shaking.

"I think Anthony will still make contact with you. But not when Alec is around," Iva said.

"What is his problem?" I asked. I was still furious.

"Isn't it obvious?" she asked.

I didn't know what she was talking about other than him being over protective and serious about everything. I didn't need a knight in shining armor!

"He treats me like I'm a child!" I said, exasperated. The smooth, less-angered Italian accent answered me. "That's because you're acting like one," Alec said behind me.

I didn't want to see him. So, instead, I kept my eyes on Iva.

"I'm going back to my room! Your work is done here, Alec; you can leave now!"

I could sense him still standing there, so I decide to escort myself. Taking my heels off and holding them, I began my walk of shame to my room. My whole night cut in half. I heard soft footsteps behind me and, of course, Alec was suddenly standing next to me.

"What part of 'I don't want to see you' don't you get!?" I said, as I raised my voice.

Alec put himself in front of me as if to stop me from walking. His mask was off and he tried to look at me, leveling his eyes with mine. I averted my eyes. I was acting truly childish now.

"Anthony was . . . well . . . he doesn't respect you! And I don't want you to be taken advantage of!" That Italian voice of his was soft and almost sweet under these circumstances. I glared at him coldly. He wasn't about to get any mercy from me!

"I don't care! Maybe I want to be taken advantage of! I need to have fun and act like a normal person!" I crossed my arms so I wouldn't punch him. I was so HOT.

"I didn't mean to embarrass you."

"Again, I don't care! Just leave me alone. Go find Iva, since she is your date tonight! Stop worrying about me and maybe you could have some fun!" My voice grew louder with each word I spoke.

"She isn't my date Aimee, we're friends. She and I don't care for each other like that," he said with a reassuring voice. But I didn't need to be reassured. I needed to be left alone.

The court was vacant as I continued to walk. Everyone young was still at the ball and enjoying the night. I could still be enjoying myself. I could hear the fountain bubbling near me. I stopped and turned too fast, and suddenly, I was in Alec's face. Clearly, I'd startled him.

"Why are you telling me this, Alec? I'm not upset about you going with Iva. I didn't even question you about it." I poked his chest with my finger.

He thought about it for a moment. "I'm telling you because I thought . . ."

"You thought what?" my eyes became narrow and focused on him.

"I don't know. I was wrong, I guess." He started backing away from me.

"You always do that! Would you just spit it out? You weren't at a loss for words with Anthony!"

I waited for him to say something, anything. But he just looked at me with such intensity that I would've kissed him if I weren't so mad. I realized he was trying to seduce me. And even though he was very good looking, with wavy brown hair, ice grey eyes, and perfectly proportioned features, it wasn't going to work. I felt that electricity come alive again. But he didn't say anything. Not a word.

"That's what I thought!" I said, as flipped my hair back. "Goodnight, Alec with no last name!" I began walking again.

"Aimee . . .," he said as he roughly touched my arm and spun me around. He pulled me close to his body. I felt his warmth as he held me close. My breathing stopped and my heart began to beat at a faster pace. He had taken me by surprise. My senses became alive, tingles and butterflies overflowed my body.

"My last name is Attias." Not that his last name mattered much to me at that moment.

All I could think of now were his lips. For a moment longer, he held my gaze. I felt a different type of fire in me. It was a hunger. I wanted him. I didn't blink, too afraid I would miss a move. He leaned his face closer to mine. I felt his breath as if to form a kiss. My heart was fluttering; I was anxious.

"How do you not remember?" he asked so softly. His breath felt sweet against my face, so close. I kept my eyes open to answer his question.

"Remember what?" I said without breathing.

"Remember this."

His lips met mine, full of passion, heat, and strength, his warm lips didn't hesitate or falter. They felt wonderful. That fire burning within me spread to the rest of my body and while it started out soft, that fire became fierce. My body instantly responded. He pushed me against the wall, holding me captive. I felt like my heart would explode.

He pulled away, watching me. Leaving my eyes closed still, I tried to catch my breath.

"What was that?" I asked, whispering. He was breathing heavy, too.

He looked frustrated and backed away from me. His eyes still held that intensity and passion. I wanted more.

Surprising myself, I told him something so not like me.

"I . . . should be going now." So many emotions filled me. I had never experienced this before. I was terrified. What was this, this fire that is deep within my soul? Being awakened?

We were just arguing, how did we end up kissing? I'm supposed to be in control! Not him! My pride was wallowing within me.

Turning my back to Alec, I began walking toward my room, a bit shaken.

"Do you want me to walk you to your room?" he asked.

I paused as I looked back at him; I thought it would be better if I went alone. With the way I was feeling, I shouldn't have him with me. I needed time to think, think about what I felt. Was this just lust or something deeper? Was I even ready or capable to trust?

"I can manage," was all I said, not looking back to see his expression.

Eight

I SAT ACROSS FROM IVA, watching her drink what looked like a juice box, but really it was blood. I was happy I couldn't see or smell it. I held the disgust from my face.

The food court was busy. It was lunchtime so the school kids and adults were out getting their doses of blood or food, and the buzz of gossip and laughter filled the room.

I was admiring a little girl who was adorable. She had brown hair pulled up in pigtails and a navy blue uniform; she was so lucky, no complications. All she had to worry about was homework. Her little girlfriends were giggling next to her. Oh, what I would give to be a kid again.

My life now held so many complications. One of them was the night of the masquerade ball. Alec's kiss, had it been a dream or reality? I could almost feel it still. Did he kiss me because of the way I looked or was it something more? In fact, it had been consuming my every thought. Why did he make things so complicated? He should have just let me kiss Anthony! I don't think Anthony's kiss would have been like Alec's. I was literally driving myself crazy! The constant reminder of Derek also lingered in my mind. I hadn't had a moment to really grasp the reality of the loss of us.

Iva glanced at me. I'm sure she saw my readable expression. She set her "juice box" down and was staring at me. I peeked up at her through the tangles of my hair.

"Yes, Iva?" I asked.

She shifted in her chair and leaned closer to me.

"I know there is something wrong and you're just not telling me." She was very observant with me. But, then again, my mood today was easy to get a read on.

"No, not really," I lied. I didn't want to talk about it.

"Aimee, I'm not dumb. I can sense it, as well as see it written all over your face." Iva was that good; I knew I couldn't pass this by her.

"Fine. Alec kissed me. Happy now?" I was a bit surprised that I'd told her so quickly; maybe it was because I was thinking about it so much and wanted to burden someone else with the information. Iva however, didn't look shocked. She sat there, calm, while my emotions were in turmoil.

"You knew about it, didn't you?" I asked.

"Yes, I did," Iva said, not denying it.

My face blushed. "He told you?"

"Yes, well, actually, I sensed something happened when I saw him later that night. I can't believe you kept it to yourself for three days."

"What did he say, exactly?"

"I knew it would happen. How do you feel about it?" Iva asked, very slyly avoiding my question; she was loyal to Alec just as much as she was to me. This was a losing battle.

"What are you, a shrink?" I asked, laughing. "I honestly don't know how I feel. He caught me off guard. And even though Derek and I are over, I still have mixed feelings. I'm trying to figure things out still."

She nodded in understanding. "Makes sense. I told him he rushed things."

"Is that why he's been avoiding me?" I asked.

"He's not exactly avoiding you. He just needs to think straight."

Wonderful, now I had to imagine what he told her. Iva was just that good. I can't believe she wouldn't spill anything about what he said. Not even a breadcrumb of information. Instead, I think she liked having a hold on me.

Iva took a sip of the juice box as she looked at me thoughtfully. I began playing with a strand of my hair as I eyed the juice box.

"How old are you and Alec?"

"Same age as you, 23," she said, taking another sip of blood.

"And what is it like being a vampire? Did it hurt when you were awakened?"

She smiled and tilted her head. Her grey eyes shined with amusement.

"All your senses are enhanced; we are fast and strong. We also have night vision. It's pretty cool. We used to talk about it all the time when we were in school." She looked sad at bringing up that memory. "It did hurt a little. But I think it was worth it."

"How does it work, being awakened?" I asked.

"Well, the elders awaken us. They are the oldest in our community. It's a whole ceremony and we drink their blood and they bite us."

I cringed at the thought of drinking blood; I most likely would have vomited right before and embarrassed my family. It took every ounce not to scrunch my nose up in disgust.

"Do you have to drink their blood? And do you struggle with wanting to kill anyone?"

Her smile grew, and she rolled her eyes. "We don't have to drink their blood, we already have the genes of our ancestors, but it's a tradition that has been passed down . . . . And I don't struggle with cravings down here, but when Alec called me to tell me he found you and that you were getting services at the hotel, that made things a bit harder. But that was simply because I'm not around humans enough. We have a subway under here, and that's usually how we travel. Only occasionally do we use the cars."

"Subways?" I asked.

"Yes, we have many communities like this all over Europe. Also in America, but we have special travels to get there."

"That's different." That interested me, traveling all over, by subways.

"Was Alec looking for me for long?" I asked.

"Yes, for six years. He never gave up on you. Neither did I. But he was braver and went looking for you after he awakened." Studying her juice box, I could tell she was in thought.

I didn't expect Alec to be the rescuer type; he was mysterious, sexy, Greek god like, with his wavy brown hair, ice grey eyes, and a body like a tennis player. Not to mention how perfect his features were. But who would have guessed a rescuer, too? I smiled at the thought of having him save me, a sexy Italian rescuer for that matter. The more I thought about it, the more I realized he was a protector. The masquerade ball had proved that.

But, I couldn't help but wonder if he would ever tell me this.

"Do you know how long he will be staying away from me?" I asked, snapping myself out of my own head.

"I do not. Please don't tell him I told you anything when you do see him. He would be mad at me. Or embarrassed. "Iva said sternly.

I was about to laugh when I heard my name being called. I glanced around; it was a man's voice. I recognized it but wasn't sure yet who it was.

"Who are you looking for?" Iva asked, puzzled.

Iva disappeared in front of me as my vision went unfocused; I felt like I was standing in a thick fog. I was engulfed in blackness. All I could hear echoing around me was my name. The returning terror filled me.

"Aimee." The man's voice was calling. I could feel the hair on my arms stand on edge.

The fog around me cleared up, as well as the blackness. I was standing in a forest. It was so beautiful, so green and lush. A stream was near; I could hear it. The sun was setting and the colors of the sky where amazing, orange and pink mixed with red. I was so caught up in the forest I almost overlooked a tree closest to me, it wasn't the tree that caught my eye, but who was standing by it. I saw him, Derek, in his khakis and white polo shirt. He was smiling coolly at me. I had almost forgotten what his face looked like.

"Derek?" I asked, unsure; fear was written all over my face.

His movement was fast. He stood in front of me; his green eyes deep like the forest. I heard another sound. Footsteps. His father emerged. His dad had the same sharp features as Derek, but something about him always scared me. His dad, Nathan, stood there and just smiled at me. His smile was sinister.

"Is this a dream?" I asked, perplexed.

"No, it's not." When Nathan spoke his voice was cold.

I felt fear growing deeper within me.

"What is going on?" I asked, backing away from them.

"Aimee, we aren't going to hurt you," Derek said.

"I don't believe you! What do you want, then?"

"We want to know where you are." A tingling sensation washed over me, like he was searching my brain for the answer. I couldn't shut him out. I wanted to scream, but nothing came out. "Hmmm, it appears you don't even know," Nathan said. His cold eyes narrowed on me.

Derek reached for me; he was inches away from me, and as he got closer, my heart was racing. I felt like I was being shaken, roughly.

My eyes became focused and it took me a moment to realize it was Iva shaking me. I was still sitting in the chair. How had I not fallen out? I quickly glanced around to see if anyone was watching me. No one even seemed to care. The court was still in its own world.

Iva was calling me from a distance; I could hear her, but all I could think about was the sudden realization that this wasn't the first time Derek had contacted me. Back at the Enclave in Greece, when I'd thought I was dreaming. I touched my face. I was startled by my sudden epiphany.

"Aimee! Can you hear me?" Iva was asking, she sounded worried. Her expression was terrified.

"I . . . I don't know what happened. I'm really scared . . . Iva, I don't know what's happening to me. Do you think I'm going crazy?" I asked in a whisper.

"Okay, calm down . . . ." Iva placed her hands on my shoulders, looking directly into my hazel eyes. "Can you tell me what you saw?" Iva asked in her same calm voice, able to collect herself so well.

I took a deep breath. "Think hard, Aimee!" I said to myself.

"I was in a forest, and Derek and his dad, Nathan, were there with me. Nathan was trying to read my thoughts; he wanted to know where I was. He couldn't find it, though, due to me not knowing where I was."

I put my face in my hands, trying to take away the images. With one fluid motion, Iva was standing and glancing down at me. I could see that warrior coming out.

"Come with me," she said, rapidly taking my hand.

The thought of the movie *Terminator* flashed into my mind. I was clearly not laughing at the situation, but I wanted to laugh at Iva saying, "Come with me if you want to live."

"Where?" I asked.

"To the bottom layer. We need to talk to someone who might know what to do."

The bottom layer? I didn't even have enough time to grasp what she was talking about. She was already pulling me to my feet.

Iva was leading me down that hallway I got lost in the first day I was here. The same earthy smell greeted us. Coming to a halt in front of the mysterious door, she pressed what I assume was a doorbell of some sort. Messy brown hair, green eyes, tan, Marcus opened the door, to my surprise, looking very hot. Literally, it was really hot down here, like we were in a boiler room. He had beads of sweat on his neck and his tank showed signs of perspiration. On someone else, I would find it dirty, but on Marcus, it looked really sexy. My smile grew, and I briefly forgot why I was actually here.

"Marcus, we need to see Teeker," Iva said, in a pushy voice. Marcus looked at me and smiled.

"What, no hello?" Marcus said.

"We don't have time!" Iva said.

"There is always time for a hello!" he said, being stubborn, with his nice crooked smile. His teeth were so white against his tan.

"Fine! Hello!" Iva said, dangerously close to losing her collected self.

"That wasn't so hard. And I can take you to him," Marcus said, pushing the door open wide so we could enter.

Inside this "bottom layer" wasn't exactly savage, but it also wasn't a place you would want to take your shoes off. The floor was black concrete, and there was dirt in some places; tree roots were creeping around the walls. It was one big open room, with caves lining the sides. The center had a large fire pit, something similar to a bonfire pit when camping, but ten times larger. They didn't mess around with the small stuff.

The werewolves were lounging around, either reading or cooking, or playing fighting games with each other. We got a few glances here and there, looks of curiosity and, by the looks of it, we are the only females there. This was confirmed when they smiled at Iva and me.

"Wait here; I'm going to tell Teeker you're here to see him," Marcus told us smoothly as he walked into a large cave. I was wondering if we were going to get attacked by the crowd of men still ogling us.

"Why are we here?" I whispered to Iva.

"To get answers. Teeker will know things that will help us."

"Who?" I asked. What kind of name was Teeker?

"An old werewolf," Iva said.

Standing and waiting made me wish that Alec were with us; at least he could protect us. Although, Iva, I'm sure, would be a good guard, also.

Moments later, Marcus came out, smiling.

"He is ready for you," Marcus said in his thick Romanian accent, which was rich sounding in the cave.

We followed him in. It was like a council room, but not as formal, with boulders as seats. I noticed the man they called Teeker immediately; old was an understatement. He was ancient looking, like he could croak at any moment. He had a small cane and a long, silver beard. His eyes were worn and tired, his skin was leathery, like he had gotten way too much sun in his glory days. How long did werewolves live? Two hundred years?

"Hello, Teeker, thank you for seeing us on short notice," Iva said.

"Aww, Aimee. I've heard much about you. Even in our world, you were a great topic," Teeker said ignoring Iva. His smile was twisted; his voice was frog-like with a thick accent of some sort. I could barely make out what he was saying to us. His breath I could smell, and it was like something had died in his mouth.

I stood even closer to Iva, trying to breathe in her perfume.

"I know why you have come; I can sense the bond right away." Teeker said.

"The bond?" I asked, confused.

"Yes, the ones who were going to turn you. It's a part of the process, once they erase your mind. It takes a great deal from that werewolf who initiates the process. That werewolf makes you connected to them, like part of a pack. I wouldn't be surprised if you've talked with them."

"They can't be the ones who captured me, though. I had been living with them for six years and they are human and they never turned me," I said.

"If they make contact with you and you think it's a dream, but it feels so real at the same time, then it's the bond, and yes, they took you," Teeker said breathlessly.

Trying to grasp that concept was hard for me. How could Derek and Norman be werewolves? I had never seen them change their forms or treat me badly. I'm not even turned! My heart felt like it was going to explode.

"What am I?" I asked.

"You are one of a kind. Genes of a vampire, but I sense something else, something stronger within you. I'm surprised the Rogues didn't turn you, it's the final stage after they erase your mind," he said, studying me.

"Which is?" I asked cautiously, almost afraid of the answer. The old man just looked at me with such sadness.

"Being bitten. Your eyes will continue to change color from hazel to honey brown along with your moods. It's almost like when we change. Our eyes change first. It's our sign, that's when we can be most dangerous, the most powerful."

Eyes change color? Signs of turning? I glanced at Iva, who was so quiet and still, she was squinting and her eyebrows rose in the way she does so perfectly.

"What would happen if I decided to be awakened?" I asked.

"I'm not sure; most Yurnlings who are taken are turned and I wouldn't know the effect it would have on you if you chose to be awakened. The Rogue who took you will try to retrieve you at all costs. As long as he lives he will always have that bond over you and he will be able to find you. I also presume he wants you as his bride."

Bride! I felt an overwhelming sickness sweep over me. If I hadn't met Alec, my fate would have been ultimately to be a werewolf. I never would have known my true identity.

"Why would he want me now? He didn't change me for all those years," I blurted out.

"That is a mystery; only he would know the reason. If you awaken I can sense you will be very strong and powerful, I'm guessing the same goes if you turn Rogue. But, then again, I can sense another power in you, if the rumors are true."

Rumors? I was the last one to find things out. I really didn't like it, either.

This old man was rambling on and I didn't know what he was talking about. Glancing over at Iva for support, I almost forgot that Marcus was in the cave with us still. He was so quiet. He watched the old man with such respect.

"Thank you for all the information, Teeker." Iva was turning to leave until the old man touched me. A wave passed through me at his touch.

His eyes became lit with something unseen.

"You have a gift. It will be quite useful once you learn how to use it," he said as he released my arm.

I wanted to ask, but Teeker had already begun walking back to his room. I wondered if Marcus would help him. But Teeker was faster than I thought was possible; he was already almost there.

My mind began to focus on "the gift" Teeker mentioned and what would happen to me. I looked at Iva. She was curious, too. Her eyes watched me. Marcus followed behind our exit.

"Marcus," Iva said, apparently not trusting him like Teeker.

"Thank you for helping us . . . well, me." I said.

"You're welcome. Anytime. Too bad you aren't turned, we could have been . . . ." He let the end of that sentence trail off. I smiled. I was dumbfounded by everything I just heard.

It was bad enough Derek was a murderer who had killed my close friend. But, to find out my family were really vampires and I'm some weird Yurnling thing and then to come to the realization that Derek was a werewolf, and Elizabeth, Derek's mother, was a werewolf was just crazy. I couldn't believe that she had lied to me. Six years. My mind was boiling with anger and confusion. Everything had become so twisted.

Making our way to the exit of this werewolf lair I began to think. Would my life ever get easier? The answer was, probably not.

"Are you okay?" Iva asked once we reached the main court area.

I thought about it for a moment. The thoughts of me not being safe at all and death most likely happening if I stayed here sent terror through my body. What about that little girl I watched today or any of those children, for that matter? If Derek Sladen found me, what would become of any of us?

"That look is dangerous; what are you thinking?" Iva asked.

"I'm putting you all at risk by me being here. I know who took me and he's invading my head. I just realized the man I love is a werewolf and his whole family were wolves. They didn't seem Rogue. They are wealthy and his mother Elizabeth is sweet and they lived in Florida. It's all so unnatural."

"Elizabeth was most likely a Yurnling also at one point. The males have to take female Yurnlings to breed with, because they don't bear baby girls, just boys. And some they just take to expand their population. Maybe Derek's family was more like leaders of their kind?" Iva said.

"So, werewolf Rogues take girl Yurnlings to breed with because they can only have boys?" I asked.

"Yes, it's why they depend on us, the Yurnlings, so much."

"What happens if they marry an already awakened vampire?" I asked.

"I don't think there has ever been a case like that, so I wouldn't know."

Derek was still present in my thoughts and the image of Krissy's murder had not been easy, either.

"Derek killed my friend. That's why I left; I witnessed it," I said quietly. I needed to tell her; it was consuming me.

Iva stopped walking; her eyes were filled with compassion.

"I know," was all she said.

How did she know? I looked at her, puzzled.

"Alec saw it also," Iva said quietly.

Of course, that's why he was on the dock. Something else that Teeker said piqued an interest in me.

The thought of having powers intrigued me, probably a little more than it should have. I wondered what my power was that the old man spoke of. And, better yet, how could I obtain it?

"The old man said something about me having a gift? Do you have one?"

"I don't, but Alec does," Iva said.

"What is it?"

"Being able to compel anyone he wishes. He told me that once." She paused, looking around the court. We stood close to the hall we just came from; being lazy, I was sitting on the floor.

"We should find your mother and tell her what we know." Iva was already helping me to my feet when she suggested that thought.

Nine

THE WORDS WALK AND SWIFTLY weren't in Iva's vocabulary. Instead, 'run like your life depended on it' was more her style. Iva ran in front of me. Her hair was swishing back and forth. I was still a little dizzy from the "bond" I had had with Derek and his father. So, trying to keep up with Iva proved to be a bit challenging.

The skinny, stuck up girl known as Beth was sitting in her usual post, the front desk. She eyeballed us as we ran toward her. She didn't look afraid, but she probably thought we suffered from some sort of crazy meltdown.

"Beth, is Rosemarie available to speak with us? It's urgent, regarding her daughter," Iva said.

"*Lady* Rosemarie," she corrected, "is in a meeting, I'm afraid. I could tell her you stopped by, though," Beth said with a smirk. She looked at us happily, gloating that she had authority over us.

"I don't care if she is in a meeting, this community or whatever you call it could be in danger," I said, tapping the glass desk. "And she is my mother."

Nothing changed with this girl; her beady eyes just narrowed on me. I wanted to punch that smirk off her face. Iva placed a hand on my shoulder, as if to calm me down. My mood had changed so quickly; maybe this old Teeker man really knew what he was talking about. I looked into Iva's eyes and they widened. That proved the eye change for me.

"Brown?" I asked

She just half smiled. My worrying started to get the better of me. I had to sit, taking deep breaths and resisting the urge to rip my hair out and scream. This uncontrollable anger really was annoying, I could flip the switch instantly on the anger part, but calming down was a bit more perplexing.

I felt aggravated as I sat, helpless, on the bench. Iva was still talking to Beth, who wasn't budging on letting us in. *What is her problem?* I asked myself. If Alec were here he would be able to get us into that room. And, just like that, as if I had spoken his name aloud, his tall form came around the corner. Beth immediately changed her expression; she was pleased to see him. But then again, what girl wasn't happy to see Alec? He did have an effect on the ladies. He didn't look at me. But he gracefully walked up to Beth and turned on the charm. I could tell he used compulsion on her. She would have done anything for him at that moment. I could see it on her face, glazed eyes and everything. Sweet! *Iva wasn't lying about that*, I thought to myself.

"Ready, ladies?" he asked, half grinning at his accomplishment. I couldn't help myself; my grin was from ear to ear. I was relieved.

"Show off," I said, under my breath. I was really happy that he was there. He looked quite sexy, as usual. I really liked the gold metal beads in his hair, they popped out when he brushed back some of his hair.

Iva and Alec stood in front of me as we approached the door. My father, Ralph, came out. We hadn't really talked at all since I'd been back and honestly I wouldn't have known what to say to him. His tall form cast a shadow over me. His grey eyes bore into mine.

"What brings you here?" He asked, amused, looking at the three of us.

"We need to see Lady Rosemarie. It's important," Iva said.

He eyed us happily.

"Her meeting just finished. The door is unlocked." He moved aside to let us pass him.

Without hesitation, Alec and Iva opened the door. Rosemarie sat at her desk, organizing the papers before her. Her face had stress written all over it. As she saw us enter, her eyebrows rose up.

"Is everything all right?" She was about to stand but Alec motioned her to stay seated.

"Aimee and I found out some things that we wanted to tell you," Iva said, motioning me to begin speaking. I went closer to her with a push from Iva. I imagined it was supposed to be an encouraging push.

"Today, while Iva and I were eating, I had a dream invasion. Derek and his dad, Nathan, came into my head and spoke to me. They are looking for me. We saw Teeker and he told us it's because of a bond I have with Nathan and his family. It happened when they erased my memory." I paused, thinking about how to phrase my next statement. "Maybe I should leave and go somewhere else so he doesn't come here again with the other Rogues," I said, breathless.

Rose sat there calm and without a hint of concern on her face. She just looked tired and stressed.

"Nathan will not be getting anywhere near us. We have high security and you most certainly will not go out and hide in some cave or wherever." She looked strained and this argument wasn't going to move forward. So I figured there was no point in continuing it.

"So, you don't see a threat with this bond thingy?" I asked.

"I don't. And once you awaken then this will no longer pose a threat to you."

Once I'm awakened? I didn't make that choice yet, and Teeker didn't know how my body would react to being awakened. Especially after my mind being erased.

"Is there anything else on your mind, Aimee?" Her eyes were soft and she was sincere. She just wasn't being very motherly. I guess six years changes people. I changed, and I still am changing.

"No ma'am. I'm sorry I wasted your time," I was looking at the ground and didn't hear her chair move; her hand lightly touched my shoulder.

"I'm here for you Aimee, we all are. Trust me when I tell you, you're safe!" She kissed my forehead and nodded at Iva and Alec. And with that, our conversation ended. *What a waste of time*, I thought.

I walked in silence as Iva and Alec were speaking to one another. My room was two doors away. My mind was in a whirl. I couldn't sleep. I had to do something about this. I didn't care what everyone would say or what they thought. Their lives could be at risk. Derek and his family already had broken in once. They could do it again. How had Derek not realized I was here, in the same place that he took me from to begin with? I looked up to see Alec standing in front of my door, still in conversation with Iva.

Alec still hadn't said anything to me. He was making me feel awkward around him, especially after that heavy kiss he planted on me nights ago. Iva was just being nice when she said he wasn't avoiding me, when in fact, he was. It was clear as glass. My heart was aching; that kiss felt more alive than any kiss or moment I ever shared with Derek.

Alec stood with his back to me. His dark brown wavy hair was in my face; I wanted to touch it. I wanted to touch him. I felt as though I could still feel his lean body pressing against me. I felt anger growing inside me, anger with myself for being so caught up in this nonsense.

"Would you like me to stay with you tonight?" Iva asked.

Alec was also looking at me.

"No, I'll be fine. Really," I said, unsure if I was trying to convince myself. I was certain I wasn't fine and I didn't want to be alone. Actually, I found that I hadn't wanted to be alone all that much since the discovery of my new life.

I could tell that Alec knew I wasn't fine; his eyes seemed to look into my soul, making me feel scrutinized under his stare.

"We both can stay with you," Alec said.

He wouldn't be alone with me. That was a fact. But I wanted him being present.

Almost like Alec knew my unspoken thoughts, he just nodded, and held my door open for me. I passed him, looking into his eyes, feeling the tingle of electricity course through my body.

Who was this Aimee? I thought. I never have been the weak one. I never needed people to be around me at all times. This clearly was not me. Things are certainly changing.

Lying in bed, I closed my eyes and tried to fall asleep, but instead, a now-familiar dizzy sensation came over me.

The classroom was empty and dimly lit. The chalkboard had that day's lesson written on it. It was being ignored because of more dominant things. Things like his soft hands caressing my arm so gently. His lips traced my jaw. Alec and I were in the empty classroom. He sat on the desk opposite me. His blue eyes took my breath away. My heart raced every time he touched me. My body ached for him. I had never felt such a strong emotion. It was more than lust. It was pure love. The kind of love that never faded, the kind of love you would die for. I sat there, soaking him in. It was the highlight of my day, seeing Alec and holding him. We would meet in secret because we knew my dad would never approve.

"School is almost over and we both will awaken together." He was telling me this wistfully, excitement lighting his features. "I know we are young, Aimee, but I knew the moment I saw you that I wanted to spend my life with you." Alec spoke confidently. I knew, for a fact, he was telling the truth. I felt it, too.

I must be dreaming! Or maybe this was a memory. My present mind was trying to make sense of it. This proved challenging because it was *Alec* with love pouring out of him. I liked it. There weren't any complications with life at this moment. Just me, him and the classroom. I wanted to be with him, not a doubt in my mind. At least this is how I was feeling.

He took my hands into his. "I love you," he said. And I could feel that he really did. I could imagine what my face looked like. Shocked, happy, complete. He then pressed his lips against mine, he tangled his hand in my hair and I wrapped myself around him, I was trying to breathe him in. My senses came alive at his touch. There was that burning within me, a fire. He kissed my neck and slowly moved down.

I woke up abruptly, gasping for air and brushing my hair away from my face. Did I actually have sex in a classroom? I wouldn't know, I guess. What a way to wake up! I was sitting up trying to even out my breathing, when a movement in the corner caused me to stiffen up.

"Did you have a bad dream?" Alec asked. His voice sounded anxious. I had forgotten that Alec was in the room with me.

Bad dream? HA. It was great; I wish I could've finished it. My eyes adjusted to the light he turned on.

"No, I had another memory," I told him. His posture became straighter, expecting me to tell him what it was about. I didn't want to tell him. I leaned back into my pillow and placed a hand over my heart. I sighed deeply. My heart was still pounding in my chest. Remembering what I had just seen, sent a shiver of happiness deep within me. I literally watched the memory unravel before me. It was a strange feeling to see yourself in the past, yet still feel every feeling and emotion I was experiencing at that point. It was intoxicating; I could live in that moment of pure bliss, and happiness.

"Do you want to talk about it?" he asked softly.

Considering that I didn't want to make things between us more awkward, I said, "I'm fine. Really tired." I scanned the room for Iva, but didn't see her.

"Iva is sleeping on your couch over there." He pointed to the other side of the room. Iva looked so peaceful. Iva really did care about me. My heart expanded at that thought and I smiled as I snuggled back into my bed, pulling the covers closer to my chin. Derek suddenly came into my mind. Actually my thoughts, is really what I should say. I stared at the ceiling.

"Did you know Derek was a werewolf that night you found me on the dock?" I don't know why that popped into my head but it did. And I knew he knew. I just wanted him to tell me.

He shifted slightly, leaning more into the chair, covering his face in his usual shadows.

"I knew a lot of things, Aimee."

"Like what?"

"Your friend Krissy is a Yurnling."

I didn't see that coming.

"Was," he corrected himself.

"Derek killed her," I said, with the memory still burning in my brain.

I had known Krissy for about a year. She was the closest friend I had since being with Derek and his family. The thought of her truly being gone was really sad to me. Alec shifted his weight.

"And how did Derek or his family not know she was a yurnling?" I asked.

"Because they knew who you were and that, if anything, they would turn her, too. But I guess things went wrong."

"Things did go wrong; she was murdered. I overheard the conversation they were having. She said she knew what he was. And then he killed her."

"I know he killed her, Aimee. I could have stopped it, but I couldn't just barge in. Krissy knew what she got into when I told her that I needed her with you," he said quietly.

I almost jumped out of bed. My eyes, I'm sure, resembled that of a deer caught in headlights. A mixture of shock, and a feeling of deep sorrow overtook me.

"What?" I said, as calmly as I could.

"Krissy was helping me out; she knew what I asked of her. She befriended you in Florida and kept an eye on you for me when I couldn't be there. I couldn't be in the sunlight."

The reality of what he just told me was sinking in slowly.

"So she was a fake friend?" I asked, even though at this point it didn't matter. I just needed closure, or so I thought. I was surprised my feelings for Derek were still there and that might be, possibly, until I broke this bond.

"No, she was loyal to you. She really cared about you. You're hard to resist. Please understand, I couldn't let them turn you, Aimee. When I found you in Florida and saw you with him . . . I could smell him a mile away! Knowing what he was and what his family wanted to do to you, I couldn't allow it . . . I'm sorry I caused you pain."

I wasn't in pain now. Just shocked that he was in Florida, the sunniest place on earth. Not to mention, he went there for me, to rescue me.

"How did you travel?"

"With difficulty; it's always sunny. Lots of tint and hiding," he said. "Can you forgive me?" His face was unreadable in the shadows.

"There is nothing to forgive, Alec. You came to save me. And you did. I can't be mad at that." Even though it hurt seeing Derek kill Krissy and most likely I would never forget it, what he did for me was romantic in a twisted way. I felt my ties slowly drift away as I looked at his silhouette. My heart expanded, a realization came to me. I still had those deep feelings for Alec within me. Hiding, and waiting to come out. They had never left me.

How was I able to have these memories now? Was it the familiar things, and being around Alec that triggered these memories?

"Do you want to know what memory I had?" I asked.

He sat quietly for a long moment before he answered me. "Only if you want to tell me," he said.

Alec was so calm and collected, I smiled to myself.

I did want to tell him now. I would tell him, then go to sleep. Hopefully.

I took a deep breath. "We were in an empty classroom," I said. The silence in the room became more evident, I think Alec even stopped breathing. He was so good at being still. Even in the shadows I could see his face in his hands. I felt happy about making him dwell on that thought. It was nice to get a reaction out of those superior ways of his.

"Goodnight, Alec." I said softly. Closing my eyes, I gave in to my need for sleep.

Ten

I WAS SITTING OUTSIDE IN THE sunlight, it was so wonderful. Iva had taken me to the sundeck, a lot of the Yurnlings would come here to soak in some sun and breathe the fresh air. It was pure bliss. I was alone today; the students were in class. I was the oldest Yurnling at this community. The decision to awaken was still something I wasn't a hundred percent sure about. I knew I didn't want to be a Rogue, but I would miss the sun. I glanced over my shoulder; Iva watched me from the inside of the viewing hall, through UV ray resistant glass. I waved at her.

The sun deck was large and open, overlooking the forest surrounding this underground community. Lounge chairs and tables scattered the surface, along with a large pool. I was surprised the deep mahogany floors didn't wither away under the direct contact with sun and rain. I sat near a huge potted tree of some sort. It offered no shade for my pale legs; they were turning a slight shade of pink. It was nice to wear shorts. I could see my reflection in the glass wall that was overlooking the forests before me.

Over the last couple of days my mind was working out the constant thoughts of Derek, Alec and my mother. I was trying to appear calm and collected when, in fact, the inside was a battle within itself. I could barely control my constant anger, it was always ready to surface at any given moment.

Alec and I hadn't talked since the night in my room, when I confessed the second memory I had, the one that was in a classroom alone with Alec. The wondering about if, in fact, I'd slept with him. How would I even begin to ask that question?

Frustrated, I stretched out like a cat on the lounge chair before I got up. The pool and Jacuzzi looked amazing and I defiantly wanted to use them at some point. It really was beautiful out. Not a cloud in the sky.

I was breathing deeply one last time before I left when a movement caught my attention. I noticed someone else outside. Marcus? HA! Iva couldn't stop me this time. Marcus was by the edge of the pool. I was a little more excited as I slyly walked over to him. He was also enjoying the sun, looking very nice without his shirt on. Boy, was he ripped. Not in a scary way, but a kick your butt way, like he would ultimately protect you from a train or something, a real Clark Kent. After admiring him for a moment longer I tapped his right shoulder and hid on the other side of the umbrella.

"I know it's you, Aimee. I saw you earlier," Marcus said, not flinching at all.

So much for my stealthy ninja skills. They cease to exist among the wolves and vampires.

This made me wonder how Derek didn't hear me when I was on the yacht, when I caught him killing my best friend, Krissy.

"How's it going?" I asked, taking a seat next to him. The sun really brought out the different brown colors in his hair.

His green eyes flashed, amused. "I should be asking you that. You know you have the scent," he said.

"The what?" I smelled myself quickly.

Marcus smiled and gave a deep chuckle. "You have a wolf scent."

"And what exactly does that smell like?" I asked, thinking about wet dog.

"Smells nice, like honey, and a warm day. Rich. It's really nice with you because it's also a bit mixed with the vamp smell. Or do you prefer the *keepers of the night*?" He laughed to himself.

Marcus was so chill, unlike Alec and Iva, who seemed to be waiting for a battle to appear in front of them, Marcus just enjoyed life, one day at a time.

"I don't care what you call me. I'm neither," I said, with a bit of an edge.

He faced his body toward me. "Are you going to change? I mean awaken?"

"I don't know what I should do. Teeker said he doesn't know what will happen to me." And, frankly, it petrified me. Everything I'm learning about myself is a nightmare.

Lightly pushing me with his shoulder, he said, "Maybe you'll be some fierce new race!"

"I did think about that. And that maybe I'd be permanently ugly or something. Who knows?" I paused, picking my chipped nail polish. "How can I smell wolfy if they only erased my mind? I'm still me."

Marcus smiled at me. "I don't . . . know if I should be the one giving you answers. I might not be right."

I just squinted at him, and made my lips into a hard line. Still the same thing, no one wants to tell me what they know.

"It's not that I don't want to tell you, Aimee, I just want to make sure the facts are true," he said, giving me a light punch in the arm.

"Sure, sure!" I said, looking at the smooth surface of the pool. "So how did you end up here?" I asked.

"Where? The pool?" he asked, sarcastic.

"You know what I'm talking about . . ."

Leaning his head back, the sun was directly on his face. "I didn't want to be Rogue; we are all born into it. Only boys are born, woman we have to take from vampire communities before they are awoken into vampires. Some weird genetic thing." Marcus sighed. "I watched my brothers tear people apart, human and vampires. Could you imagine growing up like that? I just didn't want to live like that. I didn't want to be thought of as evil and cruel. My pack was really savage; they thought I was the odd one. Some Rogues lived civilly, they still did terrible things, but they lived among humans, and weren't detected . . . I left when I was old enough, I sniffed out this community and after being certain that this was a community that accepted werewolves, I was presented to Teeker. He was the first in this pack here." His eyes softened at the mention of him. It was safe to assume he thought of him as a father figure.

I couldn't imagine living like that, or watching it. I was fortunate that I only saw Derek kill once, but still it had an effect on me.

"How old were you?" I asked.

"I was nineteen. It was the best choice I made . . . I heard about you while I lived among the Rogues. The ones who took you, I never met that pack, but they are royal, and only want the best."

I didn't know if he was paying me some weird compliment, but I decided to ignore it.

"I can't imagine what you feel like, having your memory washed away and told you were involved in a car accident, to come to find out you are a Yurnling and the last six years have been a waste of life, of not knowing the truth," Marcus said as his eyes were closed and he was taking in the warmth of the sun.

Marcus was easy to talk to. And, I felt comfortable with him.

The truth, it wasn't easy; everyday seemed to be some new thing I had to cope with. I will probably end up bald by the end of the year, from all the stress.

"It's hard, but I'm learning how to deal with it every day. My friends are great and patient," I said.

"Yeah, Iva may be stuck up toward me but she is pretty hot . . ."

I sat up swiftly, excited about this new information. I was eagerly leaning towards Marcus.

"You have a crush on her!" I said, my smile widening.

"Like it matters. She doesn't even see me."

"Ooohh, I think you're hard not to see. She isn't blind, Marcus!" I couldn't hold down the excitement in my voice.

Marcus sat up, and became serious. Which was a new look for him, and it was hard to listen when sweat was dripping from his muscled, tanned chest.

"Don't say a word! I mean it!" his eyes flashed. I remembered that I couldn't get him mad. I patted his arm.

"Your secret is safe with me, my friend!" I said.

He grinned his pearly whites at me, then relaxed back into the lounge chair.

"Well my friend I need to get going before Iva has a canary. She doesn't like me to be too far out of reach." I said as I stood.

Marcus stood also; I gave him a half hug. And got bits of sweat on my shirt. The secret would most likely kill me.

Marcus eyed me as I walked to the entrance to go back inside.

Iva met me at the door, which was engulfed by darkness. Her arms crossed and a disapproving look was written on her face. I was calmly waiting for my sentence.

"Yes, I know, don't talk to Marcus. I get that, but he is a nice guy." I put my hands on my hips. I could tell she tried not to smile at my stubborn expression but failed.

"Maybe you should be nicer to him," I told her slyly.

"And why would I do that?" Her grey eyes widened suspiciously.

"Because he is built and sexy. And you said that there are no guys you would date here, vampires that is." I said, planting the seed.

A hissing noise came out through her lips. "What exactly are you suggesting, that I run off with a Rogue?" she wasn't mad, but definitely annoyed.

"I didn't say it. And Marcus isn't a Rogue; he is a werewolf, a sexy, single, strong one for that matter," I said, leaving her in the hall. It took her moments to be next to me again.

"You are crazy," was all she said. "There may be no cute vampires, but that doesn't mean I'm going to be the first to run off with a Rogue!" Her voice was high pitched.

"Okay, and that's why you are talking about it . . ." I said.

Iva just glared at me.

I was becoming really curious about how I was before I was taken, and I needed to change the subject before Iva's patience waned.

"What was I like before . . . I was taken?" I asked. She stopped walking, deep in thought. Her eyes softened.

"You really haven't changed that much; you're still the same stubborn talkative girl I knew before. Just now you're more confused, and you have a new dark side that has been poking out." She laughed at the realization. "Your personality is still the same; you just have to figure things out now, which will take time and healing."

"Do you miss the old me?" I asked.

She tucked a strand of brown hair behind her ear; turning to face me, she smiled. "You *are* the old you, just more complicated. Sure, we have to grow as friends again, and I miss how that was, but I still feel our friendship, the connection we always had."

I agreed with her, from the first time we met again I'd felt a connection. "I feel the same way . . . you know, I'm remembering bits and pieces slowly. I had a memory about Alec the other night. He told me he loved me. I loved him, too," I said, nearly choking on the "love" part.

She closed her eyes as her grin widened. "How do you feel about it now?"

"I'm not really sure; I have always been attracted to him, physically. And I have this weird electric current run through me every time he's near. But I'm not there yet . . . . Maybe this bond thing with Derek will always hold me back from moving forward."

"Don't shut Alec out, okay? Give him a chance. I know things are hard and strange for you right now, but try."

"Your team Alec, aren't you?" I asked, laughing.

"Of course I am. He has been searching for you for six years; everyone told him to give up, that it was too late. He didn't listen; he just knew you would be okay and not Rogue. He had so much faith in you. If you saw it . . . . His determination, love and passion . . . . Listen, all I'm saying is don't give up yet."

I was considering her words. I could see Alec's determination and faith in me. Since the moment on the dock, I'd seen something in his eyes, a fire. He is still a mystery to me, a dangerous mystery. But could I give him what he deserved. My heartfelt broken, I wasn't even sure I could love. Not with this consistent anger intensifying deep within my being and not yet being done grieving for my lost relationship with Derek.

"Then you should give Marcus a chance." The words slipped out by accident.

"WHAT DOES THAT HAVE ANYTHING TO DO WITH . . . ANYTHING???" It was the first time her voice had ever became loud.

"Sorry." I almost started cracking up laughing at her expression; she wasn't exactly saying no to the idea of Marcus, and her face held the thought and she was clearly dwelling on it. The seed was planted.

Alone and bored, back in my room, I was folding some jeans, trying to stay somewhat organized. There was nothing else for me to do. A soft knock on my door startled me. Happily, I jumped up from the floor and ran to the door. I opened the door to see messy dark hair, the usual grey eyes, the boyish features. Anthony was smiling at me, looking cute in his jeans and black jacket with a tee under it, like he stepped out of a Ralph Lauren ad. He leaned on my door crossing his arms, giving me a smoldering look.

"Would you be interested in coming to a party?" he asked.

Anthony always cut to the chase, he was not a play games type of guy. It was a nice change.

"You have my attention. Where is it?" I asked, intrigued.

"On the other side of court. Anyone who's anyone will be there."

A party away from Iva and Alec's watchful eyes. I would be alone, truly. The idea piqued my interest, highly. Yet deep down, I felt a little bit guilty, considering I promised I wouldn't sneak around. That moment of guilt quickly vanished, replaced by excitement.

"You have my interest. Give me a second so I can change," I said, and his smile broadened.

Closing the door swiftly, I began rifling through some clothes on a nearby chair, which soon ended on the floor. I found a cheetah print tank top, with skinny jeans and red heels. I brushed my hair quickly. Luckily, I had straightened it so it wasn't too bad.

I opened the door; Anthony nodded in approval. I was mildly concerned about being caught. I could almost see Alec's face and hear his disapproving voice. But it was easier to ask forgiveness than ask permission. Shrugging off the thought, I happily followed Anthony.

As we walked Anthony turned to me.

"Where's your body guard tonight?" he asked, smiling. I could hear the hint of fear in his voice. He should be fearful, Alec had a dark side that I'm sure would come out when angered. I got a taste of it at the ball.

"I don't know; hopefully you aren't taking me around his room."

He chuckled. "No, I wouldn't do that."

He didn't say anything else about that night, and I was thankful; it was awkward enough. Not to mention that Alec and I basically made out in the hall when I was supposed to be angry. How *that* got twisted. I kept the laugh to myself, so I wouldn't be questioned about why I was laughing.

Glancing around, I nearly forgot what I was doing, but then again my thoughts constantly consumed me. I didn't recognize where we were. The hall we went down was in the opposite direction I usually went. Never having been on this side of the court, I noticed it was mostly young vampires, around the same age as me. It was still identical to the look of the hall that led to my bedroom, but they had their own community. Something like a college campus dorm area, except open with couches and a large flat screen TV on the far side of the room. I briefly glanced at the couples openly making out, and quickly passed a group of young vampires laughing.

I saw what looked like a keg along the back wall, but what came out was blood. I hid my disgust as a vampire poured himself a glass.

Anthony took my hand in his, and I allowed him to do so; he led me across the room. I noticed immediately a group of guys that were leaning along the back wall. As we approached them they quieted and their eyes widened at the sight of me. I casually pushed my hair back as we approached this staring group.

One blonde guy in particular was clearly shocked, and didn't hide his facial expression.

"You actually brought her? I thought you were lying."

"I knew she was bored, being cooped up in her room under lock down. We need to show her a good time," Anthony said, elbowing the blonde guy.

"I'm Eli," the blonde one said, sticking out his hand to me. I shook it and his face lit up.

"Nice to meet you." I didn't state my name, figuring he knew it already.

"Can I get you a drink?" Anthony asked.

Remembering the keg with the blood, I was a bit afraid, but didn't want to exude that.

"Umm, depends on what it is," I said, not wanting to drink blood.

The guys rose their eyebrows and smiled to each other coyly, as if in on an inside joke. Ignoring the motion, I simply gave a half smile.

"We have a special drink, it's not blood, but it's pretty good. Gives a nice buzz," Anthony said motioning for his friend to bring the drink.

His friend, some dark-haired vampire, disappeared into the crowd, returning swiftly with some kind of drink in his hand.

Praying silently, I was feeling a little skeptical about being offered a drink by a group of guys. Date rape crossed my mind.

They handed it to me. I wanted to smell it, and to be sure it didn't have some sort of pill in it or something. Not that I could smell that. It looked normal, it was clear and bubbly. Am I really being one of those dumb girls who takes drinks from random guys who thought I were cute? I guess my common sense went out of the window when I got into the car with Alec. *Here goes nothing*, I thought to myself.

I took a sip; surprisingly it was tasty, almost like cherry soda but clear, with more of a fruity taste that popped on my tongue, leaving it numb. It was actually quite a pleasant feeling.

I began to feel uncomfortable as the guys watched me like I was an experiment. I glared back at them, almost challenging them.

"How do you like it?" Eli asked me.

"It is good. What is it?" I asked, examining it once more, as if I would find out from the cup.

"We can't tell you all our secrets, now," the guy named Eli said as he laughed at me.

I didn't want to stand around being a joke of some kind to these arrogant fools. I knew those types too well. And I was sure my fake smile was usually easily read, but when dealing with brainless men, I was unreadable.

My attention shifted toward the dance floor, The music was playing loud, and a big group of people were dancing and having a good time. I watched a bit longer and was met by Anthony's hand again.

"Do you want to dance?" Anthony asked seeing my interest toward the dance floor. Did I ever.

I nodded at the group of cocky guys, and happily turned toward Anthony.

"Sure." I finished the drink; he grasped my hand and led me to the floor, more like where the other vampires were dancing.

Making our way into the middle of the crowd, almost tripping over a couple of girls who were just standing around the edges of the dancers, they just glared at me as I approached. They were clearly not happy that I was there. I simply smiled at them. In return they just rolled their beady eyes at me.

It was a remix of some sort and it was great; I was feeling like I was back in the masquerade ball, minus Alec's watchful eyes. Freedom for the first time. It felt so wonderful to be out and have freedom.

I began to feel a little nauseous as I danced. The lights began to become fuzzy and my head started to spin. Or maybe I was spinning. I was still dancing close to Anthony, his hands creeping along my waist, making me a little uncomfortable. I was so disoriented I was unable to stop him, due to the spinning. I felt on the verge of throwing up. The drink they gave me did not mesh with my stomach. Before I knew what was happening I was being led away from the dance floor. My body was completely numb, a feeling like I was floating.

The people around me disappeared, when in reality I knew they were there. My eyesight was going in and out. We ended up down a hall, which was empty. Anthony roughly pushed me against the wall, his lips moving along my neck. I was trying to push him off.

"Stop. Stop!" I was saying, but the fool wouldn't listen to me. Anthony, it would seem, tried that much harder to violate me. Thinking of Alec, I hated to admit it, but he was right. Anthony did just want to take advantage of me. But then again most guys that were young and wanted to "have fun" just wanted to have a hook up. Whatever he gave me to drink prevented me from moving, and he was stronger than me. I was alone, like I had wanted to be, and I was terrified. I could feel my heart racing inside my chest, like a bird trying to get out.

His lips pressed against mine as his hands touched me. The drink, what was it? My anger became evident and I began to feel the burning heat spread to my fingers, feeling it in the core of my chest, working its way up and out of me. I never felt this hot before, like I could be in flames. It wasn't exactly painful, but it wasn't pleasant. I felt it, like a rubber band. I could move.

"Anthony, take your hands off me!" My voice, I didn't recognize it as my own. A growl in my chest came out. Anthony stopped this time, his face emitting confusion, his eyes narrowing on me. Did he finally grasp what I was saying? Anthony truly looked afraid as he watched me.

Were my eyes brown or something else? Shaking his head, he touched my boob. That did it. All comprehension returned in full force, snapping me out of it. All my strength was pouring out of me, readying me to attack. I narrowed my eyes on Anthony, who was oblivious to my anger.

I pushed him hard and he flew across the hall we were in, hitting the wall hard, leaving the wall more than cracked. He was now was on the other side of it, in someone's bedroom.

I was in complete shock at what I just did to Anthony; yet, the fury still was burning in me, which hindered my thinking. I had never been this angered before. I wanted to rip his head off. It wasn't an exaggeration; my body instinctively moved toward his unconscious body. I was so close when strong hands grabbed me; turning, expecting to see Alec, it was Marcus.

"Calm down, Aimee!" Marcus said quietly as he was holding my arms, like he would handcuff me. It might as well be handcuffs; his grip was strong.

"Get off me!" I growled at him. Spinning myself around and out of his grip, I lunged at Marcus, who was just as fast and pinned me to the ground.

"Aimee, don't cause a scene. No one sees you at the moment. Let's keep it that way."

I stopped fighting him; the fire was ebbing away as he got off me. Marcus helped me to my feet, while Holding my wrist firmly as we walked toward the exit and passed the people enjoying themselves, clearly not aware of me, and I was grateful for that, feeling ashamed at my predicament.

"We can't talk here," he said, almost like he read my mind. "I'll take you back to your room."

He continued to hold my wrist all the way back to my room, making me feel like I was a prisoner.

"How did you find me?" I asked, happy that the drink and anger were wearing off. I was left feeling extremely nauseous.

"I was patrolling the area and I felt you."

Felt me? I thought. "What do you mean?"

"Your anger, it vibrated in the ground. As a werewolf, I am very aware of the senses and emotions of the earth. Slight emotional changes;, I can feel them. That's how I found you. I never felt something like that before, though. I could literally feel the anger, and how strong you were. I was surprised you didn't combust."

We reached my room, my mind was racing. Combust? Who was I? I felt completely lost. I'm not this angry, sinister person. I was leaning on the wall and slid down it to sit. I sat staring at the wall across from me. "Am I going crazy? I never felt that way before and . . . I pushed him really hard; I didn't even know I had that kind of strength in me."

"You are not crazy; your body is confused. Not being changed as a werewolf or a vampire has it effects on you. The two are fighting to come out. The stronger one will eventually leak out."

"But I'm not a werewolf; I mean, I don't have the same gene like I do of a vampire. And all Derek did was erase my mind," I said, anxious.

"Hmmmm, well, it seems you have something else that is giving you such an edge. Have you acted like this before?" Marcus asked.

I tried to think back. I did have anger, sometimes so strong I felt I was on fire. But I never acted on it.

"I have had that burning angry feeling before. But not to this extent," I said, as I put my face in my hands. "Do you think he's really hurt?" I glanced up at Marcus through my hair. He was smiling coolly.

"He will live . . . May have a bad headache, but he deserved what he got. Do you have any idea about the drink he gave you?"

"No," I said quietly.

"And you drank it anyway?" Marcus said, looking at my face, which probably looked as if I would cry. He changed his tone. "It's got wolf blood, that's what gives it the kick."

That was exactly what I hadn't wanted to drink, and yet I drank blood after all.

"How did they get that?" I asked.

"I'm sure they have their sources."

"Do you think that's why I acted the way I did?" hoping that was the reason for my outburst.

I leaned on my knee. Marcus's features from this angle where very nice.

"I don't know, Aimee. Like Teeker said, most Yurnlings who are captured don't stay that way; they are turned shortly after being captured. Everything about you is new."

My life seemed so complex, nothing was simple or could be explained, it was infuriating and frustrating. I started to cry out of frustration, I couldn't help it. My body began quivering. Marcus knelt down next to me, and placed a nervous hand on me.

"I don't know how it feels, but you aren't alone. You will get through this!"

My mind wandered to Alec and what he told me not to do, and he was right. Anthony wasn't any good.

"I'm such a fool!" I spoke out.

"What?"

"I ran off without thinking again. Alec told me to think before I act, and I failed."

"It's not a test, Aimee, but it's good advice. He really is loyal to you," Marcus said.

"How do you know that?"

"Because I can feel it, and, well, see it. I'm pretty sure he would do anything for you," Marcus said, smiling.

I knew Alec would if I asked, even if I didn't, I couldn't get him to leave even if I wanted him to.

"I'm so lost, Marcus. I feel like my body is being torn in two. I don't want to be either a werewolf or vampire. I want to stay *me*. And I don't even know who me is anymore. I'm so angry, and I can't control it." Passion filled my voice.

"Listen, that time will come one day, but until then, just take it one day at a time. Live for today; tomorrow will have its own worries! As for the anger, you have a lot to deal with. Learning where you came from and who you are is hard in itself, and adding the wolf and vampire to the mix just creates more fuel for the fire." His eyes were dark green, and had so much compassion in them.

Why did people believe in me so much? I didn't deserve any of it.

He wiped a tear from my cheek, and helped me stand up.

Without thinking, I gave him a hug. After a moment of uncertainty, he placed his hands on my back. He was warm and rock solid. I didn't have romantic feelings for him, but he was a friend, someone I could trust. He understood the wolf side of me I didn't, if there was a wolf side. But I couldn't deny how good looking Marcus was. Pulling away, I kissed his cheek.

"Thank you, Marcus, for the help!"

He patted my head. "You're welcome, my friend. You should get back inside before Alec or Iva find us together." He opened the door for me as I stepped in.

'"Night, Aimee! We will talk again soon," Marcus said, smiling.

I glanced around my room, and then swiftly began walking toward my bathroom, kicking off my heels as I took my clothes off. I turned the shower on and had yet another knock on the door. I put a towel around myself. What did Marcus have to say this time? Smiling as I opened the door, I saw ice grey eyes, wavy brown hair, that perfect face. Alec stood in my doorway; clearly he was shocked at the state I was in, looking down to make sure I did have a towel on.

"I'm sorry. I didn't know you were . . . well . . . ." He blushed, but didn't move or hide the admiring stare he cast at me.

"Is something wrong?" I asked.

"No, I just had a feeling, that's all, and I wanted to make sure you were all right."

He wasn't too far off; if he had come five minutes earlier he would have seen me with Marcus.

"I'm fine," I assured him.

"Okay, well, I will let you get back to your shower or whatever you were about to do." He made it sound like I was doing something secretive in my room. I smiled at this thought. I could invite him in; would it give the wrong message? As if Alec could sense what I was thinking, he said, "Can I come in?" His voice sounded uncertain, almost as if he didn't want me to say yes.

"Ummm, I guess. Just give me a second to change." I let him into the room as I ran to the bathroom, turning the shower off and putting a robe on.

He sat on his usual chair. It was becoming a ritual. Being in my room at night and him sitting on that same chair that looked so uncomfortable.

I took my usual seat on my bed. It was a safe distance.

"Aimee, I wanted to talk to you about something," he said, not looking at me.

"Okay," I said.

"About that night of the ball. You were right to want to be able to . . . do whatever you were going to do with Anthony. It wasn't my place. Just because we were together in the past doesn't mean anything, and I'm sorry."

It wasn't his place, but he was right about Anthony—he was a creeper.

"And about the kiss . . . ." He looked into my eyes.

"I don't regret it," I said quietly.

"You don't? I rushed things, and I'm sorry. It's been hard for me; you have no idea."

"I don't regret it," I said again firmly.

He sat up straighter in his chair, relief on his face.

"I don't want to make you confused," Alec said softly.

It was confusing, but the more I saw Alec and talked with him, the more my feelings grew.

"Derek was in your life for six years; you must have feelings for him still. And the bond you have with him. It's hard for me to change that."

"I do have a lot of emotions, Alec, with everything, not just Derek, but with who I am. I feel so . . . lost," I said. "But learning what Derek is, and what he was planning for me. Well it's overwhelming."

"Do you wish you were married?"

His question caught off guard a bit. I hadn't been thinking of marriage. It was way off topic. Now that he brought it up the pang in my chest came to surface. I hadn't been able to grieve fully the end of the relationship, if that's what you could even call it.

"Not now, not after I found out that Derek and his dad were the ones who took me. I am grateful for your rescue."

He hesitated before standing up and then made his way to the door. Alec was acting strange, strange as far as Alec goes, anyway. He looked back to me, hand on the knob. "It's late, and I'm sorry for bothering you." I stood up and rushed to the door, placing a hand on his wrist.

"Do you still love him?" he asked.

?This question really caught me by surprise. Did I love Derek? The answer would hurt Alec, because no matter what I told myself, that part of me longed for Derek. How do I shut off a feeling that I had for so long? I didn't know if I should answer him. This feeling I had with Alec, it was different, natural, and I could be myself. Flaws and all. The feeling with Derek was something else, I couldn't even begin to describe it.

Alec nodded,; taking my silence as his answer, he turned the knob. I pushed the door shut. He was so stubborn.

"What do you want me to say, Alec?"

"I understand, and that's why I need to leave."

"Leave where?"

"Your room." He spun around so fast, his eyes so full of fire, a hungry fire.

"It's not love I feel for Derek. What I feel with you is something natural, like I'm complete. I just . . . need . . . time." I didn't want him to leave me. I wanted to kiss him so bad, his soft lips were inches from me. I was feeling the warmth between us again. He nodded at me and opened the door; grabbing his shoulder, it took strength to turn his body to face me. Standing on my toes I reached for his face and kissed him hard.

He froze, then began giving in to me. He held me in his arms while kissing me with that same intense passion. My heart was racing, as well as my pulse.

Releasing me, he looked me levelly in the eyes, which revealed so much to me. "Goodnight, Aimee," Alec said, leaving my room.

Eleven

SOME THINGS WERE CERTAIN, I could become a werewolf, become a vampire, or just stay the way I was, which was confusing in itself. As if that wasn't complicated enough, my love life was in shambles and basically a hot mess. Derek was my ex-fiancée, and a werewolf, more known as a Rogue. His family kidnapped me to convert me to become a wolf bride, and carry on the race. I couldn't forget him due to the fact he had some twisted bond over me, where he would call me at any time, and read my thoughts. I was helplessly still in love with him, the murderous Rogue werewolf.

Then there is Alec the vampire. Apparently we were in love before my abduction, and he spent six years trying to free me, succeeding last month when he set up Derek with a Yurnling. A Yurnling is anyone who yearns to be awakened as a vampire, which you have to be born with the genes of a vampire for. Unfortunately, the Yurnling was my friend, Krissy, and she got her neck snapped by Derek.

Mixed with all this craziness were my anger surges. I had no control over them. I could be happy and the next moment a burning fire deep within me erupted like a volcano, pouring out like venom, hurting the people I care about with my hot temper. I didn't know why it happened, it seemed to be getting worse. It left me feeling horrible for the way I would snap and yell at Alec and Iva, who was apparently my bestie before I was abducted.

My feelings for Alec had been growing—or stirring, maybe they had never left. Being around him made me happy. Yes, he was infuriating at times, but I was, too. Was this feeling love, or lust?

Derek still lingered in my heart, like a dark evil, but I still wanted him. I wanted them both.

Kissing Alec the other night in my room, I was hoping I wasn't causing him more damage. Seeing him now, he smiled a little brighter, but he still didn't acknowledge the kiss. But that was Alec. The more I seemed to get to know him, the more mysterious and hard to get a solid read on he was.

There was Alec, sitting across from me. We were all in my room, on the floor; Iva sat on my right side. They were discussing how we could break the bond. I didn't see that happening. I stood, stretched and walked to my mini fridge, grabbing a bottle of water. Alec had his eyes on me, as if I was going to dash out the door. Or possibly he was admiring me. Regardless of what he was thinking as he looked at me, millions of tiny butterflies erupted in my stomach. Alec both excited me and made me unsure at the same time.

"Teeker may have an answer as to how to break the connection!" Iva said confidently.

"Maybe, but I think it's something more complex," Alec said, putting his hands through his beautiful hair. I caught myself admiring his eyes. Even though all vamps had grey eyes, his were piercing.

"Guys, I think things will be fine. Just don't tell me how to get here or where exactly I'm at and he can't find me." I was smiling like a cheese ball. As if my answer was the key.

"This connection isn't healthy for you," Alec said, concerned.

Perhaps Alec just didn't want me talking with my ex. That thought was immature of me to think, but it could be a possibility.

I flopped on my canopy bed, sprawling out.

"He hasn't tried to reach me in weeks now. Perhaps he's given up," I said.

"Unlikely. There is a purpose to everything that they do," Iva said.

"Can you reach them from your end?" Alec asked suddenly.

I'd never thought of it before.

"Like trying to read their thoughts?" I asked.

"That and just reaching them in general."

"I don't know; I haven't tried before," I said. Sitting up, they were both glaring at me. "Why are you looking at me like that?" Then realization dawned on me. "You want me to try, don't you?"

"Wouldn't hurt. And we are both here with you," Alec said with excitement in his voice.

Sure, everyone could be entertained at my expense.

"Okay." I was about to close my eyes, but they were still staring at me.

"Do you mind giving me space?" I asked, a little testy.

Diverting their eyes at each other now, they were unsuccessful with hiding their smiles from me.

Here goes nothing. Closing my eyes, I tried to relax. I focused on Derek, but nothing was happening, and I was feeling stupid. I was about to open my eyes when the familiar hazy fog appeared, the forest returned.

It was the same as I remembered it. Rich green trees surrounded me. The grass was damp, as my feet walked uncertainly toward the forest, searching for him. My heart was beating very fast; my hands began to sweat, and I was feeling sick. I really wasn't sure what to say if Derek was here.

Almost relieved, I didn't see him. The fear, however, was still in my subconscious.

"Where are you, Derek?" I spoke loud and firmly. All I heard was the birds chirping to my call.

It was dusk, and the forest gave off an almost eerie, silent vibe. Nothing seems stranger than standing alone in a Freddie Kruger forest and calling out to someone who isn't responding.

A slight, quiet movement caught my attention. I froze, stiffening instantly. A dark figure emerged from the trees. His dark cropped hair was a bit disheveled, but those eyes, there was no mistaking them.

Derek came into view, smiling, reminding me of that night on the yacht when he killed Krissy.

"You figured it out, Aimee!" he almost sounded proud.

"And your point is?" I asked coldly.

He came close to me, and he was so good looking, his sharp features mixed with his green eyes, my heart hurt a little. Be strong! My flesh was so weak.

"You might want to speak to me more nicely. You are the one who called *me*," he said, raising his eyebrows.

What was I supposed to ask him? His green eyes watched me; he wore an arrogant expression, waiting.

"You killed her," I said quietly.

His facial expression didn't change in the slightest bit.

"I did what I had to," Derek said dryly.

"Was our relationship even real?" I asked. "Yes, I believe it is."

"How could you do this to me, then? Live a lie. If I married you, never knowing any of this . . . . Were you going to change me?"

"I don't believe it's a lie; it's the way of our world, Aimee. And yes, I was going to change you after the honeymoon."

My heart skipped a beat. "Why me? And why wait so long?" I asked.

"I have wanted you for a long time, Aimee. You won't remember now, but I saw you long ago, you were out of your community with your parents at the airport. And I saw you. I already knew what you were, I could smell you, and I knew you were royal with the guard around you. There was something about you, also; I knew you would be mine."

Taking in what he said was scary, more than scary, it petrified me to the core, sending chills down my spine. It was planned, my capture. Teeker was right.

"Did you really love me?" I asked quietly.

He walked closer to me, and I let him. He put his hand on my cheek. It was familiar, yet it frightened me. My emotions were so contradictory.

"I have always loved you, Aimee. And my mother does, too. She misses you," he said coyly.

Derek was so good at making you feel desired. He knew how to get what he ultimately wanted. That's what made him so dangerous.

His hand stayed on my face, and the sick part was, I allowed it too. I would undoubtedly feel guilty later about it.

I did miss Elizabeth. And a part of me wished I could be with Derek. But that wasn't a life I wanted anymore.

"Why do you kill the innocent?"

"I can't control myself, Aimee. It's what I am. I never harmed you." His eyes were soft, and held so much strength.

My trance was broken and I stepped back away from him; I was the one who summoned him this time. I was the one in control!

"I can't be with you now, Derek. I don't want to go Rogue!"

His eyes twitched, and I could see the fury hidden behind them.

"It's already in you, can't you feel it? The anger and burning fire. It's who you are, too. You still have a lot to learn about yourself. I can help you see who you are."

"It's not what I will become!"

"Maybe not today, but I will find you. I want you. We belong together. My family is royalty, Aimee. I belong with the best. Our son will be a great ruler."

"We don't have a son, Derek!" I said, raising my voice, putting more distance between us.

"Not yet, but we will." He was so confident. And in reality he terrified me.

"No, we won't! I will break the bond!" I blurted out.

"You can't, sweetheart. And the only way you can won't happen because you're not strong enough, and I can see you love me . . . ." His smile played at his lips. "I need to be getting back now. "He leaned down to me, pressing his lips to my forehead. "We should do this again. And Aimee, I will find you. So tell Alec to be careful. He can't have you, not that it matters. He won't live long enough," Derek said softly. It sent a cold chill down my spine.

"How do you know about him?" I asked

Briefly stopping, he was near the edge of the forest." I have my sources; I know you were involved with him before me." He then disappeared into the darkness of the forest.

My mouth dropped open. He was going to kill Alec! The forest faded and I opened my eyes, vision blurred a little.

Alec and Iva hovered over me, anxious, I assumed, about what happened.

I didn't want to talk. The fact was, I did care about Derek. A part of me loved him. Alec was looking at me with concern on his face.

My heart ached for Alec. Alec was true and good, which made it easy for my feeling to grow daily. How could I tell him? I curled into a ball, hoping they would leave me alone. But they didn't. I wanted to cry, or scream. Something to relieve this deep pain that was building in my chest. I felt so numb.

"Aimee, are you all right?" Iva asked, apparently Alec was at a loss for words. I didn't answer her. How could I? I'm a traitor to my feelings. I wanted to be left alone.

"Do you want us to leave?" Alec asked. He always seemed to understand me. I thought about it and I did need to think. I just nodded. Alec had a pained expression on his face as Iva stood up and she exchanged a glance with Alec.

I heard the door shut behind them, a tear leaked out from the corner of my eye. What was I supposed to do? Derek knew about Alec; what else did he know? A sudden realization came to mind. The Enclave, the night I left Derek, it wasn't a dream, and he was looking for me. If I didn't trust Alec, Derek would ultimately have me. I closed my eyes and sobbed in silence.

After what seemed like a long time being in my room, I decided to venture out.

My hunger took me out of seclusion.

The hallway was empty as I walked alone, passing the many cream-colored hotel-looking doors, with door numbers in the center of each.

My stomach was growling as I made my way towards the pizza parlor, walking like a zombie, completely unaware of my surroundings or who was around me. I was feeling a little depressed, mixed with anxiety. Maybe being alone wasn't the best option.

Entering the main court area, which was shaped like a horseshoe, the little food boutiques captivated me. In the center were stone benches and tables, the ceiling was shaped like a dome, a bronze dome.

The vampires and Yurnlings happily enjoyed whatever happy thoughts they had. I eyed them enviously. I wished my life were like that.

I haven't spoken with my mother in a while, I thought, watching a daughter and mother pass me smiling. My father figure just basically worshiped my mom. Anything she wanted. That would drive me crazy; I would end up ditching the man.

The guy behind the counter smiled as I approached him.

"Cheese, please." The man picked a slice and put it in the oven.

"Hungry, huh?" came Alec's voice from behind me. I didn't turn to face him, still in a mood. He placed a hand on my shoulder; I flinched slightly at his touch.

"Can I join you?" he asked, uncertain.

"If you want to," I told him.

We took a seat at a table out of earshot from the cashier in the very back.

The first bite was amazing; it burned my tongue but that didn't stop me. I was starving.

I was avoiding Alec's eyes, looking at the pizza.

"Aimee, what's wrong? And don't say 'nothing'!"

"I don't want to talk about it," I said, mouth full of pizza.

"Iva and I are so worried. You have been hiding in your room all day. Did he hurt you?" he asked, lowering his voice. If only that was it. I wished that were the reason for my hiding.

Looking into Alec's eyes, how could I tell him what Derek told me? I frowned as I took a sip of my soda.

"I'm sorry. I can't tell you," I said finally.

"Don't you trust me?" He looked hurt.

"I do trust you, I just can't tell you right now."

His eyes narrowed. He reached out and touched my hand. I felt the warmth and electricity run through me. Pulling my hand back startled him.

How could I be such a traitor? I didn't deserve him. His eyes showed so much hope. Why did he do this to me?

"Why do you care so much, Alec?" I asked, even though I knew the answer already. It was petty of me. But the fact was I didn't deserve him. I should be alone in my pity party.

His eyebrows rose. "Are you being serious?" he asked.

"Yes, I am being serious! Stop pretending like everything is fine, because it's not! I'm not fine! I have changed, no matter what you and Iva think! The old Aimee you both knew is gone!" my voice was raising.

"What can I do to help?"

What didn't he get? My mood was rapidly growing, as I tried to get him to see my reasoning.

"Alec, stop! You can't help me, don't you get it?"

"I can and I will help you!" He was so confident in everything, and at this moment that was infuriating. No matter what I said he wouldn't see my reason. In the end it would kill him.

"So stop trying to get rid of me, it won't work. I'm in this with you! You have nothing to fear," Alec said.

I had everything to fear, losing Alec. Derek wasn't going to stop until he found me. I didn't even know where he was, or if he was close by.

I gave him a lopsided smile. "Why are you such a fool?" I asked.

"Because I'm a fool in love." He said it in a whisper. That took me by surprise. What could I say in response to him?

Looking at the table, I said, "No you aren't."

"I am! I have loved you from the moment we had had our first class together, and you let me borrow your pen—even before that, when I first laid eyes on you in your mother's office. I love you still; every day it burns in my chest, Aimee. I will never give up on you, on us. I know you've changed over the years, I know you were engaged. But we are meant for each other." He spoke with so much passion that my chest ached. I have been denying myself loving Alec. In truth, I knew for a while that how I feel when I'm with Alec wasn't just a like or a crush, it went deeper.

Electricity ran through me as he captured my hand. His icy eyes were so full of warmth and love.

"Why are you telling me this?" I asked, voice cracking.

"Because it's the truth and I'm tired of not telling you."

"We can't be together, Alec," I said in a whisper.

"Maybe not right now, with the things we have to fix. And we will overcome it."

"That's not why we can't be together," I said.

"Then why?" he asked.

Taking a deep breath, I couldn't bear the thought of losing him. If I had to push him away to keep him safe then I would.

"I don't feel the same way, Alec," I said, the biggest lie, it was so sour coming out of my lips.

"I don't believe you," he said.

"I'm telling the truth, Alec. You and I aren't ever going to work, not now not ever." His eyes flashed and I knew my words had struck him hard. I wanted to cry and be alone. I knew what I had to do. Standing and picking my garbage up, Alec just sat there frozen; the words were sinking in slowly, like cancer. I could see the effect it was having on him.

I turned to walk away from him but he grabbed my wrist, hard.

"I still don't believe you; you aren't protecting me by pushing me away. I can see it in your eyes." Alec said, the fact was he was hoping that's what I was doing, and he was right. I just wouldn't tell him.

"Just let me go, please," I said with agony. Alec listened and released me. I couldn't look at his face any longer, there was so much pain and confusion. He had the same expression I knew so well. *I'm doing this to protect him,* I told myself, trying to stay strong. He stayed in his chair as I left the pizza parlor.

Twelve

***I**F ONLY ALEC KNEW WHAT* DEREK told me, would he still be acting as stubborn? Yes, he would, never giving up on me. This is why I have to push him away. My options were slim, yet in my heart, I knew what had to be done. I had to find Marcus and find out how to kill a werewolf. I hoped that Alec would forgive me when the time came.

I was truly regretting everything I told him. Oh, the ugliness of lies.

Coming up to the metal door that would lead me to the wolf lair, I pushed the button, but Marcus did not answer the door. Some other handsome guy did, the same green eyes and clean haircut, chiseled features. Very nice looking.

His expression was pleasantly confused. "Are you lost?" the werewolf asked, smiling.

"No, I'm looking for Marcus. Would you tell him Aimee is looking for him?" I asked.

"Aimee?" he asked, my name playing on his lips. Testing it.

"Yes, can you please hurry?" I asked, getting annoyed. I didn't have time to flirt. My arms were crossed as I glared at this wolf.

His eyebrows raised and he nodded. He shut the door and I waited anxiously in the hall, pacing like a mad woman.

My mind was spinning. Would I be able to actually kill Derek even though I had feelings for him? The thought of him coming here—well that was not going to happen, I wouldn't let it!

I didn't want to become a werewolf or have him kill Alec. Maybe there was another way? The door opened shortly and Marcus stood there looking like a god.

"Is everything all right?" Marcus asked, full of concern.

Why did everyone ask that? The other wolf man stood next to him, curious. I shot him a look; Marcus turned to glare at the man. "She is fine, Clark." Clark clearly didn't want to leave, but eventually he walked away, sulking.

"Sorry to barge in like this, but it's important," I said.

"Come in," he said, and I followed him to the fire pit. I didn't know how they lived in such heat, I could already feel the perspiration beads on my forehead.

I sat on a rocking chair while he chose to sit on the walls that surround the fire pit. The room still was the same, like a giant bear cave, with bits of tree roots pocking out on the walls and ceiling.

His eyes were on me intently, ready for whatever I would say. "So this bond thing I have with Derek and his family . . . ." I took a deep breath. "Well, I summoned him earlier today. And I found out some things that I can't share with anyone." He nodded in understanding for me to continue. "Well, the thing is, I need your help. Derek said I couldn't break the bond, because I won't have enough strength to do it . . . Am I right to assume I would have to kill . . . him?" I asked, taking a jagged breath.

I could tell Marcus was thinking about it. "Your assumptions are correct. That is the only way, unless you decide to be awakened. Then the bond breaks."

That was an option, but that would mean Derek would still hunt me.

"How would I kill . . . a Rogue werewolf?" His eyes flashed and the realization crossed his features.

"Aimee, what do you intend to do?"

"Just answer the question."

He was hesitant. "Aimee, please don't tell me you want to hunt him." His voice was raised.

I just looked away, which was answer enough. He sighed heavily. "Please don't run off alone," he said quietly.

"Is it true that silver bullets—?"

He cut me off, laughing. "No, that is a myth. The only way is a vampire bite. Another possibility would be to cut his head off with a special metal that is usually in the shape of a sword."

Darn, no wonder Derek said I couldn't. I'm neither a vampire nor do I have a sword made of whatever metal. I began feeling dejected about the whole thing.

"You don't understand, Marcus, I don't have a choice," I said.

"There is always a choice. This is a suicide mission. I'm afraid he is right."

I leaned back into my chair. "What did you mean about not going alone?" I asked.

"Meaning don't go off and get yourself killed or turn Rogue."

A new thought came to mind, and a smile claimed my face.

"Would you help me?" I batted my lashes at him. "If I help you with Iva?"

Marcus looked shocked that I mentioned Iva, but I could see briefly the wheels turning in his good-looking face of his.

"Iva is a lost fantasy, which should be left alone," he said, scolding me. "What exactly would you have me do?"

That I wasn't sure about, maybe just be my moral support. I was thankful for Marcus even considering it at all.

"I'm not sure. If you don't want me to go alone, then come with me!" I said, trying to convince him.

He laughed." I knew it! You want to go after this guy. And you think I would go off on a suicide mission with you?" Marcus said pointing his finger at me. His voice had raised and a few passing werewolves glanced at him.

I didn't think about that part. I wouldn't want him to get harmed.

"Hey, you told me not to go alone. Remember?"

"Yes . . . but I didn't think you were really serious," Marcus said.

"So?" I asked, leaning my body towards him.

He just looked at me with an expression of utter disapproval. "So, what?"

"You know exactly what. Are you going to come with me? We can go on an adventure together."

"I don't need any more adventures," he said, agitated.

"You said you are free to go as you please; we will be a great team!" I patted his shoulder, which was stiff; he gave me a half smile.

"I don't know, Aimee," he said.

"Listen, I'm going to be planning to leave soon. Think about it." He just glared at me. I began to stand up and his warm hand gripped my wrist.

"Aimee, what about your family?" he asked.

"I am protecting them, Marcus," I said, as he released me. I escorted myself out the door, leaving him to sit and think about what I asked of him, passing the cute blonde werewolf, Clark. "Will I be seeing you again?" he asked.

Glancing over my shoulder at him, I said, "Maybe!"

He smiled at me as I left.

My mind was replaying how hard this mission was going to be, but most important I was wondering if I would be able to kill Derek.

I was almost to the main court when I got a glimpse of Iva striding toward me; she was mad looking. Actually, mad was an understatement—she was livid. Could I out run her? I thought about my chances. Slim to none.

"And where have you been?" she asked, coming to a halt in front of me. I could see she was almost shaking with fury.

"Marcus and I had some things to discuss," I said coolly.

"Oh, really! Aimee, why don't you ever listen to anyone? I used to be your best friend at one time and we used to respect each other. I do miss that!" Yup, she was mad, all right.

"I still think of you as my best friend." She was my only friend. But the feelings were there still.

She took a deep breath. "What did you need to talk to a werewolf about?" she asked coldly.

I smiled; *well this would open a can of worms*, I thought. "You."

"Me?"

"Yes. You."

Confusion crossed her beautiful face. "Why?"

"Well, he has a wolfy crush on you," I said, smiling.

Marcus would skin me alive if he heard this conversation, but at least Iva wouldn't tell him.

Iva's stunned expression was priceless. Her mouth hung open as she just narrowed her eyes on me. It was part of the truth, after all. I couldn't tell her what I was really doing, and I didn't even know for certain what I would do.

She closed her mouth. "It doesn't mean you have to sneak off and speak with him in his lair," she said.

At least she wasn't as mad and there was something in her eyes that I hadn't seen before. I knew it! She was attracted to him. Well, how could she not be? He was gorgeous. I wanted to smile, but I held it in.

"And where are you headed off to now?" she asked, a little more calmed down, and back to the same controlled Iva.

That was a good question, because I didn't know. "Nowhere in particular," I said.

"You know, I saw Alec a little while ago and he was really depressed looking. What did you say to him?"

I froze and my mouth was open, I closed it, taking a breath. I didn't see this turn of events coming. Geez it was attack Aimee day.

I flinched at the memory of what I told him. "I told him not to care about me." My smile turned into a hard line. In truth, I felt horrible, and sick even.

She looked at me, dumbfounded. "Why would you say that to him? I thought you two were on the mend."

"I can't explain it Iva, I do care about him. But I need to have space and learn things without him right now." Even saying that I could hear the lie in it. Hopefully Iva wasn't as observant as she usually was.

"I feel really bad for Alec, Aimee. You shouldn't have led him on, then."

Led him on? I wasn't . . . okay, maybe I was, but I do care about him I just couldn't tell him or Iva at the moment. Not with my plans. I didn't say anything. What could I say? Iva's eyes were searching mine. Her usually slicked-back shoulder length brown hair was loose and wavy. I liked her like this, not so uptight.

"Aimee, what are you not telling me?" she asked, still searching my eyes. Iva, I doubted, ever had a non-observant day, at least when it came to me.

Thinking fast. "I snuck out with Anthony and went to his secret party," I blurted out.

"What?" her voice was dangerous, but she was clearly taken by surprise.

"You heard me, I'm tired of being treated like I'm 12; I'm a grown woman and I can make my own choices."

"When was that?"

"A couple of nights ago. I didn't stay long because Marcus came to the rescue. Anthony drugged me, with some kind of drink made from wolf blood." That certainly got a reaction from her. She lost it in the hall. Her nostrils flared, and her eyes flashed. I want sure to be frightened or run for it.

"That is an illegal substance, they shouldn't be drinking it! I can't believe you took it from him! You have always been the one with common sense!" Iva was screaming at me, her arms flailing around looking utterly ridiculous, yet entertaining at the same time.

I reeled in my amusement and tried to put my serious face on.

"Maybe I lost it," I said back at her. "Yelling at me isn't going to change the fact that I hung out with a werewolf or a creeper like Anthony. So just forgive me and be over it."

"That simple, huh?" She was smiling a little now.

"Yes it is. We all make mistakes, and I'm not your prisoner!" I said, hands on my hips.

Iva took a deep breath. "I'm sorry for being controlling. I'll forgive you if you can forgive me."

"Of course I forgive you," I said and walked up to her and hugged her. She was stiff at first but returned the hug.

"Marcus isn't bad either. You should really give him a chance."

"Don't push it,." she said, amused now.

Alec came into my head and I felt that empty feeling in my heart, for the things I said to him. He had always been there with his hope and love and I just threw it in his face. I sucked.

"Do you think Alec will forgive me?" I asked, as we started to walk away from the wolf lair hall, crossing the court and making our way toward my room.

A few Yurnlings passed us in the hall, looking at me curiously.

"I don't know. He is in love with you, Aimee; you could probably try to kill him and he would still forgive you. You should talk to him and explain things to him," she said encouragingly.

Could I even face him ever again? I was only going to be here for a little longer. I should apologize at least; I do want to try and work out if I end up surviving this quest.

Thirteen

*S*TANDING IN THE HALL OUTSIDE my room, everything became blurry and the floor felt like it was moving, but it wasn't, I was. I gripped the wall for support. The feeling of overwhelming nausea rose.

Blackness surrounded me. It felt like eternity, but pieces of light began to seep into the darkness. It was like watching a movie; I was standing inside my mother's glass room. Everything seemed to look the same. Same lily flowers in the vases, messy desk by the door. The curtains that engulfed the large windows that overlooked the outside were velvet ivory drapes, the couches were also different, dark blue. She had definitely upgraded her couches.

That's probably why I'm so disorganized, I thought, glancing once more at her paper stacks on the desk.

My mother stood in front of me, arms crossed.

"Aimee, I already told you, no! You cannot go to that boy's party. It's unacceptable for you to be there. You will one day be the leader of this community and you can't be acting like a child."

I stood there, crossing my arms at her, and glaring, angered by her answer.

Even though I watched the scene in front of me, I could feel how the past me felt.

"It isn't fair! I'm sixteen years old and should be able to do what I want." I could feel that same anger and mood change happen so swiftly. It would seem that it was always with me.

"You are not an adult. You still have two years before you awaken, and I'm still saying *no*. End of discussion." She had her narrow eyes glaring at me. Her face was smoother, having a little fewer wrinkles, and I looked the same. I guess I hadn't aged much at all. The door suddenly opened and in came my father, with his hands on a boy's shoulder. It was Alec; he was dirty and his hair was messy, but still that same length he has it now. His blue eyes looked at me, embarrassed. His eyes held so much hurt and pain. We just locked eyes, until my dad spoke.

"This is Alec. I found him while traveling. The Rogues murdered his family. And he was left. Aimee, why don't you take him to get cleaned, then bring him to the guest housing?"

My dad had the look of don't ask questions, just do it. So I just nodded as I turned my attention to Alec.

So this was the first time I'd laid eyes on him. I could feel the butterflies in my chest and how I felt, giddy, excited. *He was the hottest thing in this place*, I thought, even though he was dirty.

I was smiling at him; Alec was blushing and not looking at me.

"I'm Aimee, by the way. Alec, was it?"

"Yes," he said.

"It's nice to meet you, Alec," I said almost crashing into the statue that was in the hall. He didn't laugh at me.

"I hope you stay," He looked up this time, meeting my glance over his shoulder.

"I have nowhere else to go." He had a nice Italian accent. I was used to it because most of the people that lived among us had Italian accents. The entire vampire race originated in Rome. Passing down the gene from our ancestors was the only way to become a vampire; no outside human could be made into a vampire. The choice to be awakened came when we were older, 18 to be exact.

We stopped in front of his door, number 264. He was looking around the hall. I opened the door for him; it was nice, with a queen size bed, flat screen TV and a mini living room. Very cozy. Alec's face reflected sadness. I'm sure losing your family was very hard and I couldn't imagine how he was feeling as I watched him.

"If you need anything, don't hesitate to call my room, I'll write it down for you. We have class the day after tomorrow, and I will help you catch up."

Alec just looked into my eyes with a depth I never felt before. "Thank you, Aimee," was all he said, but the words held tremendous warmth in them.

Shutting the door, a huge smile swept across my face. I quickly ran down the hall to look for Iva. I didn't have to look far; coming around the corner, I almost ran into her.

"Oh my gosh, you will never believe who I just met!" I said, excited.

"Brad Pitt?" she asked, sarcastic and smiling.

I wished. "No, his name is Alec and he is so cute. My father asked me to help him! His family was killed by the Rogues."

Iva's smile went into a hard line. She looked the same, a little younger, maybe, and her hair was waist length. "Brad Pitt sounds better," she said, laughing.

The dizzy, groggy sensation was lifting. I slowly opened my eyes to the present; Iva was sitting on the ground waiting patiently. I was also sitting on the ground. How this happened, I wasn't sure—maybe when I blacked out I hit the ground and Iva sat me upright.

Iva didn't say anything but just sat there. "It was the first day I met Alec," I said. I was attracted to him at first sight.

Iva had so much sympathy in her eyes.

"You were there also, talking about Brad Pitt," I said, smiling.

Iva smiled widely showing her fangs. "I remember that. It was the good old times." I could tell she went into thought as she looked past me. "You should get some sleep, though. It's been a long day," Iva said.

I was surprised she didn't press me for details, but I agreed, I did need to try to sleep. I may never get to see Alec again, and that thought scared me.

Fourteen

*L*YING IN BED, FOR WHAT seemed like a long time, sleep never came over me. After tossing and turning for the hundredth time, I kicked the sheets off of me, and wiped the sweat from my forehead, getting out of bed, frustrated. All I could think about was Alec. I just lay there reliving those few memories I had of him. My mind wandered to the pool, the pool sounded really good; hopefully I could drown some thoughts away. Rummaging through my underwear drawer, I found a totally inappropriate suit. *Perfect.* Slipping on a pretty sexy swim suit that no one would see but me felt good. Taking a towel and wrapping it around me, I peeked out my door. All clear.

The pool was empty, just as I knew it would be. It was really dark; the little lanterns that surrounded the pool and hung in the trees on the deck gave very little light.

I set my towel down and put a toe in the water, wanting to test it, in case it was cold. It was heated, sweet! I sat on the steps and leaned back, letting the water engulf my hair. The stars were so bright on this crisp late spring night. Enjoying the fresh air, I closed my eyes. My thoughts unfortunately were not disappearing, as I knew they wouldn't. But the warm water was nice against my body.

The feeling of deep sadness lingered in my chest. I knew what I had to do, but a very large part of me didn't want to. Who in their right mind would go after someone they loved, and kill them? It was a task I wasn't sure I could even accomplish.

Sitting up just enough so that my head was out of the water, I heard a noise. I had the sudden feeling someone was watching me, and I became rigid and sat up rapidly. My eyes glanced around the pool area. It was so dark that I could only make out the spots that the lanterns lit. This was not much light.

By the outskirts of the pool area was someone standing very still and quiet. My eyes were desperately trying to see who it was. My heart was beating very fast in my chest. My immediate thought was Derek. Had he found me? The shadow moved more toward the light, illuminating the face of Alec. He stood very quietly as he watched me. *Silent stalker*, I thought, and I smiled, then quickly frowned. I didn't want to discuss things at this point. I became self-conscious under his gaze.

"You scared me half to death!" I said to him. I could see his grin. He came closer and took a seat near the edge of the pool.

"Why don't you join me?" I asked, splashing the water with my hands.

I was happy to see he wasn't mad enough to really stay away from me.

"Will you please make up your mind?" he said quietly.

Confused, I just looked at him. "What do you mean?"

"Hmmmm, where do I begin? You give me mixed signals. For instance, leading me on by kissing me and looking at me like you are now. Telling me to leave you alone this evening. And yet here you are with come hither eyes on me asking me to swim with you."

He was right. I wish everything wasn't so complicated, but it was. I wanted to push him away to keep him safe, so I could leave without conflict. But the truth was that every fiber of me thought about Alec; I wanted to protect him. Yet I yearned for him, my heart needed him. He was looking at me so vulnerably.

Sensing he wasn't going to join me, I decided to get out of the pool, to wrap myself in my warm towel. As I walked out, I forgot the bikini I wore, it was a little Brazilian bathing suit that left little to the imagination. If I thought Alec's eyes went wide at the first sight of me in the dress I wore to dinner, my first night, that had nothing on this look. I knew I looked pretty darn good in it, too. He had a hard time concealing his expression. He was openly admiring my body; I don't think he ever saw me this clothesless before.

"I'm sorry for what I said; I didn't want to hurt you," I told him. I placed my towel firmly around my body and sat next to him on the lounge chair.

"I know you don't want me to be close to you, I can sense it. You're also hiding something from me. I have this gut feeling you're going to leave, with . . . *him*." I kept my face expression normal; as if he hadn't just guessed everything I was going to do. Minus the running away with Derek. I was going to kill him, or that was my plan.

"I'm not running off with *him* . . . I don't want him, Alec. He just has this weird connection with me. And I'm not the Aimee you once loved. This is who I am now. I'm truly sorry I can't remember who I was before. I was probably less moody, and stress free. That must have been nice. You're the last person I want to hurt. I want to protect your heart. In all honesty, I don't deserve you . . . Maybe I can't love," I said as I longingly looked at the stars.

"I don't believe that. I know you can love," he said confidently. "And you haven't changed much, you were moody just the same; I think that's just who you are," Alec said, laughing.

I shook my wet hair. "Watch it," I said, laughing back. Our eyes locked for a brief moment. I broke the trance and played with the end of the towel.

What could I say? My feelings for Alec grew stronger every day. Sitting here next to Alec alone, I felt the electricity sparking between us, making everything that much harder for me.

He reached out and placed his hand on top of mine, which felt warm and wonderful.

I allowed my hair to fall in my face as I closed my eyes. I wanted to give in, to forget everything I had to do. *Be strong, Aimee*, I told myself. I wanted to be held by Alec and be together. Instead for this moment I gave in a little, I rested my head on his shoulder. Alec's stiff posture relaxed a bit and he placed his arm around me. We sat like that for a while, letting the peaceful essences of the night sink in.

"Why are you so difficult?" I asked.

"How am I the one who is difficult? You're the one who can't make up your mind up," he said, chuckling.

"I still don't know what I want."

"I know that, that's why I forgive you for earlier, but I also know I mean something to you, so I wait . . .," he said, softly stroking my hair. "I also came with a message from your mother."

"Oh, yeah? And what does she want, for me to join another committee? Seeing as how much fun I had planning the last one, I can't wait. Zara is a real hoot."

Alec chuckled at that. "Yeah, Zara is a stickler for that . . . Your mother wants you to go on a trip with her."

"What? And where would we go?" This could actually postpone my trip for Derek. I sat up, glaring at him.

"She wants to take you to see some relatives in France."

"Really, and she expects me to go?" I asked, standing up.

His face was amused as he just nodded at me. "It's only for a couple of days. You would leave tomorrow and be back in two days."

I would be back and still have time to fulfill my plan.

"Well you can tell her I accept."

"Then you should get some rest because you have a long train ride tomorrow," Alec said.

I was getting really tired, no pun intended, of everyone telling me to get some sleep. Squinting my eyes at Alec and putting my hands on my hips caused my towel to fall off. His face just lit up; he was clearly enjoying himself. Getting mad now, I picked the towel up and gave him a back view of me as I stormed inside. Hearing Alec's laughing infuriating me more. I was acting like such a child

Fifteen

WHENEVER I THOUGHT ABOUT traveling, I thought about crowded spaces, no leg room on planes and, my favorite, motion sickness. Even first class flights were nothing spectacular. Yet vampire travel, that's a whole other story.

Underground traveling was an understatement. I stood on the platform, watching my mother dictate to the others about God knows what. The train was gold and sleek, looking like a bullet train, at least the shape. I'd never seen a train of this magnitude. The station itself wasn't that large, just open enough for fifty people to stand on the concrete platform. The wall behind the train was black glass, covering the ceiling as well, showing the reflection of the train.

I was close to the sliding glass doors, still, as I just admired the splendor before me. Alec wasn't lying about the subways underground.

We boarded the train and it was a mini palace suite. The carpet was sleek velvet red. The walls were gold, probably real gold. It wouldn't be a surprise to me, thinking instantly of what royalty would use, it had such an historical feeling to it.

I took a seat closest to where I was standing, which was by the door, placing my Jimmy Choo'd feet on the table across from me. My leggings were a nice choice with my long, off-the-shoulder white loose shirt. Leaning my head back, as I shut my eyes.

"Maybe you should wait till we get moving before you set up your feet," the voice of Iva said.

I knew she would be coming. I opened my eyes. So much for peace.

"I agree," said Alec. There was no escaping them. My mother finally boarded and she smiled at me and sat with the other members of the council.

"I thought this was mother daughter bonding," I said watching the council down the back of the train.

"Everything she does has to benefit something; in this case she is killing two birds with one stone," Iva said.

"Clearly," I said, keeping my feet on the table. It keeps getting better and better. I closed my eyes once again, as I leaned back in my chair, snuggling as best I could.

"So what, you're just going to tune us out?" Iva asked.

"Yup," I said, not opening my eyes, happily annoying them.

The forest returned and Derek's green eyes met me immediately. His hair was messy, which was very unusual for Derek; he always made sure he was always at his prim.

I was a bit annoyed. Derek seemed to know when to summon me. *I really wanted to sleep*, I thought darkly.

"Derek." I said coldly.

"Ahhh, Aimee."

"What do you want?" I asked, crossing my arms.

"You think you can summon me anytime you want but I can't. I miss you?" he said, cocking his head to one side.

"We spoke yesterday! And I have nothing more to say to you, wolf boy!"

"Wolf boy! You're part wolf, too." he said, smirking.

"Maybe, at least not by injection. And I'm not turning into a rogue."

"Yeah, I heard you last time . . . ." He came closer to me, tucking a strand of blonde hair behind my ear. The sick thing was I wanted him to touch me. I was yearning for the touch. I guess it's true what they say about girls liking the bad ones. Derek was as bad as they come. After watching him kill my friend Krissy, who turned out to be a Yurnling, after all Derek had done, I still had feelings for him.

"Obviously I was not clear enough!" I said as I stared Derek in the eyes and smirked.

Derek studied me. "Since when did you get so bold?"

"I dunno, maybe I'm finding myself," I said, being feisty.

"I like it. I like this new Aimee . . . you and I-"

I cut him off. "There is no 'you and I' Derek!" I poked his shoulder hard. He caught my hand and pulled me to him; my breathing faltered a little. I just glared at him, trying to hold my ground, but inside I was screaming for a kiss.

He smiled as he leaned closer to my face.

"You forget whom you're speaking to. I always win." He then pulled my face to his and kissed me. My lips responded to his as he fiercely tangled his hands in my hair. Pure adrenaline was coursing in my veins. The heat, passion, excitement I felt! I wanted him.

My flesh was so weak. I pulled back from him. "Don't do that again!" I said, my voice shaking. I wanted him too much.

"Then don't kiss me back, Aimee. You can fight me all you want, but I know you want me, too. I can feel it. Alec may be some weird love of yours but what we have is a desire that is deeper than love."

"That's where you're wrong, Derek," I said.

Derek just stared at me, astonished by my boldness. I had never talked to him like this before.

Like a bad reception, Derek began to flicker in front of me. I didn't get to say anything more because I was being shaken awake.

I tries to focus my eyes, and not make it obvious I had been talking to Derek.

"Aimee, were here!" Iva said, close to my ear.

Alec had his usual expression on, which was one I couldn't read. We all stood, ready for what lay ahead. A very robust man entered the train, briefly welcoming us. By the looks of him, he could have had a lot of battle scars. He didn't look vampire. His eyes were green. Werewolf. I found that strange.

The wolf man began leading us up a hall, which was dark, gloomy, and had an intense smell of decay. This place gave me the chills. We ended at the same kind of strong metal door. I was really curious what kind of doors these were.

Guards watched the doors closely; it was nice to see that they were doing what they were supposed to do. I also assumed they were werewolves, they stood next to the door, opening it as we crossed their paths.

The light was darker than normal, but wouldn't affect a vampire's sight. I could see the light at the end of the hall, and I almost had that same weird feeling, like I had been here before. Or maybe it was just the look on my mother's face. She was tense, yet at ease, her facial expression was different from her usual placid one.

Stepping from the hall was more of a shock. First, it was darker than normal; my eyes could barely capture the little light that the ancient-looking torches cast.

This commune had the same structure as the one I came from but seemed older, like medieval, and had a sinister feel to it. Not only that it wasn't as remodeled, but the vampires that walked around had a darker edge to them as if they went into battles or came from some. The floor was grimy and old matted carpet.

I leaned into Alec as we continued to follow the robust man.

I was studying a girl around my age that passed me. She was studying us as well. Her face was gaunt, like she hadn't had enough blood, nutrients, or sleep, or perhaps all three.

"Why do they look so different?" I asked.

"They don't live as grandly as our commune does. The Rogues constantly target them, and that takes a toll on them. They grow up fighting for their life. And they fight more than our commune ever has."

"So why are we risking being here?" I asked, my mind going back to Derek, remembering Derek's bond dream on the train.

"Your . . . Rose wants you to meet some important family," Alec said.

We continued to walk, passing some more young vampires who looked at me with glares. We all looked so clean compared to them. But what really caught my eye was the green eyes, staring at me. Werewolves, lots of them, openly were lounging around. Very unusual. I probably looked unusual, in these Jimmy Choo shoes. And I really felt out of place and awkward.

We entered a guest housing area, which was down the same halls we have, numbers on the doors as well. These doors, however, were off-white dirty, and some of the numbers were missing. Our door had a dangling number four, and thankfully Iva and I shared this room; Iva suggested Alec stay with us, too. I thought that was a good idea. I felt uncertain about this place. And Alec could have the couch. Or my bed. I doubted I would be sleeping.

Iva and I lay across the top of the bed. I was a bit skeptical about the bed, she was reading some kind of book and Alec was passed out on the couch already. So much for him being the guard.

"So who are these relatives?" I asked.

"I'm not sure. I never met them, either."

"I noticed a lot more werewolves, too. More than vampires almost. Or close to." Their court was medieval-looking with their source of light being torches and candles. Lots of them. Thankfully our bedroom was a little more up kept, but it still had the feeling that no one had stayed in this room for quite a while, and I didn't want to sleep in the sheets.

"It would appear so. It's strange, and that's why I wanted Alec to stay with us. He is pretty good in fights."

"How would you know how he fights?" I asked.

"Because I have seen it . . . we had combat training, and he overtook the trainers. He's a force to be reckoned with."

"Are all communities around like this?" I asked.

"No, this is one of the more rundown spots," Iva said as she put her book aside with a bookmark.

"This is France, they should be the most . . . you know," I said.

Iva laughed at me. "This isn't the only one in France. There are over 15 different communities in Europe."

My eyes widened.

Iva was silently laughing at me; I could tell by her expression. "I'm glad I can amuse you," I said, sarcastic.

She looked so relaxed and human. I was so used to her being uptight and polished all the time. I had an overwhelming sensation. I wanted to tell her about Derek, that he visited me again, but I was afraid she would ask about yesterday's encounter with Marcus. I knew she still wanted to know about that.

Iva stifled a yawn and stretched out on the bed.

"You look like you need sleep," I told her, just to annoy her. She smiled at me with her fangs showing. But she didn't disagree with me.

We woke up early the next morning and got dressed in silence. Alec left the room to give us privacy.

As we entered the breakfast hall, which was empty, I began to wonder if it was safe to eat the food. Iva and Alec were both on edge feeling the same way about this place. Did they even have blood for them? Even the food shops were shambled looking. I could be endangered by e coli.

Why on earth couldn't my relatives come to us?

Alec and Iva got their usual juice boxes, which I was surprised they had, and I settled for a bagel and cream cheese, feeling like it was the safest choice.

I sniffed the bagel, and Alec burst into laughter, which echoed in the empty food hall. I just looked up at him, confused.

"What is so funny?" I asked.

"Nothing," he said looking as though he might laugh again.

"You think I'm a bad liar! You're worse," I said.

He looked like he was about to answer me, but a plump little man walked up to us.

"You have been summoned by your leader, Rosemarie." We all stood immediately. "Just Aimee," he corrected himself.

Iva and Alec exchanged bewildered glances.

Just me? I didn't want to go alone. I glanced at the two of them, who also had the same expression I did. But they didn't argue.

"Okay. Lead on, little man," I said. Alec had that grin on his face again and Iva just shook her head at my comment. And the little man just ignored it.

I felt like my heart would fly out of my chest.

My mother stood by the lounge area; it was a small and shabby area. It looked as though the couches were scratching posts for cats, and smelled like it, too. She seemed unphased by the appearance of the place and just rose up at my arrival.

"Thank you, Kirk." He disappeared after his bow.

Kirk? He didn't look like a Kirk. He should have been named Waldo, but I concealed that information, seeing as to how he hadn't responded to my little man comment.

My mother looked stressed as she inhaled deeply. What indeed awaited me?

"Good morning, Aimee, I hope you slept well."

"I did," I lied.

"You must be wondering why we are here and not just having him come to us."

Him? I thought it was relatives.

"He is very ill, Aimee, and he wrote to me expressing his wish was to finally meet you," she said quietly. "A long time ago we both agreed it would be best for you not to know about him. But the circumstances changed. I'm sorry for all the lies," she said. Her face showed her sadness, and her age was apparent for the first time.

I was completely confused as to what she was talking about.

"The man we are about to see is . . ." she closed her eyes, taking a deep breath. "Is your father, your biological father."

My life was a complete mystery to me. I wasn't as shocked, because I didn't look like the man my mother was married to, and I haven't spoken more than two sentences to him since I have been back.

"But Aimee, his condition is frightening. I want you to be mentally ready. Not only was I in love with another man, he is also a werewolf."

My face now became shocked and my mouth opened. I'm truly half wolf, then. She continued to keep walking; everything around me seemed to black out.

"I'm so sorry, sorry I'm telling you now. He is a gentle, wonderful man, and I loved him deeply. I would have married him if I was allowed." My mother's eyes shone with true grief. "Ralph is a great man, too, who lets me lead the community, but my heart has always been here." She looked into my eyes, probably for signs of an outburst, but didn't see any. I felt bad that she had to live a life she didn't want.

"Are you going in the room with me?" I asked.

"If you would like."

I nodded yes to her. And she smiled and took my hand, which nearly caused me to choke. I could tell that my mother still loved this werewolf. Her eyes didn't conceal it from me.

Entering what appeared to be a hospital wing caused me to have goose bumps. I could almost smell the sick. Or maybe that it was really dirty, and there were questionable stains on the walls. I don't care how sick I was; I'd rather go somewhere else than be here. The walls were off white, a yellow tinge to them. Like someone had smoked in the halls.

A vampire in all white rounded the corner and stopped in front of my mother and me. She looked at my mother. Apparently they knew each other.

"Elecho is ready for you both," the pretty brunette vampire said solemnly. Neither of us said anything.

The woman led us down a darker hall and I became afraid. *What kind of appearance would he have?* I wondered.

She stopped in front of a door, and opened it quietly.

It was even darker inside the room she took us to. She lit a small candle that gave barely any light; I had to adjust to it. I could barely make out a bed with a shape of something in it. The nurse brought the candle next to the bed, and I held my mouth, almost gasping. It was frightening. And painful looking.

The man was in between forms, looking like a man but had what appeared to be the wolf coming out, too, he was stuck in between the transformation. It looked painful. His body was contorted awkwardly, and his right arm looked broken, without a cast. He smiled warmly to my mother; I could see the love between them never leaving. I couldn't see a resemblance between him and me due to the state he was in. His hair had grey in it, but even in this phase he looked handsome, more like his face had a warm, gentle look.

"Aimee." he said in a soft whisper; I could hear the faint French accent. If I weren't looking at him, I wouldn't have heard him.

My mother nudged me. I had to encourage my legs to move. I walked over to his bedside and took a seat in the empty chair.

"So many things to say." Feeling so much emotion for the unknown man, I took his left hand in mine. He took a deep, raspy breath. His hand was calloused and rough.

"You can start at the beginning," I encouraged him.

Even though I didn't know this man before me, I felt such compassion for him.

"You were the most beautiful baby I had ever seen; I never for an instant thought I would love something so much. I was told werewolves only had boys, which is true, never has a werewolf had a girl, but your mother was, is, a vampire. And there has never been a relationship like ours. All I know is that one look at you and I knew you would be the link that would change our races. The first true half breed." He paused, taking a deep raspy breath. "When you were taken, I almost went hunting for them myself; I soon became ill after your abduction and spent the years wasting away in this place . . .," he said, bitterly casting a loathing look around the room. "I still can't believe you aren't changed, or that they didn't keep a better hold on you."

"Would they be able to change me, being a half breed?" I asked.

"I don't know. You clearly have both genes. I suppose they can make the wolf gene more active, but I don't know. You are the first of your kind."

"They were able to erase my memories, though."

"Are they truly gone?" he asked raising an eyebrow.

"They were for a long time, but recently being back and around familiar things, certain memories have been coming back."

"Yes, the memories weren't fully washed away. How can they be when you possess the same genes as a werewolf? You are a force all its own. The ones who took you, I believe knew about you. Most werewolves and Rogue werewolves knew about this strange affair your mother and I had, or heard a rumor. The vampires all hid the secret; only a select few knew the truth about you. But to the wolves you were a hybrid, and I'm surprised they didn't try sooner." He looked into my eyes and I could see the sorrow in them as the candle flickered.

"I wish we had spent time together before this illness, and that I could have watched you grow up. You are so beautiful. I can see bits of me in you. And I'm so lucky to have a daughter. I can sense you have some gifts, do you know what they are?" he asked.

"I'm afraid I don't," I said.

"You will be great, Aimee. Have you made a decision on which gene you wish to try?" he asked. Did he think I would ever go wolf? Maybe it was a dream of his or something.

"I haven't," was all I said, not wanting to cause him more pain.

"You will be a great leader, like you mother, Rose." His eyes became distant, I could see he was fighting to stay in the present and not to wander off.

"Can I ask you something?"

His eyes flashed back to me. "Anything."

"The Rogues who took me were Derek and Nathan Sladen," I said.

He looked as though he would sit up if he could.

"What did you say?" he asked, startled.

"Um, Derek and Nathan Sladen took me," I said, unsure.

"I would have never guessed them to do such a thing to me!" he said, furious.

"Did you know them?"

"KNOW THEM?! That's an understatement. Nathan and I were very close before he went Rogue, when he took Elizabeth and began killing innocents. Never did I think he would take my child for his son; he knew about your mother and me!" he said, with venom in his voice.

I sat so still. Derek grew up knowing about me. It wasn't true that he just saw me at the airport and chose me. I could feel the anger building in my chest.

"I now have a bond with Nathan and Derek. Is there a way maybe to unlink us?" I knew the answer was death only, but I figured I would ask anyway.

His face became, if possible, more grim. "Death to them both or you awaken." The same two options. "What are you planning, Aimee?" His eyes were fierce as he watched me.

"Nothing," I said. My voice was raspy.

"I would go with you if I could. You aren't going alone, are you?" Elecho asked.

He knew what I was going to do. My mother, still in the room, was very quiet.

"I'm not going alone; I'm going with another werewolf," I said.

His lips curled into a smile. I really hoped Marcus would be going with me. Thinking about the company and help was a nice feeling of comfort.

"Who?" he asked.

"Marcus. I'm afraid I don't know his last name."

"Awwww, Marcus Cuthrow, his family was Rogue. I like him very much. Do you like him?" he asked happily.

"Not in that way; he is taken with my friend Iva, who is a vampire." His lips widened in a bigger smile. I was certain he loved that even more.

"And how does she feel?" he asked.

I almost laughed. "Iva, well, is attracted to him. But she is so uptight and won't admit what she could feel," I said.

"And I assume then, you are still taken with Alec?"

How did he know about him? Unless my mother told him. I glanced in her direction; she did tell.

"Not the same way anymore; things became more complicated," I said thinking about Derek, and how I secretly wanted him still.

Elecho, the werewolf dad of mine, I could barely look at him. I wanted to cry.

"Is there any way to help you, there isn't a cure?" I asked.

"I'm afraid not."

"What kind of illness is it?"

"A vampire bite." This is what happens? It freezes them in such a state, a painful one? And still be alive for all this time, suffering. I think I would ask to be killed.

"How much longer are you going to suffer like this?" I asked.

"I have been holding on, waiting for the day I would see you again," he said. I felt my eyes burn with tears. He began coughing uncontrollably. The nurse came in to help him.

"I think it's time to leave," she said in a nice voice.

"Wait!" my dad said in between fits. "I want you to always remember that I love you, and I'm proud of the woman you have become! And take your revenge on them, be careful, you are one of a kind," he said as the nurse was injecting him with some sedative.

My mother and I left the room in silence. Her face showed stress and grief. I never have seen her so vulnerable, not that I can remember past the time I have been back, but still, she wasn't a vulnerable person.

"Aimee, I should have known you wouldn't be staying," she said finally.

"Please don't say anything to Iva and Alec, they won't let me leave. I have to do this. Until I find them and kill them, they will always hunt me."

"I know they will," she said. "You have to know also that Alec will always come after you."

That thought had crossed my mind also.

"I do, and that's why I can't say anything to him. Derek said he was going to kill him," I said on the verge of hysterics.

"Do you love Alec?" my mother asked.

Could I really say my feelings, what I truly tried to deny?.
"I do," I said.

She just nodded in silence. I then realized I just acknowledged I was, indeed, in love with Alec.

Sixteen

THE TRAIN RIDE BACK WAS STRANGE. I was thinking about everything Elecho said to me. I'm the first hybrid, the first woman born from a female vampire who had sexual encounters with a male werewolf. What was I? Besides a hybrid? I felt more lost. And what did he mean saying I was the link? So many questions. Then the simple fact that my dad was suffering. There had to be a cure. He couldn't die like that. Somehow I would find it.

Alec and Iva didn't ask questions when I returned. Where would I even begin? My face probably showed my feelings, and they didn't want to push me. Instead, they sat across from me on the train. I knew it bugged them and they were dying to know what happened.

I liked Elecho; I could see why my mother loved him, so much passion filled him. He also exuded confidence and had a certain coolness about him. I also assume he was very good looking before the bite. I just stared out the window at the blackness that engulfed the train.

We slowed to a stop at our community, and I stood in silence as we were exiting. I could see my mother ahead of us; she was waiting for me at the main entrance to the community, and when I reached her, she pulled me aside.

"We will be waiting inside for you," Iva said softly.

I smiled at her as Alec and Iva passed me.

My mother became serious. "When are you leaving?" she asked.

I glanced at the door Iva and Alec entered. "Soon."

"Can you wait one more day so we can have dinner together?" She had so much motherly concern in her eyes.

"I could do that," I said. I wasn't planning to leave that soon.

"You have so much of your father in you. He was a free spirit, too. Always running. I see that in you. Just remember Alec, before it's too late." She touched my cheek and smiled sadly. "Are you going to come back?"

"I will, I promise," I said.

We reached Iva and Alec. My mother said goodnight to them as she passed us. I wasn't tired. There were so many thoughts in my head. I needed to speak with Marcus. How I was going to shake these two off was going to be a challenge.

"Can I meet you guys in fifteen minutes?"

They exchanged glances. "You don't want us to come with you?" Iva asked.

"There is just something I need to do alone." Iva was staring at me for answers. Surprisingly, Alec nodded. Iva was equally as shocked as me; she was clearly looking for team effort.

"We can meet at my room." I dashed away, before they could do anything more, hoping to find Marcus. Luckily, as I entered the court and made my way to the wolf lair, I didn't have to search too hard because he was almost to the hall.

"Marcus!" I shouted. He stopped as he saw me sprinting towards him. He wore an amused expression on his face.

"Hello, Aimee, how was your trip?" he asked.

Wait a minute. I wonder if he knew the story. "Did you know my father was a werewolf?" I asked.

He smiled. "Yes of course, your hot news is in my world, or at least the rumor is."

"I bet. And you never told me?" I asked.

"No, it wasn't the time to tell you, and besides you have a lot on your plate. Why add an extra thing? And it wasn't my place."

I just kept my hands on my hips as I glared at him.

"I guess . . . I wanted to tell you that I really want to leave soon. In case you want to come with me." Marcus just smiled as he looked at me.

"Ahh, Aimee, do you really think I would let you go alone?. Your dad would have my neck if he were able to. I'm sure he would have gone with you."

"He told me he would have," I said.

His eyebrows rose. "You told him?"

"Not exactly, he just knew somehow," I said.

"Oh," was all Marcus said.

"So, I'll see you soon? Ooh, he said something else too."

"What was that?" he asked curiously; his Romanian accent was so sexy.

"He asked if we were involved. He's like, 'Marcus is a great man,'" I said with a smile.

"And what did you say?"

"I said your heart belongs to someone else." I laughed at his expression, which was clearly taken back. I punched his arm.

"Goodnight, Marcus. I'll see you soon." I left him with his mouth open.

Approaching my room, I saw only Alec standing there. Alec was a true Greek god, with his hair in perfect waves around his face; he was leaning against the wall arms crossed over his perfect chest. His tennis player build was very nice. Grey eyes on me.

"Where is Iva?" I asked smoothly.

"She was hungry; she will meet up with us later," he said. "Do you want to go for a walk?" his Italian accent still sent a shiver down my spine. I love accents.

"A walk?" I asked.

"Yes, I would like to walk with you." His eyes held a certain intimacy in them.

"Okay," I said.

I didn't know where he was taking me, but it was nice just having a normal time together.

We passed many rooms going in the opposite direction of the main court area or the area where all the young vampires live, where Anthony had taken me. I saw a simple door heavily tinted. It was outside. He opened the door for me; my eyes tried to take in everything. It was beautiful. Flowers and a pond in the middle. A garden, a large one. Must have been at least twelve acres, with trees lining the edges. It was like the movie *A Secret Garden*; it had a certain mystical feel to it.

"What is this place?" I asked, awestruck.

"Just a place every age likes to come and enjoy. The Yurnlings get to enjoy it in the sun."

"It's beautiful, Alec," I said. We followed the path in silence.

"How was meeting your relative?" Alec asked, looking at the stars.

I knew he would ask me. He was too curious to deny himself.

"It was interesting. Did you know about my dad?" I asked casually.

"Dad?"

"That my biological dad is a werewolf," I said. He stopped walking and just froze. I was right in assuming that he didn't know.

"What?" he asked.

"I guess you didn't know then. His name is Elecho, and he is very ill. He was bitten by a vampire," I said. "I can see the love between my mom and Elecho still burns." Alec was watching me.

"Some things never change with time." He looked at the ground. "How do you feel about it?"

"Well, for one thing, I never thought of my mom as being rebellious and falling in love with a wolf," I said, laughing bitterly. "It's sad, I feel bad for them. All the secrecy." Alec took my hand in his as we walked. It was romantic and sweet.

"I don't want us to be like that, Aimee," he said quietly.

"Like what?"

"Waiting till it's too late to be together. I can feel it, you being distant. I know you are planning to leave, and leave me in the process."

I stopped under a tree, facing him. "Alec, I want us to be together, too. Just not right now. I have to figure things out. That doesn't change how I feel about you."

"And how do you feel about me?" he asked.

"I love you. I felt it the day I met you, the instant you touched me. A connection. I knew I could trust you, even though at the time

I didn't know you." I could feel his pulse racing; it was vibrating into his hands.

"You love me?" he asked.

"Yes. And that's why I'm telling you we have to wait to be together, so I can figure out *me* first."

His icy grey eyes looked into mine with such intensity. He pulled me closer to him and smothered my lips with his, so soft at first and then intense. We stumbled as we lay in the grass, just holding tight to each other. His lips caressed my neck. I could feel the fangs grazing softly, lingering on my neck. His desire was there; his self-control pulled him back to my lips, hovering over me he just brushed my hair from my face.

"I love you so much it hurts," he said.

I touched his face and brought him closer to me. We lay entwined together, watching each other, studying each other's features. "These last six years have been so hard."

I brushed his silky hair back. The gold beads stood out, and I touched them.

"Why do you wear these?" I asked.

"You put them in my hair, after the movie *Troy* came out; you had that crush on Orlando Bloom. I used to be jealous of him."

"And you kept them in?"

"Yes, because it was a piece of you," Alec said. I didn't know what to say to that. Instead, I kissed him.

"Did we ever go farther than kissing?" I asked, quietly, embarrassed about not knowing.

He smiled and just stroked my face. "No, we planned on it, but you were taken first."

A part of me was happy, relieved, because I would want to remember the first time. Alec continued to watch my face, then he rolled over to his side. Our heads were close together as we stargazed. It really was a beautiful night. Why did my life have to be filled with so much confusion and worry? I wished I could lie like this for a long time.

Seventeen

TAKING A SHOWER WAS VERY therapeutic, as the hot water rushed over my body, washing away the stress and worry. Briefly forgetting Alec and Derek was what I really needed. Turning the shower off and wrapping a warm puffy towel around my chest, I allowed my hair to drip around me as I wiped the steamed mirror. My reflection was blurry as it became steamed again. But slowly the mirror unfogged, and I recognized the girl in the mirror, the same blonde hair, plump pink lips, hazel eyes. Hidden away for no one to see was my anger, the small chance I could become Rogue if my attempt to kill Derek failed. My mission was a suicide one. Yet looking at my eyes, I wanted revenge, I want to be free of this bond. But that tiny speck of guilt in my heart, my feeling for Derek, was still there.

My eyesight became hazy, I felt like the ground was moving around me. Startled, I sat down. The room became less dizzy. Immediately I was sucked into another bond dream, unlike the previous ones, where it was in a forest, this was in Elizabeth Sladen's kitchen. Her kitchen was light and happy. Pale blue walls, the color of the sky, her large Island in the middle. Marble counter tops. A true gourmet kitchen.

Off to the side was her living room that overlooked the ocean with the wraparound porch. It was one of the most breathtaking views in Palm Beach.

I was not expecting to see Elizabeth come into the kitchen. She was as beautiful as ever; her hair was pulled in a loose pony tail, so you could see how proportioned her face was. Her stunning light green eyes that always filled with so much compassion toward me now held sadness. She took a seat on a closer stool that sat around the island.

"Hello, Aimee," she said softly.

I didn't say anything to her at first; I just studied her.

"Elizabeth," I said finally.

"It feels so long since I have seen you, and yet it was only a month ago you ran away from us."

"Derek didn't leave me a choice," I said.

Her smile faltered a bit. "What Derek did or didn't do is in the past now, doesn't make a difference . . . . Why can't you come home? You are like a daughter to me. Don't you care about my feelings?"

"I did care about your feelings, but that is in the past, too, now. I won't turn Rogue like your family. I won't kill innocents."

"Aimee, it's who we are. We were once great rulers. I believe Rogues are still . . . . Refusing to live in a vampire community doesn't make us evil. We don't want to bow down to vampires," she said passionately.

"It's not who I am. I will never be that," I said.

"You already have it in you . . . . Derek will never give up on you. He will find you."

"Speaking of that, where is Derek now?"

"He doesn't know about us meeting right now. He doesn't want me meddling in his affairs. But I really miss you, and had to see you for myself. Don't you miss me?"

She completely avoided my question.

"The only thing I miss is being innocent to the whole Rogue and vampire stuff," I said stiffly. "You were once like me, you know. Do you remember?" I asked her. Her face was in thought for a moment.

"It doesn't matter what I was, this is my life now."

"Do you really wish upon me having my life stripped away to become a monster?" I asked.

"You are going to be a monster either way, Aimee . . . my son's happiness matters to me, and he chose you," she said.

This conversation was really going nowhere. I sighed. Elizabeth's eyes widened on something behind me. She got up, growling.

"Derek!" she screamed. Derek appeared almost as quickly as she had said his name. Derek bounded into the kitchen, face in worry. He stopped abruptly, eyes narrowing. I stepped to the side so I could see what threat was behind me.

My eyes widened in shock. Under the shade of the trees was a wolf. His eyes just showed through the fur. I had never seen what a Rogue looked like. Well, like any werewolf in general, it was truly scary. Skin rough like leather, deep greyish brown, eyes bloodshot, snouts protruding but standing like a human; he was built like the hulk but a little leaner, more adapted to speed. When the Rogue looked at me, I could have sworn it smiled, as if to assure me I was going to be fine.

Derek, on the other hand, was baring his teeth.

"You know you aren't supposed to cross bonds," Derek said ferociously. The Rogue just stood there, staring menacingly at them both, taunting them.

Before anything could happen, the kitchen became hazy and my bathroom appeared before my eyes. I was on the ground, towel still wrapped around me. I put my hands through my wet hair, wondering what the heck just happened. I didn't know other Rogues could cross paths in bond dreams. I'm sure they could fight, too, then. And I missed it! I really wanted to know what happened.

I quickly stood up and raced to my closet to throw on something. A pair of leggings and a long striped shirt and I was ready.

I didn't know who to talk to first, Alec, Iva or maybe Marcus.

I most likely looked crazy running down the hall. Whenever I needed someone; it would seem that no one was around. What the heck? I didn't even know where Alec or Iva's rooms were. Feeling dejected, I sat on a random bench, my back to a storefront. I closed my eyes, pressing my temples with my index fingers.

Okay, relax, Aimee, try and remember what happened. Keeping my eyes closed to recap everything, I nearly screamed when I was lightly tapped.

Iva's curious eyes were on me.

"Is everything all right? You look paler than normal."

"You won't believe what happened." I began to tell her about Elizabeth and the mysterious Rogue. Her face remained the same. Not shocked at all.

"It has to be someone you know," she said.

"You think so? I could have sworn the Rogue smiled at me."

"That would explain it. Why else would it be there? Do you think Marcus would?"

How come I didn't think of that, genius? I thought. "Good thinking, we should go talk to him," I said, turning to find Marcus, but Iva grabbed my shirt.

"Not now. There are other things to discuss right now."

"What is more important than this?" I threw my hands in the air, startling a group of girl Yurnlings. Iva was calm and collected as usual.

"Then tell me what we need to talk about," I said sarcastically.

"Have you finished your tantrum?"

I just glared at her, arms crossed. "Clearly."

"Come on, we can't talk here. Let's go to my room."

"Lead on, then," I said.

I don't know how it was possible, but I had never been to Iva's room before; it was down the same hall as my room.

It was smaller than mine and the bed was a simple sleigh bed, with a couch in the corner. It was cozy and intimate. I wasn't expecting it to be girlie, but you wouldn't know that anyone lived in the room because, unlike my room, it was pristine.

I ran and jumped on her bed. Iva smiled at me. "So what is so important that you had to tell me here?"

Her eyes became glassy as she turned to me.

"I'll tell you when I get back; I left something in the hall."

She was acting really strange. Iva wasn't the normal Iva. Something was definitely wrong. I stood up without distracting her. She was close to the door. How would I leave the room? Iva sensed me and I didn't even see her coming. She had me pressed to the ground, hands on my shoulders.

"Iva, what is wrong with you?" I said, trying to breathe. Her glassy eyes were vacant. She was being compelled, I assumed. I had never seen what it looked like, but this had to be compulsion.

"You are to stay here," Iva said.

I was afraid as I was gasping for air.

"What do you plan on doing with me, then?" I said, in between gasps.

Iva was still pinning me down. All she said was, "You will stay here."

"Fine, I will stay. Can you get off me now?" She hesitated, but got up. Where was my super strength I had had with Anthony? Maybe because it's Iva and I didn't want to hurt her. But this wasn't Iva my friend, it was compelled Iva. Iva didn't wait another moment; she was gone from the room, very fast. Vampire speed.

I already knew the door would be locked yet, I ran to it, turning the handle. Yep, locked. Who would compel her? Better question: who would lock me up?

I paced the door about a million times. What was I going to do? Did Alec know I was here?

I began looking for a vent of some sort. Of course, one was in the middle of the room on the ceiling. But I had nothing tall enough to reach it. This is just my luck.

Entering the bathroom, I saw just a vent that was so small my arm would not fit. *Great.*

How did I get in this mess?

Giving up, I lay on Iva's bed. Or was this even her room? I just stared at the ceiling, as though it would help me.

Eighteen

SO IT WAS OFFICIAL, being locked in a room with no windows, check; alone and going crazy, check. I had no idea how long I had been in this room. It seemed like forever, but most likely a day or two. I also realized there was no clock or phone. How long would I be here? Iva hadn't even checked on me. Instead, I had been staring at the ceiling, at the air vent the only exit in this room. The room was pretty torn up out of anger. I was hungry, too. The tiny mini bar had a few snacks in it, but not enough to fill me. Was I going to starve? Alec had to be thinking about me. Wouldn't he be concerned about me? The sound in the room became a hum; my thoughts were tuned out also. I began hearing voices. They became loud, as though I had turned up the volume.

"Are you sure you haven't seen Aimee?" It was Alec.

"No, I haven't, last I saw her was . . . I can't remember," Iva said.

"She wouldn't just leave. I checked her room earlier and she wasn't there. Rosemarie hasn't been available. Don't you find it strange?" Alec's voice was saying.

"Alec I think you are thinking about things too much. Everything is fine. When Aimee wants to be seen she will turn up."

Alec, I'm not okay! I thought loudly in my head. I was going mental. Hearing voices was sure sign of it.

"Aimee? Is that you?" he asked. Was I imagining him hearing me?

I couldn't hold that thought much longer and I felt the snap of sound turn off. It was bizarre feeling, like a balloon snapping.

Did Alec really hear my thoughts just now?

Okay, so my options were . . . I had none. Besides the vent . . . .

I got off the bed and started to search the room for anything tall. The closet was empty and there was obviously no convenient ladder anywhere. My eyes fell on the dresser. It would be tall enough if I put a chair on top. I might die trying to get into the vent, but I had to try.

The dresser wasn't as light as I thought it would be and I almost pulled a muscle. *What the heck!*

With great difficulty, I managed to wiggle it close enough. I stood on top of the dresser to measure the distance I had left. I needed just an extra foot to get enough height. I jumped off onto the bed. And heard a crunch noise. Lying on the bed, I hung my head off the bed to check to see what crunched. It was some kind of device. Reaching for it, I burnt my finger. It was really hot. What is it? It looked like some kind of tracking device but larger, the size of an iPad. It stood on a stand. Was I truly being monitored? I really had to escape. Very dangerously, I pulled the chair on top of the dresser. I was pretty scared to stand on the chair. I began to balance myself on this contraption I built. It wobbled a bit under my unsteady feet. But fortunately I was able to push the vent open. Dust went in my face and I almost fell off the chair, coughing and gagging. Dust was my nemesis.

Glad I wore leggings because they were so flexible, I pulled myself into the vent. It was a long silver old tunnel, and it was dark. *I can do this!* Sure, I didn't know where it led and I would have to try to be quiet. I know vamps have acute senses and would be able to hear me clanking above their heads.

I began crawling in the very confined space. Luckily, I wasn't claustrophobic, because then I would surely perish in here.

Glancing into some vents as I passed, I looked for my room. I knew I was only a few doors from it. I was hoping I had gone the right way. My breathing was getting heavier and the smell was awful; I would die of mold poisoning if I stayed any longer. And my knees were crying in pain. I was also driving myself crazy with the complaining. Anyone would shoot me. I was annoying myself.

I had to get out of this air vent. I reached the next opening and took the vent cover off. Peeking my head down, I saw it was empty. That's one good thing. Problem, I never thought about how I was going to get down. Would I break my leg from the fall? Why does this stuff happen to me?

Putting my feet first and holding onto the rims, I dangled for a moment. If someone were to come back to their room and see me dangling from the ceiling it would be quite comical.

Taking a deep breath, I released my hold, anticipating my fall.

The fall didn't break my leg as far as I knew. I landed on my feet surprisingly, it didn't hurt, but it was still uncomfortable. Making a jog to the door and opening it, quickly glancing out the door, the hall was empty.

Do I take a chance and go to my room or make a run for Alec? I didn't think my room would be smart; for all I knew Iva could be there. I ran down the hall passing some young vampires that jumped out of my way, giving me a death stare as I passed them.

The main court was busy with Yurnlings; I guess it was lunchtime. Alec where are you? Why was he never around when I needed him? Well, that wasn't true, he was always around. I slowed to a walk and began swiftly making my way to my mom's office area. She would know what to do.

Sitting straight in her chair, with such a smug face, I saw Beth at a distance; she was at her usual spot, the front desk by the koi pond.

Reaching her, she glanced up at me; her smug expression was irritating.

"Beth, I need to see my mother," I told her. Her lips curled into a smile; it wasn't a friendly one, more like the one you would punch in the face for being irritating.

"She is unavailable," she said happily.

"I don't care, this is important!" I said, slamming my fist on her glass desk.

She flinched. "I'm sorry. I can leave her a message."

Not good enough. I ignored her and walked toward the door. Beth was at the door first, of course, vampire speed. Her smile broadened. I felt that same fire in my chest and creeping in my skin. Everything that I'd gone through the last couple days really was building. My temper was boiling. Beth touched my arm and set me off. Back slapping her, she flew backward and hit her desk.

I stood there, frozen for a moment, mouth ajar, completely shocked at what I'd just done. It felt good.

Again my crazy strength had come out of nowhere. I didn't check to see if she was okay; instead I rushed inside the room, making my way to my mom's office. It was quiet in the hall, an unusual quiet.

I reached her office, anxious, but her room . . . she wasn't there. The lounge area was vacant. Scanning the room for anything unusual I didn't notice anything. What is going on? My arm hairs began to prickle up. Something wasn't right.

Alec, I thought. Maybe he could hear me. "I'm in my mom's office. Please, if you hear me. Come to me." I thought really hard, focusing on him. I didn't know if it worked or not; I might actually be going crazy. I walked to my mom's desk and found a planner. Opening the planner I looked for today's date. She was supposed to have a meeting in this room today. I heard the door open and I didn't even have time to hide. I looked stunned, more or less like a fool; it was Alec. Cautiously, I stayed where I stood.

"Aimee?" he said, unsure.

I blinked a couple times before coming to my senses.

"Alec, are you okay?" I asked. He looked at me, confused.

"Yes, why wouldn't I be? What about you, you have been gone for days! I have been so worried. And your mother, she disappeared. I have been asking to see her but she apparently has been busy."

"She's not here," I said, stating the obvious. "Iva was compelled and trapped me in a room."

"Iva?" he said, shocked.

"Yes, I escaped through an air vent . . . . Did you hear me call you?" I asked.

He smiled. "I thought it was my imagination, but I listened to it."

"So you really heard me?" I said, excited.

"I believe so."

"Cool. I just thought hard about you, then I heard you talking, and I don't know, I gave it a shot, but couldn't keep it long."

"I heard you then and this time, very clearly. It was like you were in my head."

So I may be slight crazy but it was worth finding Alec. How was this even possible?

"We need to find my mom. Something is seriously wrong!" I said.

"I know. I feel something is wrong," Alec said.

"Where is Iva?" I asked.

He shrugged. "I don't know. I saw her yesterday and this morning, but that's it."

"What do we do?" I asked, he came to me and hugged me.

"We find your mom. But first we need to go somewhere safe," Alec said.

Nineteen

I NEVER WOULD HAVE THOUGHT this day would ever come into existence. Who would have thought that Alec would take me to the werewolf lair? He must have been really desperate.

Finding Marcus wasn't hard; he was sitting by the fire pit, his hair was messy, and his shirt really defined his muscles. I was greeted with a huge bear hug, which was so unlike Marcus. I was surprised that Alec didn't kill him on the spot.

Alec explained pretty quickly what was going on, and Marcus was eager to help us.

Catching my eye, Clark, the sandy blonde wolf who had given me a hard time waved at me as we passed him. Alec shot him a death glare. Poor Clark, he frowned and glanced away.

I poked Alec hard in the side. "Be nice!" I said.

Entering Marcus's little cave room, we saw it was clean, relatively speaking, and had a puffy bed in the corner, a bed fit for a bear, and

I plopped myself onto it. It was so soft and comfy. I snuggled into his pillow, and it smelled really nice; luckily his sheets were clean.

Alec and Marcus were discussing options as I was going in and out of sleep. It was hard not to fall asleep.

They prodded me awake to feed me some kind of meat that the wolves made down here and it was good. I could have been eating rat for all I knew. But when you're hungry, anything is good, and I was too afraid to ask what it was.

After I stuffed myself, and was feeling like a cow, Alec came and sat on the bed close to me.

"Aimee, the wolves haven't seen your mom the last couple of days. Your dad is even missing," Alec said.

Elecho entered my mind, the wolf that was my biological father. The only female, me, to be born from a werewolf. A hybrid, the first of my kind.

"He isn't my dad," I said suddenly.

Alec raised his eyebrows. "My father is a werewolf," I said fast.

I could see that thought processing through Alec's mind. "Yes, you told me already Aimee . . . . Don't you remember?" Alec said.

I sat staring at them both. I *was* losing my mind.

"It explains the mood swings you have, and the eye color change," Alec said, not sarcastically, which surprised me. "And you don't look like Ralph, your vampire dad."

Yes, finding that out about myself was eye opening, yet very useful. I finally could start putting myself back together. I decided to change the subject, due to the awkward silence that was suffocating me.

"So, what do we do?" I asked.

Marcus came stealthily and sat on the edge of the bed. His tight black shirt was *extra* tight. His green eyes studied me.

"We have a few ideas on where we can search, but this community expands very wide. There's the train, but we don't know if she is still in the community or has left," Alec said, then glanced back at Marcus. "We should check the train first. Marcus, you will be able to smell any new scents, I presume?"

Marcus nodded at this arrangement. "We should hurry, the longer we wait—"Marcus didn't finish. I knew he feared the worst.

I bolted up out of his bed and Alec placed his hand on my shoulder and pushed me back down.

I looked up at him, confused. "Aren't I going?" I asked.

"No, you need to stay here, and be safe." Alec said.

"Oh, no I'm not! I'm going, too!" I said, standing and pushing his hands away.

I glared at them both as if daring them to challenge me. They didn't say anything more. I smiled in victory as I followed Alec and Marcus.

"Stop smiling," Alec said.

"Is it bothering you?" I asked happily, wanting it to.

"What do you think?" he said.

"I think you just got told," I said, laughing.

Alec just rolled his eyes at me.

We didn't go out the usual exit; instead, Marcus led us down a new path. It was more like a tunnel; lanterns were hanging from the dark ceiling, it looked like dirt, but was probably mixed with concrete. Luckily, I wore my moccasins slippers, and not sandals. The tunnel looked to go a long distance, maybe because I could barely see in front of me.

"This leads to the train station?" I asked.

"Yes, it also will take us anywhere we need to go undetected," Marcus said.

"Do you think the person who compelled Iva took my mom? And I thought you were the only one who could compel," I asked, looking at Alec.

"Some vampires have the same abilities. Whoever compelled Iva was strong; I couldn't sense any completion left on her when I spoke to her this morning. I don't think she remembers anything," Alec said.

"Do you think it's safe for her to be wandering around? What if they get her again?" I asked, concerned.

"We need to keep you safe first, and find Rose. Iva isn't the target," Alec said, and took my hand in his as we walked farther down this tunnel.

The air was getting cooler as we reached the train station, also brighter. Everything seemed not to have changed since our arrival back from the small trip. The gold train still was there and was eerily quiet. Marcus immediately became on guard; without a glance, he asked us to stay as he quietly approached the train to inspect it.

Alec was pacing around the station, being impatient as usual. He was making me nervous.

Why couldn't he just relax? "Alec . . ." I stopped; soft footsteps caught my attention, I heard the door open, the normal entrance door. Without hesitation, Alec spun me around pressing me against the wall, hiding me in the darkness.

My heart began pounding in my chest.

Who came out was someone I wasn't expecting to see: Beth, walked out, looking around. *Why was she here*, I thought. Her slender body was masked in a black knee-length trench coat and a pair of heels. Weird combination. She waited as though she expected someone.

The door opened a second time, A man soon came from behind her, tapping her arm lightly, she smiled and he kissed her. I couldn't make out the man. He was too much in shadow from his cloak.

My breathing almost stopped; I was afraid to be seen. Alec was so still, like a statue. He held me tightly to his body, and sparks of electricity came alive.

They spoke to each other but I couldn't hear them, wishing I had vamp ears. I was sure Alec would tell me. Remembering that Marcus was on the train still, I was silently praying that they didn't board. After a few moments, they gave each other another soft kiss and he left first. Beth soon followed.

Being sure they were truly gone Alec released me, still aware of everything. His eyes scanned the station cautiously. Why had Beth been here?

My eyes were wide as I tried to calm myself. "What did they say to each other?" I asked.

Alec thought for a moment. "The man said that the plans were coming together, and no one suspects anything. And soon she will be gone . . . I'm not sure who the man was. As far as Beth goes, she's in on whatever is going on."

Beth. I could hardly believe she was capable to be a part of this. I was now not feeling guilty about the push earlier, not that I had felt guilty to begin with.

I started to feel stressed. Waiting for what felt like a long while, Marcus finally got off the train. I relaxed a bit. He jogged to us, face serious.

"It hasn't been used since at least a few days ago, I'm assuming your trip, because your scent was on board still." Marcus said, running his hands through his hair.

"Were you able to make out the man that was out here just now?" I asked Marcus, hoping he was looking out the window.

"Unfortunately, I had to stay hidden, the vampires would have sensed me," Marcus said.

"What do we do now?" I asked.

Alec and Marcus exchanged glances.

The floor began to move, and the familiar blurry vision came over me. The same lush forest appeared before my eyes. I waited impatiently for my vision to stop being hazy. I felt really agitated.

Great this is exactly what I need right now!

"I know you are here Derek," I said, aggravated.

Derek crept behind me and my reflexes instinctively kicked in, causing me to jump to the side and out of his reach. Derek wasn't expecting that from me, and looked pleasantly surprised.

"Can't you just leave me alone?" I asked impatiently, as I tapped my foot.

His green eyes lingered on me for a moment longer before he spoke.

"You know I can't stay away from you. God, you're so beautiful! Maybe this separation was a good thing; your spirit is so strong now, like a new fire has grown inside of you. I like it."

"You didn't think I was beautiful before?' I asked, arms crossed, I knew it was irrelevant but I still wondered.

"I always have, but your being has changed so much. I can't wait to change you," he said in his confident way.

"I'm sorry, but you won't be." I smiled at him.

"You would be surprised as to what plans I have." His eyes gave him away. I could see a flicker of something in them.

I knew it, he was coming for me. I needed to get out of this dream, needed to find my mother, and leave before Alec was killed by Derek.

"Well, actually, Derek, you would be surprised with the plans I have for you, too."

Just like in Elizabeth's bond dream, I saw the same Rogue lingering by the trees. Watching me. I froze. Derek turned and, seeing the Rogue, became rigid, his eyes flashed that honey brown, and he changed right in front of me, his clothes ripping off his changing body. Bounding for the Rogue in the forest, I just watched in horror at the scene that unfolded in front of me.

I felt like I was being sucked backwards, feeling really dizzy, my eyes fluttered open. Alec was holding me close to him. His sent was so sweet, I couldn't place the smell. It reminded me of cinnamon mixed with apples.

"Marcus," I said and Alec looked at me startled that I said Marcus. I ignored Alec's facial expression and released myself from his arms.

"There has been an unknown Rogue appearing in my bond dreams. Derek changed in front of me to his Rogue werewolf, and charged the other Rogue. How is that even possible?" I asked, still a little disoriented. The room was spinning slightly.

Marcus looked at me for a long moment, thinking. I could see the crease form between his eyebrows. "There are a few werewolves who could invade another bond dream, but they have to be either related or have some kind of link. Did they fight?" Marcus asked.

"Well, they charged each other, but I didn't get to see anything more. Can you die in the bond dream?"

"No, you can't, it just our psyches. But still, it's very powerful. I'm not sure what that could do to your mind."

My mind was spinning now, who was the Rogue? And did Derek get injured? A part of me didn't want him to get harmed, which was quite ironic seeing that I was going to kill him.

"What the crust!" I said aloud. causing both of them to just look at me.

"What the *crust*?" Alec asked, raising his eyebrows.

"Sorry, I just can't believe the things that are happing to us, that's all." I said. flailing my arms. An idea suddenly popped into my head.

"Alec, you know how I called you earlier?" I asked.

His eyes sparked with a light. I knew Alec knew what I was going to say.

"Do you think it would work on your mother?" he asked.

"I don't know, I could try. Wouldn't hurt. But should we go back to the tunnel?" I asked.

"Yeah, that's smart." Marcus said. We swiftly walked back to the safety of the tunnel.

"I'm not sure how to do it exactly, it just sort of happened last time." They just stared at me. "Can you not stare at me?" I told them. Alec raised his eyebrows in that perfect arch he always did, but listened and turned, nudging Marcus in the side.

Putting my pointer fingers to my temples and pressing on them, I focused hard on my mother. "Mom? Where are you?" I asked, waiting, but nothing happened. I waited a few moments. It didn't work, maybe it had just been luck last time. I felt a little discouraged by my failure.

I sighed heavily, opening my eyes. "I don't know how I did it. Maybe we are better connected, Alec." Alec smiled at that.

Alec pulled me to my feet and Marcus began leading us back up the dark and dirty tunnel.

My ears began to bother me, I pressed on them. It felt like they had become clogged. The sound began far away, like I had a head cold. "Aimee? Are you still there? I think I'm going crazy." It was my mom. I almost laughed.

"You aren't going crazy Mom! I can hear you! Where are you?" I asked.

"No, Aimee it's not safe, so many things happened. We have been betrayed. I heard you are locked up."

"I'm safe, please just tell me!" I heard nothing but silence for a long while.

"I'm chained to a table. I don't know where, it looks like a basement."

"We will find you, okay!?"

"Be careful!"

The volume turned up again and the same weird sensation came over me, like my ears popping, as if I was on a plane.

A huge smile spread across my face.

"What happened?" Alec asked.

"She thought she was going crazy; that's why she didn't respond to me. She is chained to a table in a basement. She doesn't know where, though. And she says we all are betrayed," I said, almost breathless.

"Can you see where she is?" Marcus asked.

"No, it's just blackness, and our voices."

The boys just stood in front of me, dumbfounded about what just happened. Alec faced Marcus.

"Does 'basements' sound familiar?" Alec asked Marcus.

Marcus ran his hands through his messy hair, closing his eyes. "There are a couple, they were used to torture . . . werewolves, well, the Rogue ones . . . . If she says we are all betrayed, I know what that means. Rogues are going to be coming."

I could feel the color drain from my face.

I'd had a feeling that's what she meant. Derek made it clear, also. My stomach twisted. I needed to leave, but all I could think about was Alec. I looked into his icy grey eyes, the ones I fell in love with all over again. I had to protect him.

Marcus, like he sensed my thoughts, stared right into my eyes, and he nodded.

"There is a basement close to where we are now, Aimee; if things go . . . wrong, you need to leave," Marcus said. I gulped.

We began jogging to the next destination, which was the basement, hopefully the right one. Everything around was a blur of darkness as I was so focused on what lay ahead of us. My breathing became heavier as we began going deeper underground.

As we approached a door, Alec stopped me. I already knew what he was going to tell me. "I think you should stay here." His eyes held so much love for me. I knew he was my protector. But I wanted to go to. I looked at Marcus for support, and got none.

"Thanks guys."

Alec dropped my hands, leaving me in the dark tunnel. It was probably more dangerous in here than in the basement. I took my seat on the dirt floor. How dare they leave me here? Uggg. And how long was I supposed to wait? I'm the worst at being patient, sitting here was going to be worse than torture. The darkness also sent chills up my spine; I was terrified of what could be lurking around the bends in these tunnels. My mind was my worst enemy at the moment.

After what felt like a long while, I became more anxious. Shouldn't they be out by now? I began staring at the door, like they would be coming out any moment with my mother.

Just breathe! Everything is fine. It just feels longer because I'm waiting.

My patience level was becoming nil.

Deciding to maybe peek in on Alec wouldn't hurt; he would just tell me it was fine. Allowing my mind to go blank, I focused on Alec. I didn't think I would get used to the sound turning off. "Alec, did you find her?" I asked.

Silence, the horrible silence. I sighed deeply.

Then, out of nowhere, an ear-piercing wailing met my ears. I didn't expect to hear screaming; it was agonizing, I almost turned it off. It caused me to jump.

"Aimee." His voice was shaking. He couldn't say anything more. That was enough for me. Alec was in excruciating pain. I had to find him.

Coming back to the tunnel, I was already standing. Exhaling, I opened the door, slowly peeking in first. It was really quiet, and the same darkness greeted me with open arms. My stomach dropped, my pulse quickened.

I didn't see anyone. It was a concrete hall, but had the same look as the wolf lair, with tree roots poking out here and there, looking like snakes in this very dimly lit area. I didn't see any brighter lights down the hall, either.

Fast-walking down the hall, I didn't exactly know where to go. I could hear my own heart beating even more wildly than before. It was so still down here. Almost too still; wouldn't I hear them being tortured?

Was I too late? My pace slowed as I approached what appeared to look like doors. My ears picked up on a soft thud of a door closing, sounding horrifically close, Following footsteps a little further down the hall, with haste, I stopped walking to hide in an alcove to conceal myself in the blanket of darkness. My breathing was jagged and I covered my mouth.

I could hear them talking among themselves. Two men were approaching and they weren't vampires. I glanced around the corner, catching a small glimpse of them. Their hair was to the shoulders, lying around their faces, and their eyes were already a honey color—something about them was evil and cold. They were, I was assuming, Rogues, but in human form. *OH GOD, they will smell me!* Each step, they were coming closer, closer. Suddenly, the footsteps stopped abruptly, turning down another hall, I assumed. My breathing was pure adrenaline; I could feel that same fire burning in my chest, growing hotter each moment.

Pushing myself forward was a little harder than I imagined; my body wanted to retreat back to the safety of the tunnel.

Coming to the crossroads, I glanced in both directions, and decided to stay on the same path. I could see a row of wooden doors. Reaching the first wooden door, hesitating briefly, I placed my ear to it. I heard muffled breathing. My heart sped up again, terrified. I wasn't a warrior, of any kind, what could I possibly help with? I twisted the knob slowly, praying that there weren't any Rogues inside, The door wasn't locked, to my advantage.

The scene in front of me was surreal. My mind went back to the night when Krissy died at Derek's hand. Even though this was a different scene, I still had that terrified feeling. I didn't see Alec anywhere in this dark dungeon; it looked like it was from the renaissance period, giving me the feeling of utter horror. A floating chandelier of candles that dangled from the arched ceiling was the only source of light.

Marcus was tied from hanging chains, his feet dangling close to the ground; he had purple bruises across his face. He didn't see me.

My mother, thankfully, was alive, but her eyes were closed and she was lying on a table, strapped to it. From what I could see she wasn't beaten. Alec, where was Alec? I was trying to control the panic inside of me.

I ran swiftly over to Marcus, first, thinking he could help.

"Marcus." His eyes fluttered open. "Are you all right? Anything broken?" His eyes bore into mine.

"Aimee you need to leave us. If they find you, you're the one they want. There are Rogues here."

"I know. I saw some before I got to you. I'm not leaving you!" I said fiercely. "Where is Alec?" I asked.

His face became grimmer. "I don't know, they took him somewhere else. I'm sorry I failed you."

"No, you didn't. Did you see where the keys were?" I asked. holding his gaze.

"Last I saw them, they were on the guard."

"Aimee?" my mother called me faintly.

I was immediately by her side. "I'm here and going to get you out."

"No, you don't understand. It is you they want. Ralph betrayed us. Your stepdad! This whole time, he and Beth were . . . listen to me, he's the one who let the Rogues in and take you . . ." The doors suddenly burst open and two Rogues stood in front of us, in their human forms. Derek never resembled these two guys. They were dirty and had a wild look in their eyes. I was shaking slightly, but I think it was with fury.

My fire grew inside of me, spreading to my fingers. Was it pure horror, or something else. Marcus just hung there, watching me. There was nothing he could do.

They smiled at me, a twisted look on their dirty faces. It turned my blood cold. My chest continued to burn with the fury, I could feel the fire creeping up. It felt stronger and hotter. I touched my arm to make sure I wasn't on fire. This feeling was different than the time with Anthony. Almost like my body became ready.

"Awwwww, look who we have here! That was easier than I thought," the sandy blonde-haired Rogue said. The other Rogue laughed, merciless.

"You have nowhere to go, little one. We aren't going to hurt you. Just come with us," the second Rogue said, in what he probably thought was his soothing voice. It wasn't working on me.

Yeah, that's exactly what I was going to do buddy, go with you.

They came closer to me, unthreatened. If only they could pay attention to the vibrating earth under my feet from all my anger boiling within me. Marcus was looking at me and his face held it all, he could see it in my eyes and his mouth hung open, a small smile playing at the corners of his lips.

The blonde unknowing Rogue placed a hand on me, which made me smile. Which was a bit crazy. I wanted to hurt them. More than that, I wanted to kill them.

"Don't touch me!" I said. They laughed like I was a cute child. And they both grabbed my arm this time.

Everything happened so fast—one swift motion, unlike my usual pace, I was fast, so fast, faster than a vampire. I twisted his arm back, cracking it, and flipped him over me, cracking his head on the floor. I didn't have time to think. The other rogue looked at me in shock but charged me full speed.

I saw a chain on the table. I snatched it up so smoothly and swung it over my head like a lasso and whipped him clear in the face, sliding out of the way, as if I was sliding into home plate. He growled in pain and was changing into a wolf in front of my eyes. His back went rigid, clothes tearing at the seams, teeth bared, eyes bloodshot. His cold glare rested on me. Snarls escaped his lips.

Thinking fast, I saw a metal-like sword, I picked it up and braced myself for the attack.

The Rogue didn't see what was in my hand as he lunged for me; I jumped and was surprised how high I went, landing like a cat away from the Rogue. He snarled in outrage. He couldn't hide the surprise on his face.

"You are making this difficult."

"Then maybe you should leave; your friend is still unconscious. Take the hint."

He smiled and came at me. I swung the sword with such a force I cut his arm off, He shrieked so loud as he held his bleeding stub. His eyes changed. I could see he was going to kill me. I could feel the anger pouring out of him.

The fool of a Rogue came charging with such speed he almost took me off guard, but my arms were ready; like swinging a baseball bat I took his head off with one sweep. I could feel the blood splatter on my face from the impact of my blade. This was the sword that could kill a Rogue, the only metal that could pierce one. In a stance like a samurai I stood up. Glancing at the Rogue, I beheaded his comrade, still unconscious on the floor. I turned my gaze to Marcus.

Marcus face was in shock as he watched me, awe in his eyes. My mother made a subtle noise; I almost forgot she was in the room with us.

I bent down, searching the guy's jacket, practically turning it inside out; finally, I felt the keys. I ran to Marcus and it took a little bit to find the right one but I finally unlocked him. He fell to the ground, shaking a bit. Marcus rubbed his wrists.

I helped him up. "Aimee, I have never seen anything like you before. It's true what they say. Hybrid!" I smiled and ran to my mother, unlocking her and helping her up, the blood on my hands staining her dress. I had forgotten about the blood. What did I look like, a monster? She appeared to be at a loss for words.

"Are you okay, Mom?" I asked.

She nodded. "Yes. Aimee they will kill Alec if you don't find him—you need to hurry."

Marcus had a stone expression on his face. "Do you know where they would take him?" he asked.

"I don't. I'll stay here and you two go find Alec. These guards were the ones watching us. I doubt anyone will know they are missing."

"I can't leave you here!" I said fiercely.

"I will be fine. Go find him. If you see Ralph, Just capture him, I would like to kill him myself," she said with a dark expression.

Marcus touched my arm; he had a blade in his hand also. "Come on."

Scurrying out the door, it was luckily clear in the hall.... We jogged down the hall, and I could feel it, the fire was still in me, as well as the adrenaline pumping through me. I was praying silently that Alec was alive still, and that I wouldn't lose this fire.

"Aimee, your eyes scared the crap out of me. They didn't turn the honey brown like a regular wolf. They were purple. I have never seen that color purple before on anybody. I think you scared those Rogues. They weren't expecting it." He was smiling. "Derek won't be expecting it either."

"What color are my eyes right now?" I asked, he quickly glanced at me.

"They are soft, light purple, I can feel the fire in you still. Hold on to it!" he said.

Reaching what looked like a dead end, we slowed our pace, listening for any sound that would point us in the next direction. We didn't have to wait that long. We both froze when we heard screaming echoing down the hall. It was horrible, tortured sound. He pushed me forward. *Please be alive.*

Reaching the door, Marcus turned to me.

"Aimee—"

"Just kick it open, we can't exactly walk in there," I said. Marcus nodded in agreement.

Kicking the door in wasn't as hard as I thought it would be, we both did it easily. The room was large, looking the same as the last dungeon we came from, the same arched ceiling, with those eerie chandeliers that had cob webs all over them.

I spotted Ralph hovering over Alec. His face had no sign of shock. Beth, his accomplice, stood close by along with two Rogues; they all looked at me, not even noticing Marcus. Alec was covered in blood, his face was slashed. They were torturing him. I almost ran to them; Marcus held my wrist. We both side glanced at each other.

"Hello Aimee. What a nice surprise. Derek will be happy you are well," Ralph said.

I wanted to tear his smile off his face. The same anger returned, burning a little brighter.

Ralph then took a hot poker and stuck it through Alec's shoulder. My face went paler than usual. I felt sick.

Alec was screaming in agony. I clenched my fists so I wouldn't explode.

"Don't touch him again," I said dangerously, shaking in anger.

Ralph smiled. "And what exactly are you going to do? Nothing. you are nothing but a Yurnling.... Why everyone is so obsessed with you is beyond me." He sneered.

"Why would you sell out your own race for Rogues?" I asked.

"Aww, it was for one, you, not the whole race! He wanted you so bad. You returning nearly ruined everything. With you and your mother gone, I could make Beth the leader and we could rule over everyone, Rogues included. That was part of the deal. Seems an unfair deal, all of that for you. He almost ruined it!" Ralph said, stabbing Alec once more.

So that's what this was about, me; somehow in Ralph's twisted head, he thought the Rogues would actually listen to him, bow down to him. Ralph was so wrong. His ignorance would cost him his life along with everyone else's.

The heat was stronger this time, more potent. I shouldn't have promised anything to my mom, meaning her killing Ralph. I might not be able to control myself.

Beth stood there, looking happy; I wanted to knock the smile off her face, too. Marcus stood close to me, hand still around my wrist.

"Retain them," Ralph said motioning to the two Rogues in the room.

Marcus and I glanced at each other. Our swords were hidden. The two Rogues came at us, they were in their changed form already, Bloodshot eyes, hulking size, grey, leathery skin....

Marcus pushed the table at them as he grabbed his sword. I didn't have time to watch them fight, my own Rogue approached me. Same twisted smile. I felt the flash in my eyes, my speed he didn't see coming, thanks to his underestimating me. The table that was supposed to trip the Rogues, I leapt onto, almost stunning myself. The Rogue was almost to me, teeth bared, growling, claws reaching for me. I was too quick for him. I swung the sword in the same circular motion, and his head came clean off; he was clearly not expecting it, his facial expression, even in death, was pure shock.

I pushed his dead-weight body off the table. Marcus had just taken his opponent's head off, blood was splattered on Marcus's arms. I wondered why he didn't change into a werewolf; his eyes were honey colored as he smiled at me, full of confidence.

Ralph just stood there watching me, eyes narrowed. Before I could move or say anything, Beth came charging at Marcus, fangs bared at him, it was like I watched it in slow motion. She was going to bite him. My legs moved before I realized what I was doing. I reached her before Marcus could move, shoving my blade deep into her heart. I had an almost pleasure, bloodlust, hunger, satisfaction course through me. Maybe it was the wolf side of me that longed for death, or maybe I just loathed her.

She gasped as I pulled my sword out, the light in her grey eyes flickering out.

I didn't know how to kill a vamp, but clearly this would hinder her if not kill her. I didn't bother watching her fall to the ground. Turning around, fire was burning in Ralph's eyes as he held a dagger to Alec's throat. His rage was all over his face. The dagger was shaking mildly. He must have really cared for this wench, Beth.

"You want to fight, old man? What is your great plan now?" I asked Ralph, antagonizing him.

His eyes narrowed more on me.

"You won't be able to fight if he's dead. Some things never change. I could see it all over your face. You may be deadly now, but if I kill him you will be nothing!"

I froze, feeling less cocky. Would it ruin me, losing Alec? I cared for him deeply, love was a stronger bond.

Ralph was right, I couldn't bear to lose Alec. That was the reason for me to run away and hunt Derek in the first place. What could I do now? I was weighing my options. They were few. Marcus was also thinking, I could see the crease between his eyebrows.

I put my sword down, slowly, as did Marcus. Backing away, I took a deep breath. I noticed there was a door behind Ralph. Ralph was so distracted with me he didn't see it open or hear it. Seeing my mother's head peek around the corner was quite comical. Holding my smile proved easier than I thought, with my blood boiling still.

I decided to distract Ralph.

"So that's your great idea? Kill Alec?" I said, sneering at him.

"It will still work; you are alive. And I will deliver you to Derek Sladen myself!" Ralph said, so confident. *How could this man truly betray everyone, my mother included?* He didn't seem like that type. But then again it was always the silent ones to be aware of.

My mother, stealthy like a true ninja, better than me, I must add, pulled out her dagger and stabbed him in the back. Pure shock shone on his face this time, as she dug deeper into his flesh. A gross spluttering of blood dribbled out his mouth, as his eyes rolled back in his sockets. A sickening gurgling escaped his lips. I had to look away to hold in the vomit. My fury power was dwindling away; the old squeamish Aimee was returning.

"You would have to go through me first, honey!" my mom said, smiling. Ralph fell to the ground. I pulled Alec away from Ralph's blood pool and untied him. His eyes were focusing on me. He had that same awed expression that Marcus had had earlier.

I pulled him up and wrapped myself around him and kissed him. His lips responded instantly, despite how tired and hurt he was. I didn't want to break away.

"You came for me?" he asked.

Would he actually think I wouldn't?

"Are you joking? You think I would leave you here?" I said. His face was looking at me, unsure for a moment. He looked more afraid than anything of making me mad.

"No, I knew you would eventually come rescue me," He said with a smile., It looked painful. His face had a bruise and a slash on it. "But I thought you would get your mother out of here first," he said, resting his hand on my shoulder.

"Yeah, my mother, Miss Warrior Princess over there, wanted to stay behind," I said, laughing. My mother half smiled at my comment, once more becoming the leader. When Alec turned his head, I could have sworn she winked at me. It happened too fast for me to really comprehend it.

"I've never seen anything like what you did tonight. And you're not even changed yet. Can you imagine what you will be like if you are awakened?" he said, starting to sound like Marcus.

"Amazing!" my mother said, interrupting. She was clearly amused.

"Your eyes were purple!" Alec said.

"What are they now?" I asked.

"Hazel," he said softly. And he brought his lips to mine again. I noticed his wounds weren't healing.

"I thought vampires heal?" I asked.

"We aren't immortal. Unlike the werewolves, who have a different kind of life expectancy, both races heal fast but not when they use a special metal that hinders the healing process."

"What special metal is it?" I asked.

"Mercury. It has an effect on werewolves and vampires. It's the only way to kill a werewolf," Alec said.

Marcus caught my eye as he passed me.

"Marcus, why didn't you change? You stayed human," I said.

Marcus smiled. "I have great control over my emotions. I wouldn't be of use as a werewolf; it's hard to control my emotions. Everything is enhanced."

Alec was weak even just standing there. My mother touched his arm. "We need to take him to the hospital wing." My mother said gently. Marcus put his arm around Alec for support.

Alec cast a glance over his shoulder, smiling in his seductive way, and looking so helpless.

Twenty

S*INCE THE RECENT EVENTS* that unfolded in my life, I was in a crazy swirl of emotions. I'd come to find out I was some weird Hybrid crossover, with the genes of a vampire and also a werewolf. I was the first of my kind and not to mention the first female to be born from a fathering male werewolf. Some weird gene thing, which is why Rogue werewolves capture female Yurnlings to breed with them, to keep their race thriving; only problem was, they erased their previous lives, and were told nothing but lies. That's what happened to me. For six years, I believed I'd lost my mother in a car accident and I just had severe head trauma, to finding out my mother is alive and a leader at a vampire community.

Not to mention the man I was engaged to was the reason for my kidnapping. Derek, the Rogue werewolf, the one I still love.

I couldn't forget Alec, the one who fought for me, searching, determined to bring me back to this underworld of vampires, his unyielding love. My feelings for him burned deep in my soul, a new kind of fire, hungry, lust, that I desire. I never loved a man more than

Alec, even my feelings for Derek were nothing compared to those for Alec. It's overwhelming, considering I have been getting glimpses of my past, which include Alec, and seeing that those feelings never left. They were buried, hidden, until they came pouring out. I can't tell Alec my true feelings; my mission was to leave very soon, and hunt the man I still love, the piece of me I wish I could forget and move on from: Derek.

I found out through recent activities that I can fight, not only fight, but also that I was stronger and faster than any Rogue werewolf or Vampire, and I'm not even awakened or turned into wolf yet.

The genes somehow conflict with each other, causing bursts of emerging powers. Those powers could change and become more potent, if in fact I choose to be either one. And I didn't think I was going to choose, it was complicated enough being somewhat regular.

My mind was spinning as I looked at the apple in my hand. White walls surrounded me as I was sitting in Alec's hospital room, keeping an eye on his healing. He looked so peaceful

I finally gave in, taking a bit of an extremely juicy apple, almost getting juice on Alec's bed. He was healing nicely. His shoulder was bandaged; he looked so helpless. I leaned forward and kissed him. He was already awake at the touch, his grey eyes on me.

"You don't need to stay here with me," he said, and his Italian accent still made me smile.

"It's okay for you to be concerned about me, but not vice versa?" I asked.

He smiled. "How is your mom doing?"

"She is surprisingly good. You know she moved my real dad, Elecho, here. He is down the hall, actually."

"Really?" Alec asked, astonished.

"Yeah, she loves him and wants to take care of him." I still believe there is a cure. Not sure how I would find it. But I know it can be done. It had to.

"What are you thinking about?" Alec asked. I couldn't tell him my thoughts.

"Just that I'm happy we all are okay."

He reached for my hand and squeezed it. "You are an amazing woman! Definitely a force all your own. Do you even want to be awakened?" he asked.

Leaning back in my chair, I have been contemplating this idea for the last couple of months.

"I don't know. Part of me does. But the other part still wants to be this." I said, pointing at myself. He nodded in understanding.

"You don't need to make any choices yet, or ever, for that matter," Alec said. I nodded in agreement.

"Is Marcus okay?" Alec asked.

"Yes. I'm going to visit him in a bit."

The door opened and Iva entered slowly, freezing in the doorway. She had such grief on her face. "Aimee, I didn't mean to lock you in a room. I didn't even know I was compelled. I didn't even know I was doing it! Please forgive me!" She took a seat next to me. Her grey eyes filled with tears.

"Iva, it's okay. I knew it wasn't you!" I said, patting her hands that were resting on my chair armrest. She looked relieved.

I stood, releasing Alec's hand. He looked at me questioningly.

"What's wrong?" he asked.

"I need to visit Marcus," I said, kissing Alec's forehead. He smiled at me.

"I'll be back soon. Iva, make sure he doesn't pull anything."

"Don't worry, he won't be escaping me." Iva said, smiling with fangs.

Closing the door behind me, I nearly bumped into the nurse as I exited the room. Her wild curly black hair poked in all directions.

"Sorry," I told her. She just shook her head at me.

Marcus' room was down the hall; he was lying on his bed arms crossed with a pissed expression on his face I entered the room. I almost laughed at the sight.

"How are you feeling, my friend?" I asked taking a seat next to him.

He just squinted his eyes at me, annoyed. "I'm perfectly fine; I don't know why I have to be in here. And why aren't you next to me?" he asked.

"They checked me out, they didn't see any reason to keep me," I said, patting his shoulder.

His green eyes were watching the TV. "How's Alec?" he asked.

I wanted to laugh at how concerned Alec and Marcus had become with each other.

"He is surviving. Iva came by to apologize for locking me in a room."

"Hmmm." A smile played on his lips. "So are we still on for escaping and killing some more Rogues?" he asked on a darker note.

"Yes, as soon as you're released . . . ." I snapped my head toward Marcus. "You didn't say anything to Alec, right?" I asked.

"If I had, you would clearly know, because you would be locked in a room again," he said, laughing.

That was true. "I will come back soon and check on you. I'm going to pay my dad a visit."

"Dad?"

My mom had him moved here a few days ago."

Marcus smiled, and nodded in understanding. "How is your mom?" he asked.

"She seems all right. I didn't realize how strong she was."

"Where do you think you get it from?"

I smiled at that thought. I gave him a salute as I stood up to exit his room.

Marcus just glared at me, annoyed with his predicament.

"Sure thing, I will just be waiting here."

I had knots turning in my stomach, from nerves. I knew I didn't have anything to be nervous about visiting my dad, especially after the Rogues. Yet I had a feeling of uncertainty.

Coming up to his room, the nurse acknowledged me, opening the door for me. His room was dark, and the nurse lit a candle and set it next to his side of the bed. Elecho was still in that twisted position, in between changing phases, that looked so painful. His right arm still contorted, bending backward, his skin had the hint of a grayish tint.

I took a seat on a wooden stool that was close to his bed. A sigh slipped from me.

"My daughter, "he said. "I heard you took out the Rogues," he said in a proud voice. His eyes, which I could barely see due to the darkness, looked a little brighter.

"I did. I still don't know where the strength came from," I said trying to brush it off.

"You're a hybrid, Aimee. You were born stronger than all of us."

"Even before I change? I'm a Yurnling! "I said, flailing my arms around. I was trying to make sense of everything, and my mind was on overload.

"I don't know what you are, Hybrid or something else, but you're not a Yurnling. You have both genes. Can a Yurnling do what you did? I think not!" he said, clearly enjoying himself.

I shrugged, not that he could see me in the dim light.

My mind drifted to another hot topic, the bond dream with Elizabeth and Derek. A thought crossed my mind. "In my bond dream . . . ." Elecho smiled very slightly, which was enough to signal me. *I knew it.* "It was *you*, wasn't it? In the dream with me?" I asked.

"Yes, what else do I have to do but lie around here and be bored to death? I wanted to give them something to get upset about." His smile grew.

Watching my father wither in pain and in this frozen state made me really sad. I tried not to let it get to me, but couldn't help it. I turned away from Elecho, my father.

"There has to be a cure! You can't die like this. So slow and painful."

"I wouldn't know. Don't worry about me," he said softly.

I laughed at that. "That's an understatement . . . I never thought that Ralph would let the Rogues in and give me up for his power. Or do that to Mom," I said.

"He was underestimated. People do strange things for love and power."

"That sounds about right," I said.

"I can tell you one thing though, Derek doesn't know what's coming." He smiled wider.

The nurse popped her head in, allowing more light to enter the room. She glanced between both of us.

"I think Elecho needs his rest after his travel here." Elecho made a face.

I rose from the stool.

"I'm happy you're here . . . Dad," I said. His breathing stopped for a moment and I could see pure joy on his face, mixed with tears.

Standing in the hall outside my dad's door, I felt a new mixture of emotions cross over me. I was so happy to have everyone I cared about alive, yet I was sad about leaving. When the time came, would

Awaken Me

I be able to kill Derek? I still had feelings for him. Knowing that by killing Derek, I would destroy his mother, as well as a piece of me was unsettling. I guess when it came I would face it.

A very tall and beautiful woman with black hair approached me.

"Aimee?" she asked, grey eyes watching me thoughtfully.

"Yes?" I said.

"Rosemarie asked to speak with you. She's in the court waiting." The woman bowed her head a little and departed from me.

Making my way through the hospital wing, dodging nearly getting bumped into, I hadn't realized before how busy it really was. I managed to leave it a bit slower than anticipated.

My mother sat on a bench alone. Her hair was in a tight bun and she wore a shiny grey dress. Silk, most likely. Her hazel eyes watched me as I came closer. The court was full of life, everyone was out and about.

"Aimee. How is everyone doing?" she asked.

"Bored, but good." I said, looking into her eyes, I felt so much warmth. "Are you holding up okay?" I asked.

She smiled. "Yes, as best I can." We sat next to each other, just watching the people walk around us.

"Can I ask you something?" I said.

She nodded.

"Why aren't your eyes grey?"

"I'm not sure. They were grey when I first was awakened, but after your birth they turned hazel; my original eye color was blue."

That's interesting. Who knows why my life is so complex.

"Are you still going to hunt Derek?" she asked quietly. The subject of the day or, better yet, my life.

I averted my eyes. "I have to. He won't stop until he gets me. I can't live like that," I said venomously.

"I know you can't, and I'm proud of you," she said lifting my chin up gently. Her eyes were soft, mixed with that looming sadness. "We never had our dinner. I'm going to still host a big banquet. I'm thinking tomorrow night."

"And I'm thinking I will be there!" I said, smiling.

"I hope our relationship continues to flourish," she said, eyes on me.

"Me, too!" I reached for her hand and held it ;she was delicate. We both sighed. Sitting with my mom was the first normal thing we had done together. Things went in slow motion; I was just wishing I could forget everything I have to do.

Closing my eyes, I leaned my head on my mom's shoulder.

I could have sat like this with my mother for a long while, until a thought crossed my mind.

I wondered if there was someone who knew how to cure a vampire bite. I wondered if a very old werewolf knew a way. Sitting up and brushing the blonde strands of hair away from my eyes, my mother glanced at me curiously.

"Mom, I will see you at the banquet tomorrow!" I said, standing up.

Her expression was uncertain, filled with concern. "Is everything okay, Aimee?" she asked.

"Yes, everything is fine," I said as I leaned down to kiss her forehead.

The question was, would this werewolf give me the answers I wanted, needed to hear?

I walked down that long hall, with the same flickering lights. Reaching the very strong metal door, I rang the bell, not surprised that it was the same wolf from before. His broad grin met me, looking sheepish; Clark's handsome features were nice to look at.

"Aimee, what can I do for you today?" the good-looking wolf named Clark asked as he leaned against the door.

"I need to see Teeker," I said.

Clark's expression faltered a bit. His eyebrows rose.

"Teeker?" His amused expression was starting to bother me.

"Yes . . . now can you please bring me to him!" my patience was dwindling.

"All right, I'm only messing with you." Clark said, gesturing a sign of peace. I walked in pushing past him.

I was guessing today was the wolf down time; most of the lounge around the fire pit area was being occupied. As I came into their vision they all narrowed their eyes at me. I received a lot of grins. Clark shot them all a warning look.

"I heard what you did to those Rogues." His smile crept up the sides of his lips.

"Hmmm," Was all I managed to say.

"I think it's pretty hot. You're nice to look at and also can kick some major—"

Clark stopped suddenly and I almost ran into the back of him. Glancing around him, I saw Teeker, with his grey beard and weary eyes.

Clark cleared his throat. "Aimee came by to see you."

Teeker raised his hand to silence Clark. Teeker was eyeing me.

"Come with me . . . ." Clark and I started to follow Teeker. "Just Aimee!" Teeker said, very softly.

Clark looked disappointed yet again. He seemed to be shooed off a lot. Teeker and I continued to walk.

We didn't go to Teeker's room; instead we ended up near the fire pit, across from the wolves, still out of ear shot of them.

Teeker took a seat on a rocking chair, paying close attention to me.

"Why have you come?" he asked with his whimsical Romanian voice.

He sure didn't play around. "My father is dying from a vampire bite, very slowly."

"You want to know if there is a cure," Teeker said while he watched me.

I wondered if everyone around here could read minds. "Ummm, yes," I said slowly.

He smiled and pulled lightly the end of his beard. Sighing. "There was one werewolf who claimed to have been cured."

"And?" I asked.

"I'm not sure if it's just a myth. I don't want to give you false hope. "His eyes became softer.

"If there was some chance, any, I will find a way to help him. He can't stay like that forever," I said fiercely.

Teeker gave me a soft smile, twisting the end of his beard between his spider-like fingers.

"The vampire who bit him would have to feed him their blood. Or something along those lines. The man who claimed to have been bitten was crazy. I'm not sure I believe him. I wish I had more knowledge for you."

If that's what I had to do, Teeker was right. It was impossible. That vampire could be dead or clear across the world. My mind played with those thoughts.

"Out of curiosity, have you decided what side you will choose?" Teeker asked.

Side? Honestly I didn't want either. I was afraid what would happen to me.

"I haven't. Not sure if I'm going to change at all."

He smiled. "You will choose, I'm sure. You will be great . . . ."

"How can I choose? The last time I spoke to you, you said you didn't know what would happen if I chose to be awakened. And now, knowing I have both genes, werewolf and vampire, I don't want to risk my sanity."

"The genes are already conflicting with each other. That's why you are so dangerous, truly one of a kind. Usually normal yurnlings don't have any vampire side come out until awoken, werewolves breed with female Yurnlings, soon turned werewolves, and the son that's born is wolf already. But you, your mother is a vampire and father is a wolf. Hybrid. What becomes of you is a mystery. I'm certainly interested in seeing what happens."

Was this some kind of joke to these people?

"What, I'm a science experiment?" I said, raising my voice.

"No, you're just an unusual case." he said, grinning. My jaw almost hit the floor. Teeker had missing teeth; how had I not seen that the last time I saw him?

My mind quickly refocused, I was thinking about my dad again. Before I could say anything, Teeker answered my unspoken thought. "I don't know, Aimee, about being healed from a vampire bite. Like I told you, the wolf who spoke of it was crazy." He patted my hand gently.

He nodded at Clark, who stood a distance away, and Clark scurried over as fast as he could. "I hope my information has been somewhat useful."

That was my cue to leave, and I felt more frustrated than anything else. *What a waste of time.*

Clark chuckled as he led me back to the exit.

"What's so funny?" I asked in a deadly voice.

"Your expression. You look pissed."

In reality, I was pissed, really pissed. "I'm not pissed; I just have a setback, that's all," I said, crossing my arms.

"Sure thing," Clark said, not believing me. He held the door open for me as I walked past him. "It was nice seeing you again; come back anytime," Clark said with a boyish grin.

I gave him a half smile as I departed. What a waste of time; I'd learned nothing from the old timer.

Twenty-One

S** PRAWLED OUT ON MY BED,** I watched Iva; she was going through my closet, determined to find something for me to wear. I was feeling so lazy, and didn't want to look. She held up a couple of options but I shook my head. I wanted to go to dinner in sweat pants, actually. Iva's dress was hanging over my chair. It was a pretty, pale blue dress with spaghetti straps. All I wanted to do was sleep and not move from the bed. I was feeling dejected about my dad and leaving Alec soon, as well as plain exhaustion from the fight.

"I'm going like this," I told her.

Iva practically yelled at me.

"You are not! You have many dresses in here and you will look beautiful when I'm done with you!" she said fiercely.

I just laid my head back on my pillow.

"How about this one?" Her Italian accent sounded stronger than ever. She held up a form-fitting knee length purple dress. Halter style top. It was pretty; I had forgotten about it.

"That will work," I said. I liked purple.

"Well, get up, we have your hair and makeup to do still."

This new Iva was annoying me. She was so determined to make things right between us, even though I told her I forgave her.

I didn't move fast enough and she threw a pillow at me.

"Okay, okay, I'm getting up!" I said, snapping at her.

Sitting on the toilet seat so she could beautify me, I was zoning in and out of trances. My mind still wondered about everything that was coming.

"Are you even listening to me?" Iva said, bringing me back to earth.

"Hmmm," I said. I didn't even know she was speaking to me at all.

"I said, are you going to look at your face now? Wait one more second," she said, keeping me still to touch up something.

I didn't see what I looked like, and honestly I didn't care. I was still tired.

She examined my face before asking me to look in the mirror for the second time. Turning my head, I didn't recognize me. She had done a dark purple smoky eye and my hair was in light curls. I looked pretty; she had done a great job.

"Looks great, Iva! Thanks!" I said. She was happy with her work, too. She left me to get dressed and returned, holding my purple dress. Her smile was wider than ever, showing her fangs.

She helped me slip on my black Jimmy Choos, even though I told her I could do it. But she never listens. There was a soft knock at my door, and Iva swiftly answered it. Marcus was standing there, looking handsome in his black suit. He was smiling as he looked at Iva. Wait, what did I miss? Marcus asked Iva to go with him and she said yes? I was extremely confused. Iva blushed as she looked at me.

"I asked Marcus to go to dinner with us, I mean with me." she said. Marcus just watched her with stars in his eyes. Oh lord.

We stepped into the hall and my eyes locked with Alec's. His hair was brushed back and his soft lips were smiling at me.

"They let you out?" I asked.

He shrugged. "It's just dinner. I'm not going hunting for Rogues anytime soon."

Marcus and I glanced at each other.

Alec studied my face for another moment then looked at what I was wearing. I knew I looked good in the dress, it was tight and it was very sexy. Alec sighed. He took my hand possessively.

As soon as we entered through the large wooden French doors to the banquet room, I was immediately summoned to the stage. My entourage escorted me toward my mother.

The room was delicately decorated, yet very elaborate. Purple seemed to be the theme, large purple flower bouquets, all shades, with gold accents. It was very beautiful, and smelled fresh.

My mother smiled at me as I walked up the steps. Her long evening gown was really elegant, long sleeves, a powder blue that hung on her perfectly. Her hair was loose around her face. I didn't know her hair was wavy. It was pretty. She immediately greeted Alec, Marcus and Iva with a kiss on the cheek.

Taking our seats, I sat in between my mother and Alec. The same little man went up to the microphone. I wondered if he was going to grovel again, like he did at the last banquet.

He cleared his voice. "Good evening, ladies and gentleman. Tonight we have the privilege to hear the leader of our community, Rosemarie Bazile." So that was my last name. I mean, I remember hearing it when my mother was introduced, but why didn't I ever ask what it was? It's French. My mother didn't have a strong accent and I never would have guessed the French part. But seeing that my dad was living in France, it made sense.

My mother gracefully rose from her throne-like seat to stand in front of the microphone and the crowd started to clap. It was so loud as the noise echoed around me.

"Thank you. As you know, I was abducted by my ex-husband to be murdered by Rogues, in exchange for my daughter to be taken again by the Rogues. Thanks to my daughter, Aimee, and Alec and Marcus, they found me and stopped my ex-husband's plan to corrupt our world . . . . My daughter was never formally introduced back to the community." My mother turned to me and Alec squeezed my hand.

"She wants you to go." Alec whispered, nudging me. I could feel my face going paler, but I rose as steadily as I could.

Walking to my mom, I took her hand. Mine were sweating. The crowd clapped as I took my place beside her. My mother watched me, so proud. Was I supposed to say something? I was hoping I didn't have to. I wasn't much for public speaking and could throw up from anxiety.

"My daughter, Aimee Bazile." The crowd went wild. I was so afraid to look at the faces before me. My mother continued to speak, but my ears tuned her out, Alec was by my side to bring me back to my seat. His face became blurry, I blinked a couple of times before he completely disappeared and the hazy green forest returned. *Not now*, I thought.

The forest was dark, and the crickets grew loud. Why was it a forest he always took me to? I glanced around, waiting for Derek to appear. This time I saw a woman. Elizabeth? She came walking out of the forest.

"Elizabeth?" I asked.

"Aimee, I don't have much time." She was acting weird, she was scared.

"What's wrong?" I said, coming closer to her. She just looked around the forest.

"I thought about what you said, about . . . everything. I don't want Derek to take your life away. He will kill you if you don't choose him. I fear for you. I know you won't change!"

"You don't have to say anything more, Elizabeth." I took her hands in mine. "You are risking a lot telling me this."

The sadness was in her eyes. "I truly do care about you, no matter what you think of me! I must go now. I can hear Nathan coming into the kitchen." She just squeezed my hands in hers; a tear escaped her eyes.

As the forest disappeared the banquet appeared. Alec was calmly by my side, waiting. My mother was anxiously watching me. Blinking a few times, I looked ahead of me. I didn't have any more time, it was running out. I had to leave. She was warning me. This was my sign.

"Aimee?" Alec asked me. I didn't know what expression I had on my face, but I'm sure it wasn't a happy one.

"I'm okay. Sorry." Was that all I said? I couldn't say anything more.

Marcus knew what I was thinking, I could tell by the look in his eyes.

Alec reached under the table and took my hand in his, giving it a soft squeeze.

After dinner, Alec was speaking to my mother and I made eye contact with Marcus, who understood my meaning. I walked away from earshot from the people around me.

"Let me guess, you want to leave?" he said.

"Yes, Elizabeth, Derek's mother, came to warn me basically. I have to get away from here and find him."

"I know. When?" he asked, concerned.

"Tomorrow. Meet me in front of the coffee shop around noon."

"Okay." He reached out and held my shoulders. "Everything will be okay! After seeing you fight, I'm not worried."

"I just hope I can actually pull through," I said, looking at the ground. "I still have feelings for him," I said quietly.

"Well of course you would, six years is a long time. But you will do it!" Marcus said, full of confidence.

Alec and Iva came up to us, smiling. Iva even gave Marcus a touch on his shoulder. I couldn't hold my smile back. And she glared at me.

"Come on Aimee, let's get out of here," Alec said, whispering in my ear. My heart nearly stopped beating.

Alec didn't need to tell me twice.

"Goodnight, guys," I said to Iva and Marcus. Marcus winked at me.

Holding hands, we took a stroll through the very elaborate court.

Hearing soft footsteps from my heels, we walked across the black granite floors.

"Are you tired?" Alec asked. Tired? Ha, if he only knew I wouldn't be sleeping tonight, but packing.

"I'm fine."

He stopped walking and held me in his arms, looking me straight in the eyes. "I wish I could read your thoughts," he said. I was thankful he couldn't.

"And what exactly did you want to hear in my head? Right now it's just a jumble of thoughts. Messy," I said.

"Then maybe I could understand you better." He then began leading me to my room.

Standing outside of my room, he leaned in to kiss me. I braced myself for it, excitement; it was so warm and electric. I pulled away and looked into his grey eyes. His pale skin was so soft, mixing beautifully with his dark brown wavy hair. I couldn't hold back any longer, I reached out and caressed his tresses. So soft and silky under my fingers. He pressed his lips to mine again.

We somehow ended up on the bed. The kissing was getting hot. Pushing himself off and taking a breath, he leaned on his arm so he could see my face. I realized his shirt was off, and his perfect muscles met my fingers as I traced them.

"I can't...." I felt stupid for wanting to tell him no sex, at least in modern times. Being 23 and a virgin was unheard of. But I couldn't do it and leave tomorrow to go off to hunt my ex. It would cause us both damage.

"It's okay, Aimee, I don't want to push you. When you're ready." he said softly. It was hard for me to hold onto self-control. I wanted him so badly that it hurt.

"I love you!" I told him, shocked it came out. But I had to tell him. It built in my chest ready to burst.

"I love you too . . . I want to marry you!" he said. I smiled at the thought. I could see us getting married, having a life together with complete happiness. But only if I made it out alive from the trip to hunt Derek.

"Oh, yeah?" I said, snuggling into his side.

"Yes, I'm positive. If I had it my way I would marry you tonight. I know I'm not rich and don't have anything to offer you, but I will always be here for you," he said.

Was this a proposal?

"Are you proposing to me?" I asked, laughing a little.

He sat up and got off the bed, getting down on one knee. He looked so sexy in his black suit pants. "Aimee Bazile, I promise to love you and protect you till I breathe my last breath. Will you marry me?" He was serious. My mouth dropped open. He shifted uneasily. "You can think about it," he said. He stood up, smiling at me. "I will always wait for you." He kissed my forehead; I sat up and threw myself on him kissing him passionately.

His eyes were lit up as he looked at me. "Think about it," he said. Standing up, he gave me one last kiss, putting his shirt on as he exited my room.

I couldn't do this; I didn't want to leave him. I couldn't leave him. I want to marry him and forget about Derek the Rogue who was hunting me! Throwing myself onto the bed I thought, *why is my life so complicated, why?* Tears filled my eyes and I couldn't control them any longer, they'd built up inside for so long.

Twenty-Two

I **WOKE UP EARLY HOLDING** my sheets close to my body, I didn't want to get up. Sluggishly, I got out of bed. My closet was full of dresses, useless to me now. My book bag was lying in the back of the closet. *That, I can use.* I grabbed the essentials, toothbrush, hairbrush, underwear, jeans and shirts. Nothing fancy. I was literally holding back tears. Just the thought of Alec, Alec and his perfect chiseled chest, soft kisses, love, devotion. Why was I leaving? Oh yes, to hunt Derek, the man I still loved also. My life at the moment pretty much sucked.

A soft knock on the door startled me. Glancing out the peephole I was surprised to see my mother standing there.

Without hesitation I opened the door for her to come in.

"I hope you were planning to say good bye before leaving today," she said as she sat on my bed. She inspected my book bag. "This is all you're taking?"

"Yes, I can't bring everything. And I'm coming back, hopefully soon . . . ." I picked up the book bag and placed it on the chair, Alec's chair. I frowned at that thought.

"Can I give you money?" my mom asked. I pulled out the five-carat yellow canary diamond. It was sparkling; I had it hidden away in my drawer. My mom gasped as she saw it. I'd always admired it. It was beautiful.

"I think I'll have plenty once I pawn the ring. What do you think?" I asked.

She placed the ring in her palm.

"He has good taste."

I felt the frown creep up the corners of my lips. "He has money. And I picked it out." Looking at it now made me feel sick; it was a stupid, materialistic thing to spend so much on something. It was so insignificant.

"The ring shouldn't matter; it's who I was going to spend my life with," I said as I brushed my sandy blonde hair out of my face and tucked it behind my ear. My mom placed a hand on my shoulder. I tensed for a moment. My eyes had begun to prickle with tears. Just the thought of Alec. What was I going to do?

"I don't know if I can do this," I whispered as I sat next to my mother.

"You can and you will! It's going to be hard. Those feelings don't turn off," she said soothingly, patting my hand. The gesture alone was awkward for her.

"No, I know I'm going to kill Derek . . . ." I think, hoping I did have that strength. "I meant leave Alec, without telling him . . . I'm lying to him," I said, tears escaping my eyes.

"He is smart, Aimee; do you really think he doesn't sense it coming?" "I know he does. He looks at me with such depth, like he's trying to extract that information from me. I don't want to leave him." I flopped backward on the bed and turned over to bury my face in the sheets. Peeking up from the sheets, my mom had an amused expression. She tapped my butt.

"It will work out. You two are meant for each other. Be strong. You will be great!" I smiled up at her. She was stroking my hair.

"Time to get up. You have a long journey ahead of you, and I suspect Marcus is already waiting for you."

She was right. I did have a long journey ahead of me, and knowing Marcus, he was waiting for me.

The hall was empty as we walked, holding hands. It was a funny feeling, this bond that was growing between my mother and me. Who would have thought? Certainly not me. I would miss my mom, too.

The halls were growing louder as we approached the main court. The school was on lunch break and the Yurnlings all gathered in their little groups talking and laughing. I was holding down the envy I was feeling bubbling in my chest.

A muscular figure captured my eye bringing me back to the present. Marcus stood at our meeting spot; he was watching the crowds with such alertness, his green eyes instantly spotting me, tilting his head to the side.

Iva popped into my head; I wished I could say goodbye to her.

I didn't even realize I'd stopped walking. I was briefly frozen.

"Aimee?" my mother asked.

"Fine, I'm fine," I said, taking a deep breath.

My mom kissed my cheek and hugged me tight. "I love my little girl!" she whispered in my ear. I was getting choked up. Who was this sensitive woman hugging me?

"I love you, too, Mom!" I said; even hearing those words come out of my mouth startled me. Our embrace lasted a moment or so longer.

She released first and I just gawked at her.

"I'll see you soon," my mother said, as she gracefully walked away from me.

Marcus smiled as I swiftly walked up to him. I'm sure my eyes were red from crying. He brushed a stray hair away from my face; he had worry in his features.

"You okay?" he asked. His green eyes bored into mine, so much concern.

I just nodded. "Okay, let's go. We have to hurry," I said, anxious.

I seriously felt like I was in a spy movie, dodging anyone that would recognize me. Marcus was very stealthy, putting my so-called ninja skills to shame.

We made it undetected to the elevator and I sighed as I placed my hand against the metal wall. Neither of us said anything. I could feel the tension growing.

The doors opened and we, in sync, sprinted through the garage, our feet hitting the concrete with such haste.

Marcus sighed in anger. "I will meet you outside the garage, okay? The car is in the other garage. Just make your way to the end. I'll see you in five." He squeezed my shoulder. Marcus jogged away and I was walking swiftly up the tunnel. I could hear my feet echo in the garage, a soft patter. The light was growing brighter as I was closer to it. It was so sunny. I was eager to be in the warm sun.

I was actually leaving undetected, which seemed unusual. I didn't see it being this easy. I thought "too soon." The tiny hairs on my arm started to prickle. My heart rate started to quicken in my chest, in the distance behind me I heard the elevator door open. I didn't need to glance back, I already knew it was Alec or it would be him, he had a knack for finding me.

I began running as fast as I could to the sunlight, knowing he couldn't touch me once I was outside. My breathing nearly stopped. I was so close. My legs burned as I pushed them further.

Alec was fast; I could feel him getting closer to me. I didn't dare turn around to see how close.

"AIMEE!" he shouted. He was gathering speed. *So close*, I thought, *almost there, a foot away*. I could almost feel his breath on my skin; without thinking I dove into the sunlight. Dirt sprayed in my face, literally a mouthful, I wanted to gag, but I stood up, with as much grace as I could.

I glanced around the area I landed in. Lucky it was dirt and not concrete.

"*Aimee?* How could you do this to *me?*" he said.

I brushed the dirt off my hands and turned to face the man I love. His grey eyes were watching me and filled with so much hurt. He stood before me, full of confusion. What could I possibly say to him, to help this situation?

I took a deep breath. "I have to, Alec."

"I thought you loved me." His Italian accent was sweet as it caressed my senses.

"I do love you, that's why I'm leaving," I said. I tried to shake my feelings for the moment.

Confusion crossed his face. "That doesn't make any sense!"

"I will always be hunted, Alec! I need to fix things, and keep you safe."

"Are you crazy? Being here is safe! I'll protect you!"

"No one can protect me, but myself. I'm sorry, I really am," I said, sounding a bit on the crazy side.

"You were going to leave without saying a word to me!" Alec sounded more hurt than angry.

"Would you have tried to stop me?" I asked.

He thought about it a moment. "That's not the point. What about Iva? You just run away and not think about anyone else? What about your mother?" He was so good looking, even when angry. Alec was standing on the edge of the garage in the shade separating us. I was eternally grateful for the barrier.

"My mom knows. I told her. As for Iva . . . she will forgive me. How did you know that I left?"

"I had a feeling something was wrong. I went by your room and you weren't there."

"So you came here?" I asked.

"Yes. And I was right!"

He did know me that well. I didn't have him fooled at all.

Alec began pacing the edge of the tunnel, covered in the protection of the shade, running his hands through his wavy brown hair. His eyes flashed toward mine.

The deep heady engine came around the corner, and right on cue, Marcus pulled up in a Mercedes SL600. Sleek and black. I was silently thanking God. Marcus came to a fast stop, wheels still spinning, causing the dirt around me to become alive and like a cloud, engulfing me.

I couldn't look at Alec's face any longer. I turned from him, opening the car door. Marcus' face went pale as he got a glimpse of Alec, through the cloud of dirt.

"How could you do this, Marcus?" Alec was yelling over the engine.

Marcus looked at me unhappy at the pain written all over Alec's face.

"I'm sorry, truly I am!" Marcus said.

Turning for the last time to face Alec, I said, "I love you with all my heart, Alec, remember that!" Blinking back tears, I sat in the car shutting the door. Tears blurred my vision. Marcus peeled the car around to do a 180, the engine revving. I looked out the back window; Alec was visible through the cloud of dirt. Anger burned his features, mixed with sadness now.

What have I done?

"Am I doing the right thing?" I asked, facing forward.

"I think so?" He reached over and squeezed my hand. "Where to?"

I thought a moment. Somewhere that Alec can't get to me easily, and far away from the ones I love. "Florida," I said.

This would definitely be an adventure to remember. How would I find a cure for my dad in Florida, and protect the man I love? I sighed. My life would never be easy, but did I really want that?

The road ahead was unknown as we drove over the hill. To protect Alec, the man I love, I chased a man I once loved. The Rogue werewolf, Derek, who abducted me to change me and make me his prize of a wolf bride, the one who would give him a new breed of a child. What would become of him, or me?

The fire was starting to burn a little more fiercely; I could feel it in my core. I was ready. Yes, Aimee, I do believe destiny finds a way to bring you back onto its course.

"Florida?" Marcus asked.

"Yes."

"Florida it is, boss lady." Boss lady. I guess, in a way I am the boss.

Acknowledgements

†

THIS BOOK IS DEDICATED TO, first, God, for giving me an imagination, and without God I am nothing . . . . There are some very special people in my life who have worked endlessly with me on this book. My husband and best friend, Joel, who has given me unconditional support and understanding. My parents, Joyce and Stephen McGuirk, who have always told me to shoot for the stars, and never give up anything I start, to push through the hardest times. Lauren Christian and Jillyn Feldman, who created my book cover; without their help I would have lost my sanity. My sister, Aimee, who I named my character after! For my other really close friends, Lauren N., Ashton, and Melloni, who believed that my idea was great and helped me refine it. I'm grateful for all of you, and love you all!